GW0065794Ø

MARGOT'S SECRET

ROBERTA KAGAN

ISBN (eBook): 978-1-957207-60-5
ISBN (Paperback): 978-1-957207-61-2
ISBN (Hardcover): 978-1-957207-62-9
ISBN (Large Print): 978-1-957207-63-6

Title Production by The Book Whisperer

DISCLAIMER

This is a work of fiction. Names, characters, businesses, places, events, and incidents are either the products of the author's imagination or used in a fictitious manner. Any resemblance to actual persons, living or dead, or actual events is purely coincidental.

PROLOGUE

Anyone sitting across from the tall, handsome man that evening would probably have found him charming, but not her. She knew better. She knew what he was, and she didn't trust him. In fact, she was terrified of him. Experience had taught her that Nazis could pretend to be charming, but beneath that debonair exterior lay a monster. If it was at all possible, she would have something to say that would cause him to lose interest in her quickly. After all, she had many secrets and must be sure he never found them. Watching him as he spoke to the host, she decided he was a man who was used to having his way. He expected it. And for some unexplained reason, which she couldn't quite understand, he had become fascinated with her almost immediately after meeting her.

The host led them to the corner of the restaurant, where they sat at a very private table with a white tablecloth. "Is this table acceptable?" the host asked the man in a voice that denoted his eagerness to please.

"It is," the man said. The host pulled the chair out for the woman, and she sat down. Then, a waiter appeared almost immediately. The Nazi ordered a bottle of Riesling wine. Then, smiling at her, he said, "I only buy German products. I drink German wine and, of course,

German beer. I eat German food. My clothes and my auto are all made right here in the fatherland. We are fortunate to live in such a country. Don't you agree?"

"Yes, of course," she said nervously.

"And much of the time, we have free labor to produce our goods. But, of course, that is the way it should be. Aryans are superior to all others; therefore, others have been put here on earth to serve us."

The woman wanted to say something that she knew would anger him about the slave labor, but she held her tongue. She knew she dared not because if she questioned him, that would allow him to feel free to question her. *Just agree with him and be quiet.*

"You are a beautiful woman," he said, glancing from her face to her breasts. Then he added, "has anyone ever told you that you would look lovely in blue?"

"I'm sorry? I don't know what you mean. I have two dresses; both are black, and I bought both of them to wear to work. I don't have money to waste on clothes," she said, then she thought she was probably a bit too rude.

"I am sorry. I didn't mean to insult you. Of course, you look stunning in your black dress tonight. However, blue is your color. I was just saying that you should wear it."

She nodded. "I'll remember that the next time I go shopping."

"Ahh, and when is that?"

"I don't shop much. Like I said." She tried to keep her tone soft and kind, so she wouldn't come off as bitter or angry. "You see, I need every Reichsmark I earn just to get by."

"Well, I can understand that. And so instead of you shopping alone, I think we should go shopping. You and I."

"Once again, I must say that I really don't have the time or the money. I'm sorry." Her tone was cold and abrupt again. *He is so insistent that it's hard not to be rude.*

Nothing she did or said seemed to discourage him or to cause his interest in her to wane. In fact, if anything, he was watching her even more closely, and he seemed to be even more intrigued. "Please don't be insulted. I want to do something nice for you. I want to take you shopping. I am not planning on having you pay for anything. It would all be my treat."

Be nice. He means well. I must try not to anger him. The owner of the restaurant where I am employed likes him. So, he could cause me lots of problems at work. He has the power to get me fired, and I had such a hard time finding this job. "How kind you are. I don't know when I'll have the time, but I will consider it," she said as sincerely as she could.

"Am I kind? Is that really how you see me, *Fräulein*? Or is it something else?" He laughed loud and hard. Loud enough that the other guests in the restaurant turned to look at them. He seemed oblivious. After he stopped laughing, he looked directly into her eyes. She felt a shiver run through her. Then he said softly, "I am going to tell you something about myself, *Fräulein*. I am going to give you a little insight into my character. I don't do that often. But I like you, so I want you to know me for who I am." He smiled, and his blue eyes glowed. "The reason I am eventually successful in everything I do is because I am the kind of man who goes for what he wants. And, no matter the price, I always get what I go after." His gaze was so intense that she had to turn away. But even this didn't stop him. "Since the first time I saw you, I knew you were the girl for me. And now, I can think of nothing else. I know we hardly know each other, but you must believe me when I tell you that you have become the center of my world. I want you. My desire for you is so strong that I can hardly contain it," he whispered. "If I could, I would lift you to his table and take you right here with everyone watching."

The powerful and frightening way he delivered those words shocked her. *He's a Nazi, an SS Officer. I would die if he tried to do that to me. Oh, dear God, this man is the last thing I need in my life right now. I'm trying to start over and somehow survive by hiding in plain sight, and now this.* Her heart was beating rapidly. She was afraid of him, and her fear must have shown on her face because he took her hand and smiled. Then he said, "Don't be afraid of me, my dear. I would never hurt you. I won't do anything you don't want me to do. That means I will never force you. I don't want you that way. I will do whatever it takes to make you want me too. If I am to have you, to really have you, then you must come to me. And believe me, you will come to me because I will do whatever it takes to make sure that you love me so much you won't be able to rest until you have me. You'll see, my sweet *Fräulein*, I know what I want, and I know how to get it."

CHAPTER 1

The streets were slick with rainwater. It had been a dark gray day, raining on and off for hours. Even now, as night descended upon Berlin, it was still possible to see the angry charcoal-colored rain clouds hanging like a premonition in the sky.

Somewhere in the distance, the roar of the siren from a Gestapo automobile alarm reverberated, shattering the city. Margot shivered at the sound and hid behind a building until the black automobile of death raced by. *Are they looking for me? Or are they here in the Jewish sector of town looking to arrest some poor, innocent Jewish family?* She sighed out loud. *What has become of Germany? I can't recognize this place as the same homeland where I spent my childhood. Berlin has become akin to a living hell. And soon, the Gestapo, the demons of that hell, will be looking for me.*

I am in trouble. I must hurry and get to the doctor. And the only doctor I could ever trust right now would be Ben. Oh, Ben. I know, for his sake, I should stay far away from him. He's a Jew, and he has enough trouble just trying to stay alive. But I need help. If I don't get help soon, my unborn child will die. I might die, too. In fact, it might already be too late. And I guess that wouldn't be the worst thing that could happen. I'm sick at heart and tired of trying to survive. But I know it would kill Max if I died. I don't know where to go or what to do next.

Blood trickled down Margot's legs. She felt the blood. It was like a warm stream of liquid pain and terror running down the cold flesh of her thighs and calves. She was tired, and her stomach was cramping, but she knew she must not stop moving. So, she mustered all of her strength and ran through the streets of Berlin. *I'm leaving a trail of blood behind me. They can find me by following the blood, just like a morbid tale of Kinder- und Hausmärchen, Hanzel and Gretel, with their bits of bread.* She thought about the fairy tale and how her mother had told her and her sisters the story when they were little girls. She remembered how scared she had been for the two children captured by the witch. But her mother had assured her and her sisters that it was only a fairy tale. What was happening to her right now was not a fairy tale. These monsters were heartless, and they were real. They were made of flesh and blood, but they were not human. A sharp pain shot through her belly, followed by a gush of blood. Sinking her to her knees, she thought, *I've got to get up. I must not stop moving, or they will find me for sure. They are like sniffing dogs.*

The last word Max said to me was, "Run." He told me to run. As long as I can move, I must do what Max told me. He is the only person in my old world who can be trusted. If my sister Trudy is telling the truth about my past, my mother and father lied to me. They should have told me that they adopted me as a baby and that my birth mother was Jewish. I know they didn't tell me because they believed it was for my own good. But somehow, Trudy found out. And I know that she's always hated me. I have no doubt that my own sister, Trudy, is my enemy. She is one of them. She's a Nazi through and through. Her heart is evil. And now things have really gotten out of hand. Trudy's husband, Rudolf, is dead. I am sure that makes my sister very angry. And to make matters even worse, he was a Nazi officer, and Max killed him. If Trudy called the police and told them that she knows for a fact that I am Jewish and she says that I am responsible for Rudy's death, they would be hunting for me right now. There is no doubt that they would believe her. I can't take the risk of being found. I must find a safe place to hide. But where? There is danger lurking around every corner, and the pain in my belly is getting so bad that I can hardly go on. I feel like I am going to drop dead any minute. My baby, my poor unborn baby, is suffering. Rudy was a bastard to the end. With every drop of blood I shed, I am getting closer to losing my baby. If I haven't already. Her mind was whirling. She felt hot tears run down her cheeks as she thought of her life with Max and their son Erik. *Erik, my son, my darling little boy, is dead. It's all my fault he's dead because I trusted Rudy and my sister. I didn't believe that they could do what they did. But they killed my little boy. What more can these Nazis take from me?* She wanted to lie down on the pavement and just lie there and weep. But, if, by some miracle, the child she carried was still alive, she knew she must do whatever she could to protect it. *I can't let go. I can't give up. I must find a hiding place. A place where I can safely lie down and rest, but where? Where? Who would take in a woman who is bleeding like this? The Nazis are always watching, and everyone is always afraid for their own safety. I can't blame them.*

As she moved through the alleyways of bombed-out Berlin, the rain began again. It started as a light drizzle. She felt it in her hair and her face. Then thunder roared, lightning flashed, and the rain came down in sheets. *It is good because it will wash away the blood on the streets,* she thought, as the water ran over her face and into her eyes. In the rays of light as each lightning flash cast down from the sky like the weapon of an angry God, the bombed-out buildings and the rubble on the ground cast an eerie picture of Berlin. It was now a mass of rubble and had once been a beautiful and vibrant city.

Margot Kraus had no idea how long she had been running or how she'd gotten to the Jewish sector, but she found herself there. The streets were empty. *I came here on instinct without thinking. I came because I knew I couldn't go home, so the only person I could go to was Ben. I must try to find Ben.* She knew which house was Ben's. She'd been there many times before. When she was a girl in school, she and Ben were classmates. They had worked on many science projects together in his father's study. Later, when she was married, her son, Erik, had whooping cough followed by seizures. Ben was a doctor who began treating her son. Poor sweet little Erik had been diagnosed with epilepsy, and the Nazis considered that to be a mental illness. The only treatment the Nazis approved for mental illness was euthanasia.

Margot put her hand under her extended belly as she climbed the stairs in front of Ben's house. She was about to ring the doorbell when a woman called out from across the street. "Don't ring that bell." The woman said in a warning tone.

Margot turned around abruptly. Her hand dropped to her side. She didn't touch the bell. But when she saw the woman, she remembered her. The woman was old. In fact, to Margot, she looked ancient. Her hair was white, and her thin, pale skin was a map of wrinkles. It had been years since the last time Margot had seen this woman, but somehow, she looked exactly the same. Margot watched the old woman limp across the street as the rain fell, drenching her hair and clothes. *Why is she coming across the street to talk to me?* Margot wondered.

Then, a sad and brief smile came over Margot's face as she was transported back to when she and Ben discussed Margot meeting this woman. Ben had told Margot that the woman's name was Frau Feiner, and she was a yenta. Margot asked Ben what 'yenta' meant. "A nosey woman who's always in everyone else's business. But Frau Feiner has a good heart. She just loves gossip." He had said, and then the two of them had laughed about it. That day seemed like a million years ago. So much has happened since. Margot had encountered Frau Feiner a few more times, and she found that it was true that the old woman was a real busy body who knew everything about everyone in the neighborhood. And what she didn't know about her neighbors, she was always in the process of trying to find out. She had no qualms about sharing everyone's private affairs. Whenever Margot happened to see her, she always had some juicy news about someone that Margot didn't even know. "She tells me the most private things. I have to admit, it makes me a little uncomfortable," Margot remembered saying to Ben.

"She doesn't mean any harm. She just talks too much," Ben had said.

"It sort of seems almost malicious."

"Nah, she's just a gossip. Ask her. She'll tell you she has a heart of gold."

Margot laughed.

"Really," Ben said. "Just ask her. She'll tell you. She'll say she'd give you the shirt off her back. But only for juicy information."

They had both laughed. But that was then. Margot wasn't laughing now. She was desperate. She closed her eyes and remembered long ago when Frau Feiner had been bold enough to ask questions about every aspect of her life. Margot had been offended. This woman had some nerve, that was for sure. Ben had certainly been right about that, and right now, Margot was hoping that Ben had also been correct when he declared that Frau Feiner had a heart of gold.

The rain was falling in sheets like the angels in heaven were weeping, and a heavy fog had set in. It was almost impossible to see directly in front of you. Frau Feiner ignored the rain and the mist as she walked towards Margot. "Come with me. We must hurry," she said. "It's better if we get out of here before anyone sees you."

Margot followed Frau Feiner across the street and up the stairs. Then, Frau Feiner opened the heavy wooden door to her house, and Margot followed her inside.

"Sit down," the old woman said.

"I couldn't. I'm soaking wet. I'll ruin your furniture."

"You're not only soaked, but you're bleeding too. Sit down. I don't worry so much about the furniture. At my age, and with the Nazis stalking me, I figure the furniture is going to outlive me. The Nazis are going to take it, anyway. So, they should have it with blood stains and maybe some mold. They deserve that. Why should they have my furniture in good condition? I hope they choke on it. *Nu?*"

Margot nodded and sat down.

Margot smiled. She'd been around Ben long enough to know that the word '*Nu*' meant many things. It could mean 'so' or 'right.' In this case, it meant 'right?'

"Yes, right," Margot said.

"What are you doing here? You came to the Jewish sector of town to look for Ben. You were going to knock on the door of his house. Why?" Frau Feiner asked as she filled her teakettle and put it on the stove to boil. She was as bold as Margot remembered. She asked whatever questions came to her mind. "I'm making you some tea, by the way. You need something hot."

"Oh, that's not necessary," Margot said. "What I need is to find Ben."

"Necessary or not, you'll drink it. It's hot, and it's good for you," Frau Feiner said.

Margot smiled. "Thank you. I appreciate it."

"Of course. You're a friend of Ben's. I remember you. What a good boy he is, and what a good doctor. He's helped plenty of people here in our neighborhood. He never turns away a person who is in need. And you need a doctor."

"Yes, Ben has always been a dear friend of mine. We've known each other for many years. Since we were children still in school."

"So you are here in our neighborhood because you came to ask Ben to help you?" The old woman sighed. "You're very pale. You must be losing a lot of blood."

"I think I'm having a miscarriage."

"I think so too. You're right. You do need a doctor right away."

"That's why I came here to find Ben," Margot said. She was in terrible pain, but she knew she must not lose patience with the old woman, or Frau Feiner might just throw her out without helping her find Ben. And she felt that if anyone knew where Ben was, it was Frau Feiner.

"What should I do?" Frau Feiner was not speaking to Margot. She was talking aloud to herself. "What kind of person would I be if I let this young girl die? Could I live with myself if I did such a thing?" She paced the floor and continued to speak. "But then again, if I tell her where Ben is, he could be in danger." She shook her head and began wringing her hands. Then, she began to speak under her breath in Yiddish. Margot spoke a little Yiddish because of Ben, but she had no idea what the old woman was saying. She couldn't be sure but thought it might be a prayer.

Frau Feiner began to rock back and forth. Margot could see that she was distraught. "Frau Feiner," Margot said softly. "You told me not to knock on the door at Ben's house. Why? Is Ben not living there anymore? Please don't tell me he's been arrested or, God forbid, worse."

"No, I am not saying he was arrested, and as far as I know, he's not dead. But the reason I came out and told you not to knock on the door over there is because he's not living there anymore. A young couple lives there now. They're Nazis. They fly a Nazi flag in the front of their home. This neighborhood is changing. There are Nazis living in most of these homes now. Most of my Jewish neighbors are gone. The Gestapo have taken them away. Only I am still here. I don't know why they've not taken me yet. But I think it will happen soon. I've thought of going away, but I have nowhere to go. No one will take me in. No one will risk themselves for an old, unimportant woman like me. So, it turns out that I am an old Jew waiting for whatever fate has in store for me."

Margot was frightened by Frau Feiner's words. She had not been to the Jewish sector of town in a long time, and she was shocked and horrified by what was happening there. Even so, she knew she must find Ben, or her unborn child would surely die. "I hate to ask you this again, but I must. My life and the life of my baby depend on you. Please, I beg you to tell me where I can find Ben."

"I can't tell you anything else. I don't know anything more than I have already told you." Frau Feiner seemed to close up like a turtle going into a shell.

"Please, I know you know where he is, and I know it's hard for you to trust me, but you must believe me. I promise you that I will never do anything to hurt Ben. Never."

"How should I know if I can trust you? There are devils everywhere, watching and waiting for an opportunity to seize a Jew. If I told you what you want to know, and it caused harm to Ben, I could never forgive myself. I know you say you and Ben are friends. But I had plenty of friends who were *goyim* before the Nazis came. You know what the word '*goyim*' means?"

"I think so."

"It means a Non-Jew. I thought these people were my friends. But when Hitler came into power, they turned on the Jews like rabid dogs. I'm sure you know that there are rewards for turning Jews in, and people need the money. They need the food. Not that it's right. It's never right. But there are also some of them that are just cruel. How do I know which one you are?"

"I am none of them. I would never turn you or Ben into the Gestapo. Don't you remember how close Ben and I were? You saw us together many times. We were best friends. In fact, one time, you and I were talking, and you implied that you thought Ben and I were lovers. Remember that? You must remember that. You said you thought that my son was Ben's child? I'm sure you can recall the little blond-haired boy with me the last time I came here to see Ben?" Margot thought of Erik and choked back hot tears.

"Ah yes, of course. I remember everything. But I also know that you're a *shiksa*. You're not one of us. And so many of your people have turned on us."

"I can't speak for them. I can only speak for myself. And I would never do that. Now, you said that you remember everything. So you must remember my little boy?" Margot said as the words caught in her throat. "That little boy with the blond hair?"

"Yes, of course. I told you that I remember. You were walking with the child on your way to Ben's house the last time I saw you. But it was a long time ago."

"Yes, that's right. And do you know what happened to my son? That sweet little boy with the blonde hair?"

"No, what happened?"

"The Nazis murdered him?"

"*Oy, Gut in Himmel.* God in heaven. He was just a child."

"Yes, he was just an innocent child. So, if you think I am one of them, you'd better think again. I hate the Nazis. I hate them with all my heart. If I could, I would kill them all with my bare hands." She was crying now. "And as far as my being a shiksa is concerned, well, actually, that might not be true. My bloodline is questionable. I'm not sure if I am a *shiksa*, as you say, or not. My sister, or at least the girl who I was raised to believe was my sister, just told me that she had known all along that my parents adopted me. According to her, my mother was Jewish."

"*Oy,* what a mess I am in! I want to help you. I want to believe you, but I don't know what to do," the old woman said, standing up and walking away from Margot. She paced the room for a few moments and then shook her head. "I am sorry, but I just can't take the risk. I can't put Ben in danger, so I can't help you. Ben is gone. That's all I know. You should go now. I can't do anything more for you. I'm sorry. I wish you good luck."

Margot let out a heart-wrenching sob. "I am begging you to tell me where he is. If you don't, I am going to die, and my child will die too. You are my only chance, my only lifeline. Please help me; I must find him." A sharp spasm of pain shot through her, and she gripped her belly.

"I cannot tell you what I don't know." Frau Feiner said, looking away for a moment. But then she turned back, and her eyes were filled with sympathy. "I lost a baby once," she moaned softly. "Many years ago. I never told anyone this."

"Then you know what kind of pain I am feeling. Please, Frau Feiner. I know that you know where I can find Ben. I need his help. And I swear to you, I swear on my child's life that I would never do anything to hurt him."

"I'm sorry. I don't want to be cruel. But I cannot help you. Take my advice. If you don't want to hurt Ben, just leave here now. If you try to find him, you might put him in danger."

The tea kettle whistled. The old woman stood up and stretched her back. Then she walked slowly to the kitchen to turn off the stove. She did not pour the water into cups, and Margot knew she would not give her any tea. It was obvious that Frau Feiner had decided that it was best if Margot left her house before she was overcome with pity for her. After she turned off the stove, Frau Feiner straightened her back with resolve, then she turned and headed back into the living room. She was planning to escort Margot out the door. But when she entered the room, she saw that Margot was on the floor, unconscious.

"*Oy*, dear God. Is she dead?" Frau Feiner said to herself. "Margot, Margot…" Frau Feiner said, shaking Margot's arm. But there was no answer. Margot lay curled up in a ball like a kitten. Blood had started to pool on the floor around Margot's midsection. *There is a lot of blood.* Frau Feiner balled up her fist and shoved it into her mouth to stifle a scream. How am I going to dispose of a dead body? I am not strong enough to lift her. This is a nightmare. Not only is there a dead body in my living room, but it's the body of a young pregnant *shiksa*. She says she's a Jew. But she was living as a *shiksa*. And the Germans probably don't know anything about her being a Jew. All I know is if the Gestapo found out she died here, I would surely be blamed for her death. Maybe she's not dead. Maybe I can get someone to help me get her out of here.

CHAPTER 2

Rudy's dead body lay on the floor in a pool of dark blood that was soaking into the expensive wool rug that Trudy had been so proud to own. It was a horrifying sight for Max. He had murdered a superior officer. There was no excuse he could give that would clear him of this crime. He was desperate because he knew he would need Trudy's cooperation to evade arrest. *She is in love with me. I must use her feelings for me to force her to help me. She's going to have to lie if I am going to get away with killing Rudy. Otherwise, I am going to face a harsh punishment.*

Trudy looked across the room at Max. Her face was pale as she gazed into Max's eyes. "He's dead," she said, and she was shaking so hard that her teeth were chattering.

"Yes. I know," Max said. He, too, was in shock at what he'd done. But Rudy had forced his hand. If he had not shot Rudy, Rudy would have killed his wife, Margot. He loved Margot and couldn't let that happen, no matter what the consequences to him might be.

"You killed him," Trudy said, more shocked than accusing.

Max nodded. "Yes." He looked down at the Nazi uniform he wore, and he wished he could tear it off and then shred it into bits. But he'd joined the Party because Rudy had insisted and had given him hope that the Party would be able to give his son Erik the medical help he needed. Max had never really trusted the Nazis. He'd always felt that they were ruthless and vicious. And after he'd joined, he had learned that he was right. The Party was filled with murderers. The Nazis thought of compassion as a weakness. They killed innocent people. And no one cared. No one said a word. But this was different. They would care about this because this was the murder of one of their own, a Nazi officer who was a member of Hitler's Death's Head Unit. Max was a nobody, an underling. He was inconsequential to the Party and had only worked at a simple job in the postal service. They wouldn't take kindly to what he'd done. He would be severely punished. Probably sent to a camp for political prisoners or criminals. He would surely suffer because the men who worked in those places tended to be masters of torture. So, as he stood there looking at the dead body, he felt sick to his stomach, not only because of what might happen to him but also because this was the first time he had personally witnessed a murder. And he was the killer.

Trudy seemed to change suddenly. Her face looked distorted and angry. She glared at him. "You killed Rudy for Margot. You would do anything for Margot. It's always been that way," Trudy said. Max was pretty sure he heard the disgust in her voice. He knew he must find a way to win her over. He must make her believe there was a chance for her to be his woman now that Margot was gone and Rudy was dead.

"I'm sorry," he said softly. His voice was cracking, and he found he could hardly speak.

"Why did you do it? Don't lie to me. I know why you did it. You did it for Margot."

"Yes. I'll admit that I did. But I also did it for my son. The Nazis killed my Erik, my little boy. And Rudy played a big part in that. If only he had told me the truth," Max said. Then he turned on Trudy. "How about you, Trudy? Why didn't you tell me? You knew what they would do to Erik, didn't you? You knew, and you didn't tell me. Why would you do that? How could you let them murder my child? I would never have let them do that to your child." Then he walked over to where she stood and took her hand. "I wouldn't have let them do that to you because I care about you," he lied, knowing these words would warm her heart and keep her quiet about his crime.

"I didn't know what they were going to do to Erik until it was too late. I swear to you, I didn't know. I would never have let it happen if I did. You must believe me, Max. You know how I feel about you. When Margot called me earlier today and told me what happened to Erik, she was insane with grief. I could understand her feelings, but what shocked me was that she was blaming me. She said she thought I knew that the doctors at the hospital planned to euthanize her son, and no matter what I said, there was no convincing her otherwise. You must believe me, Max. I would have told you what they were planning if I knew," she lied.

"And what was all of this about Margot being Jewish.? Please explain what you said about Margot having been adopted?"

"It's true. She's not my biological sister. She was adopted by my parents at birth. Her mother was a Jewish prostitute who had an affair with my crazy uncle Alex. I'm sure you remember him. He's my father's brother, the one who died."

"I know who he is."

"Well, as far as Margot being Jewish, I swear it is true."

"How do you know this?" he asked.

"I overheard my parents talking. It was years ago. They didn't know I heard them. But I did. The reason I kept this secret for so long was because of you. I wanted to protect you. I was afraid that if Rudy found out that you had married a Jew, he would have had you arrested. I couldn't let that happen."

"This seems so farfetched. I know you and Margot never got along. But this?"

"I know you don't believe me. But you can call my mother. She knows the truth. She'll have to tell you that it's true."

"Your father has been sick. This is the last thing your mother needs to worry about. I don't want to get Adelaide involved in all of this. If I call her, I would have to tell her that Margot has run away and that Rudy is dead. More importantly, we don't know what we will tell the police yet. So, I am not ready to try to explain what happened. And besides, if the police found out that your parents had adopted a Jewish child, they might be in trouble. Until things cool down, I think it's best not to tell your parents anything. Besides, none of that matters right now. What matters right now is that we must get rid of this body and think of some plausible story to tell the police. We must come up with something that they will believe."

"Yes, we must think of a way to keep them from knowing that you had anything to do with this, Max," she said.

"So you do still care for me?" he said. Then he looked into her eyes.

"I've always been in love with you, Max. You know that."

"I know," he said. His throat was dry, and his Adam's apple bobbed. He hated to lie, but it was the only way. "I've always been in love with you, too."

Trudy let out a sigh. "I've waited my whole life to hear you say those words," she said. "You don't know how hard it's been for me, being in love with you and watching you with my sister."

"I can imagine. It's been hard for me too. But we can change things now." He tried to smile. Then he added, "Trudy, there is not time for us to just stand around here and talk. We must get busy clearing away the evidence. Come on, let's go into the living room and clean up."

Rudy's eyes were wide open, and he was staring straight ahead. Trudy looked down at his face and shivered. Then she glanced over at Max. "This is the first time I've ever seen a dead body that had been murdered. I mean, I've seen dead bodies before, but not like this. Not with all this blood and the smell of gunpowder…" Trudy said, her eyes wide. "I'm so scared. I'm so scared."

"Yes, I realize that. But you must calm down. You said that you want to protect me. You do, don't you?" He gripped her arm and looked into her eyes. She was clearly terrified. "Trudy, listen to me. You don't want the police to take me away. Do you?"

"No, no, I don't. I want to protect and keep you with me forever, Max."

"All right then. We must think logically right now. We both agree that because Rudy was a Nazi officer, if the police find out that I killed him, I'll be sent away. And neither of us wants that. We want to be together, right?" he said.

"Yes."

Max nodded. *Trudy has always been in love with me. I must convince her there is a chance for her and me to be together because if she believes she has a chance with me, she will keep her mouth shut. I am going to have to play at being her lover for a while. During that time, I will go out and search for Margot. Once I find Margot, I'll find a way for Margot and me to run away from here together. This nonsense about her being a Jew makes no difference to me. I don't care about that at all. I love her. I always have, and right now, I just want my wife back. We've lost our child, and I'll never get over it. And I know for certain that Trudy and her husband both knew that Erik was going to be murdered in the euthanasia program. The Nazis promised us that they could cure our little boy's epilepsy, but I believe that Rudy knew that they never planned to help Erik. They planned to euthanize him. Our child is gone, and there is nothing I can do for him anymore. But, if I can just find Margot, we can start over again.*

"I never loved Rudy, not really. I think you know that," Trudy admitted as she turned away from Rudy's unseeing gaze. "But it's hard to believe that he's really gone. It's hard to look at his dead body and not think that he will be all right. I know that sounds crazy, but it all seems like a bad dream. Look at him lying there, Max. He was such a powerful man. You know something? I know this might sound silly, but I didn't think he could die. I thought that, somehow, he was too powerful. You didn't know him the way I did. Rudy was so strong. He was such a hard man," Trudy said. For a moment, it seemed to Max that Trudy was genuinely upset that Rudy was dead. Max was worried. If she was feeling grief, she might turn him in. He tried to think of something to say, but she didn't wait for Max to speak. She walked over to Max and looked up into his eyes. "I'm scared, Max." She put her arms around his neck. Instinctively, he started to pull away, but then he remembered that he must do whatever it took to convince her he was in love with her. Her body was trembling as she shot a quick glance back at Rudy. Then she asked, "What will happen to me now? I don't know how to begin to live without Rudy. Do you think the Party will make me move out of this house?"

"I don't know," Max admitted.

"The Party only gave us the house because of Rudy's position. And as you know, we were supposed to move to a new house on the grounds of Dachau on the outskirts of Munich. He had just received that promotion into the Death's Head Unit, and because of it, we were going to receive a lovely new home. But now that he's not here anymore, I won't be moving to that new house in Munich without him. I am afraid they'll put me on the street. He left a little money, but not much. He spent it as fast as he earned it."

Max nodded. The immediate situation at hand distracted him from what Trudy was saying. He couldn't think about Trudy's house right now. He had to figure out what to do with the body. And even so, the very idea of her agreeing to live at Dachau and of Rudy being a part of a terrible organization like the Death's Head Unit made him sick. He paced as he thought for a moment. "I think we should bury the body and pretend that Rudy has run away."

"Really? Is that what you think we should do? We could get caught."

"Well, if the police think you're waiting for Rudy to return, they might allow you to stay here at this house, at least for a while. During that time, we can figure out a place for you to stay."

"I'm not sure that they would allow it. I never really know what they will do. A new family has already been scheduled to move here in June because that was when Rudy and I were supposed to leave. I am afraid that even if they let me stay for now, they will throw me out in June for sure. Don't you think so? Where will I go? I have no place to go. What will become of me?" Trudy asked. She was distraught, but her tone was also suggestive.

Max looked at her as if he were watching her like an actress in a play, detached from the situation. *She is pathetic. Even now, she is thinking of only herself. She doesn't care that her husband is dead. But what did I expect? She didn't care when her little girl died, either. She played the grieving mother for a few days and then returned to her old self. I know she doesn't care about Margot, but she does care about me.* Trudy was pacing the floor, wringing her hands together. "I must hurry and call the police," she said. "If I don't call them and they find out somehow, I could be blamed for all this."

Max studied her. She was easy to figure out. As long as he remembered that she would always put her own needs first, he could control her. *If I tell her not to call the police, I believe she will listen. I don't want to call them until I have come up with something convincing to tell them that doesn't point a finger at Margot or me. Trudy could easily get flustered, and since she hates Margot, she could turn the tables on her. I know Trudy would be happy to tell the police that Margot was somehow responsible for Rudy's death.*

Most importantly, I need to be sure that Trudy doesn't send the police out searching for Margot. So, until I can come up with a feasible plan, I must convince Trudy to stay quiet. "Trudy, don't call anyone just yet. Do you trust me?" he said.

She shrugged. "I want to, Max. I want to trust you."

"All right. Listen, because I have an idea I think you might really like." He managed a quick smile, but his lips were trembling. "And, since you and I have never really given things between us a chance because of the circumstances…well…maybe this is the right time. "

Her face lit up. Her eyes glowed as she stared at him. Trudy reacted to his words just as he knew she would. He hated to be manipulative. He'd never been one to lie or manipulate. But now, with Margot's safety hanging in the balance and his possible arrest lurking around every corner, he had to make sure Trudy was on his side. The only way to do that was to tell Trudy what she wanted to hear.

He smiled at her warmly. Then he took her hands as if she were his long-lost love. She stared into his eyes as he said softly and tenderly, "If you are forced to leave this house, perhaps you would consider moving in with me." A smile lit up her entire face. Max could see she was happy, regardless of all the pain and trouble she had caused him and Margot. *I hate her,* he thought, *but I need her on my side right now. Most of all, I need her to be quiet about what happened until I can find Margot and think of a way for Margot and me to get out of here safely.*

"Oh, Max, really?" She was taken in by his proposal. Trudy did not even consider that he might be using her. All she knew was that her long-awaited dream was finally coming true, and she would do anything to make sure that nothing spoiled it.

"Yes, really, I am quite serious," he said. "of course. I would love to have you living with me."

She smiled. "I would love to live with you. I've always wanted us to be together. I've always known I was the right one for you, not Margot."

"I know, Trudy. I know you have always felt that way. And I realize now that I was wrong to have chosen Margot over you. You were the right choice for me," he said, his lips quivering as he smiled at her.

"So, let's get Margot out of the way. I can have her arrested. I will tell the police what I know about her mother being Jewish. That would get her out of our way for good."

He was nervous. This was what he was afraid of. "Yes, but it might get me arrested, too. Don't forget that it's illegal for an Aryan to marry a Jew. I might get put away for this. You wouldn't want that, now, would you?"

"Oh no, not that," she said. "But we could tell them that you didn't know."

"They would want proof. And if I couldn't convince them, they would send me to prison. Then you and I would never be together."

She nodded. "No, that must not happen."

"So the best thing for us to do is let Margot go. I told her to run, and I am sure she will never return to Berlin after what happened here today."

"Yes, I think you might be right."

"I know I am," he said, squeezing her hands. "But we must handle this situation before we can even think about the future. You and I must bury Rudy in the yard tonight after dark."

"Bury him in the yard?" she said, and he could feel her shaking.

"Well, we can't just leave him here like this, can we?"

"We could try to run away. We could leave Berlin."

"And if we got caught, the fact that we tried to run would make us look very guilty. Don't you agree?"

"Yes, I suppose you're right."

"I know I am," he said.

"All right. I'll do whatever I can to help."

CHAPTER 3

I t seemed that it would remain bright outside forever. It seemed that night would never come. Rudy's body lay out in the open in the middle of the living room. If anyone came to the door, Trudy knew she must not open it. After the shooting, Trudy quickly drew the living room shades. But even so, someone might be able to see inside, and Max was anxious as he waited for the cover of darkness. Trudy was on edge as well. To add to Max's nervousness, Trudy was talking incessantly. In response to her, he just nodded his head. She asked him questions, trying to engage him in a conversation, but he couldn't think to answer. His mind was ticking like a time bomb. He was worried not only about what they were about to do but also about Margot and the baby, and he was silently praying that they were somewhere safe.

"What if we can't dig a hole deep enough?" Trudy asked. "A body is big. How are we going to drag him to the yard? He's not light."

Max shrugged and shook his head as if to say he had no idea what he would do next.

"What if we are caught digging?" Trudy was wringing her hands. "What if one of my neighbors walks by and sees us in the yard? People go out after dark here. We might be seen. Then what?"

She repeated the same questions, rephrasing them in hopes of receiving an answer she felt comfortable with. But Max was lost in his own worries, and he wasn't able to comfort her. Finally, after a long time and far too many questions, he reached his tolerance limit. In an angry, deep, quiet voice, he said, "Please, Trudy. Stop asking questions that I have no answers to. We are doing what we must do. Worrying and wondering what will happen isn't going to help. Just be quiet for a while and let me think. I need to think. It's been a horrific day, and my mind is cluttered."

When night finally enveloped the city like a tomb of darkness, Max turned to Trudy, who was biting her polished nails, and said, "All right. Let's go. We'll dig the hole first, then once we've finished digging, we'll come back and drag the body into the yard."

She nodded and followed him. "Do you have two shovels?" he asked.

"I don't know where they are," she answered. "I have never worked in the yard. We have Jews who Rudy brought from one of the prison camps to do the landscaping."

"Is the shed open, or do I need a key?"

"I don't know. Honestly, I don't. Like I said, I don't know anything about it."

Max grunted in frustration. He knew he shouldn't blame her. After all, this had been her way of life, and he understood that. How could he expect her to know these things? "Wait here," he said. Then he walked over to the shed. It was unlocked. Inside, there were several shovels. He took two and then headed back to Trudy. He handed her one. She almost dropped it. "It's heavy," she said. She could hardly hold it up. Then she dropped the shovel and said, "Ouch."

"What?" Max asked, a nervous sweat dripping down his face.

"I got a splinter."

"Forget it for now. I'll get it out for you when this is all over," he said in frustration. Then, he began to attempt to dig. It started to drizzle, but Max was determined. He fought against the hard ground, forcing his shovel into the earth with all his strength. But after two hours of strenuous effort, he finally realized it would be impossible. Trudy was no help. It wasn't that she didn't want to help. She wasn't strong enough; he couldn't break through this hard ground alone. If he were to dig this grave, he would need more men, and that was out of the question. He finally had to accept that the ground was too hard to dig deep enough. Max sat down on a rock and put his head in his hands. He was spent. His body was aching. It was close to midnight, and he had accomplished nothing. Trudy walked over to him, and for the first time, he noticed she was still wearing the dress and high heels she had worn when he arrived. He grunted in anger and frustration. He wanted to yell at her, to blame her for everything. But he just sat there with his head still buried in his hands.

"What are we ever going to do?" she asked. He could hear her teeth chattering. "I think we should run away tonight."

"No, I can't do that," Max said firmly. *I will never leave Berlin without Margot.*

"But Max," Trudy said, and he could hear from her voice that she was crying. "I am afraid. When Rudy doesn't show up to work tomorrow, the police will come here looking for him. They will want to talk to me. When they come in the house, they will see his body and the blood, and then what?" Trudy was shaking. "I am so afraid. What if they think I killed him? I can't go to one of those prisons. I just can't. I would die there for sure."

He nodded. But said nothing.

"Well, how would you feel if they found out that it was you who killed him? They could take you away," she said. Her voice told him she was irritated with him for not finding a solution. He had not answered her questions or tried to comfort her, either.

He knew he'd pushed her too far. She might be contemplating turning him in. He had to stop treating her so coldly, even though he was far too nervous right now to carry on the pretense of caring for her. He wanted to say, "Go ahead, turn me in. I am tired, and I don't have the strength to coddle you. I'm sorry, but your needs are just not that important to me." But he remained silent, reminding himself that he had to find Margot. He had to help her, and the only way he could do that was to survive. So, he had to give Trudy what she needed: his attention and affection. "Trudy, darling," he managed to say, "I know you are afraid. But I know you want us to be together, don't you?"

"Of course."

"Well then, we must find a way to keep the police from finding out the truth about what happened here. Or they will take me away. Then there will be no chance for us."

"Oh. I know," she moaned.

He stood up and put his arms around her. "You would never tell on me, would you?"

"Never, no, Max, never. I can't let them take you. I just can't."

"All right then. We need a new plan. We can't bury him. So, we have to find another way. Now, give me a minute to think."

"I love you, Max. I would protect you with my life."

"Let's hope it doesn't come to that. Now, shhh, let me think," Max said. Several moments passed in silence. Trudy paced back and forth. Then Max said, "Come on, let's go inside. I am pretty sure I have a plan that should work."

"What about the shovels?" she asked.

He nodded. "You're right. We can't just leave them out. Wait here." He carried the shovels back to the shed and returned them to where he had found them. Then he motioned for Trudy to follow him back inside the house.

Trudy walked beside Max as they entered the house. He closed the door behind them and locked it. Then he turned to her and said, "All right. Here is what we are going to do."

She walked over to a chair in the living room and sat down.

"We are going to call the police and tell them that Rudy committed suicide."

"Suicide, but why?"

"Well, we will say he did it because he was distraught. He had been asking you for a divorce, but you didn't want to divorce him because you are a good German wife. We'll say that he admitted to you that he was having an affair with my wife, Margot, and she wanted a divorce from me, too. But because Rudy could not get a divorce and marry her, she broke up with him, and then she left me and left the country. Before he died, Rudy accidentally happened to mention to you that he thought Margot went to France. If you would give him a divorce, he was planning to follow her. You were adamant about not giving him the divorce. Instead, you told him that you wanted more children. Aryan children because you are a good German hausfrau. You see what a good light this will put you in? This is the way the Party encourages women to behave. Yes?"

"Yes, you're right. And it sounds good," she admitted.

"Anyway, back to the plan. Rudy was so distraught at Margot's leaving him that he shot himself. You were in the kitchen when it happened. When you heard the shot, you ran to the living room and found him dead. That's when you called me."

"Why would I call you and not the police?"

"Because Rudy was cheating with my wife, and you were so distraught that you didn't know what else to do. You were beside yourself with grief at losing your beloved husband. So, you weren't thinking straight."

"Yes," she agreed.

"When you called me and told me what happened, Margot was already gone. I felt bad for you because I had lost my wife. Even though she didn't die, she was gone, and I knew how hard it was to lose a spouse. So, I came over right away, and then together we called the police."

"Yes. That makes sense," she said. "That's why Rudy's body is still lying on the ground."

"Exactly."

"I think this sounds good."

"Yes, I think so, too."

"Before we call, I'll wipe my prints off the gun and put it in Rudy's hand. So, it looks like he shot himself," Max said.

"Yes, that's a good idea," she admitted.

"I don't know if the Nazi Party will make you leave this house or not. I don't know what they are going to do. We'll just have to wait and see. No matter what, right now, we have to hide any trace of evidence before we call," he said.

"If they force me to leave here, I will move in with you."

"Yes," he said, trying to hide the dread in his voice. "You'll move in with me."

There was a moment of silence. Then Trudy smiled, "Max…" she

28

said. "You know, I've always wanted nice things. As you know, our parents were poor, and we grew up struggling. I finally had money and a beautiful place to live after I married Rudy," she said. Then, softly, she added, "I know this might sound crazy to you, but I would gladly give up this house to be with you. You could be right; this might have happened just so we could finally have a chance to be together. It could be an answer to my prayers. I've been praying that someday you and I would be together."

He closed his eyes and nodded. *This woman is so repulsive to me. I sincerely doubt that this nightmare we are living in is an answer to a prayer. But Trudy is so self-centered that she actually believes God would orchestrate something so horrible just for her happiness.*

"You're thinking of Margot, aren't you?" she said, glaring at him and not waiting for his answer. "But, take my advice. Forget about her. She's a Jew; besides that, I guess she probably has left Berlin. In fact, I wouldn't be surprised if she had left Germany by now. She might actually be in France. Who knows? But with all that's happened, I am sure she wouldn't dare return here. Not even for you. So, that's good for us. We can finally see what life would be like if she wasn't in the way. You and I are both Aryan. We both think the same way and come from the same background. When you were young, you were attracted to my sister. But she's gone now, and you and I have a chance to be a real couple."

His mouth was dry as he swallowed hard. His Adam's apple bobbing. "Yes, that's right. You're right."

"Do you still love her? Tell me you don't. Tell me that you can see that the two of you never belonged together," Trudy said. "Now that you know that she's a Jew and she has caused all of these problems for you. You must be able to see that you will be better off without her."

He shot a glance at her. *I must remember that it's essential that I convince her that I don't care at all about Margot anymore. If she thinks I still have any feelings for Margot, she'll have Margot hunted down.* "I must admit, after all, Margot and I have been through, the magic in our relationship has faded. I can honestly say I am no longer in love with her." He couldn't look directly into Trudy's eyes. He was afraid she would see he was lying, so he looked down at his shoes.

Then he added, "Trudy, I guess you might say that I don't feel for her what I have been feeling for you lately."

"Oh, Max, I didn't know."

"I know. However, I don't hate her. I hope you don't either. After all, she may no longer be the love of my life, but she was the mother of my son, and because of that, I hope she will escape safely. It would mean a lot to me. Just knowing she's safe would make it easier for us to build our own lives together."

"Have you been feeling these things for me for a while?"

"Yes," he said. Even the sound of her voice had begun to disgust him.

"You should have told me."

"I didn't want to have an affair. Even when you approached me about it, I couldn't do it. I have too much respect for you to have an affair. Do you understand? I wanted something more than that."

She nodded and smiled. "You've always been a decent man, Max. That was what attracted me to you. And you just wait and see. I promise you that you're going to be so happy with me. I'll make sure of it. I've been waiting for what seems like a lifetime for you to see that we were meant for each other. And I promise I will do whatever I need to do to show you that I am the one for you." Then she winked, "And, just to let you know…" She put her hand on his penis. He instinctively drew away from her, but she didn't notice. She just giggled, "You weren't expecting that, were you?" she asked.

"No, I was hardly expecting that." He let out an uncomfortable laugh.

"Well, you just wait and see what happens once you and I make love. I can promise you that after you and I are lovers, you won't ever think of any other woman again."

He nodded. It was an awkward moment for him, and he tried to smile. "Now, let's get back to this situation at hand. We must take care of this right now. There is a dead man on the ground, and that's our most important concern at the moment. Yes?"

She nodded.

"All right, let's focus our attention on getting this right so that neither of us gets arrested for this crime."

"You're right."

"The first thing we have to do is take care of the gun, wipe the prints, and all that. Then we'll take care of everything else."

"Yes, all right. So, what do you want me to do?"

"Just stay here and wait. I'll do all of it. I'll let you know when I've finished clearing away any evidence, and then it will be your turn to handle things. You will have to call the police."

"I'll be waiting right here. And Max?"

"Yes?"

"I know that this is a terrible time to say this. I mean, with all the bad things that happened, the death of my daughter, the death of your son, Rudy, and then Margot being Jewish, all of it. But regardless of all of these terrible things, I must tell you, I'm happy. For the first time in my life, I'm truly happy."

He nodded. "Good, that's good." He was feeling sick to his stomach as he walked out of the room.

Max cleaned his prints off of the gun. It was his gun. After all, Margot had brought it with her. It was the gun that he'd used to kill Rudy. He tucked it into his pocket and thought for a moment. And realized that it would be much better if Rudy was found holding his own gun.

He returned to the living room, but Trudy had left the room and was now sitting at the table in the kitchen. "Trudy," he called out to her.

"Yes?"

"Does Rudy keep a gun in the house?" He knew that Rudy probably kept several guns in the house.

"Yes, of course, he does. There's a pistol in his desk drawer upstairs in his study."

"All right," Max said. Trudy entered the living room, and Max handed her the cloth he'd used to clean the prints of his own gun. Then, he said, "Go and get Rudy's gun for me. Make sure you pick it up with this cloth. Don't touch it with your bare hands. I want to make sure you don't leave any prints on it. By the way, before you go and get the gun, do you have any gloves?"

"Yes, mine or Rudy's?"

"Rudy's."

"I'll get them for you."

She brought him a pair of black leather gloves. He slipped them on. They were a bit snug, but they fit well enough to keep his fingerprints off the gun. "Now, go and get me the gun." He instructed.

She nodded. In a few moments, she returned with a pistol in her hand. He looked at it. It was, as he suspected, the same kind of pistol as the one he had used to kill Rudy. "Good," he said, taking Rudy's pistol from her trembling hand. Then he wrapped Rudy's fingers around the trigger.

"Why did you do that?" Trudy asked. "Why did you need his gun? It's the same kind of gun as yours, right?"

"Yes, but just in case, I don't want them to find out that it was my gun that was used in the shooting. It's better if it was his own gun. Especially since we want them to believe that he committed suicide."

"But why would he have done a thing like this in the middle of our living room? Wouldn't he have done it in his study where he could be alone?"

"Perhaps he had an argument with Margot right here in the living room, and that was when she left him. That's what we will tell the police about what happened. You will say you overheard Rudy and Margot arguing about her leaving him. You will say you heard her tell him she was seeing another man."

"So, let me get this straight. We are going to tell the police that Margot left you, and then she left Rudy, too. Is that right?"

"Yes, we'll say she left both of us for someone else. A new man. And you have no idea who that man is. She never mentioned any names. But you think from what you overheard, he was French, and she has gone to Paris."

"To Paris."

"Yes, to Paris." He nodded. Then he remembered how much Trudy hated her sister. "Listen, I know you hate Margot, and you would just as soon see her burn for this crime. But if you want me, you remember what I said about Margot getting away. I don't love her anymore, but she is the mother of my child. So, you must not do anything to set the police on Margot's trail. You must promise me that you are going to say everything exactly the way I told you to and that you will let Margot go. Let her be gone. If you do this and do it right, it will be you and I from now on."

"Yes." She sighed. "You and I from now on. Just as it always should have been from the beginning, Max."

"Exactly. Now, don't forget a word of what we discussed. It's very important that you don't veer from the plan at all. One mistake, one wrong statement from you, could cost us dearly. You must keep your head about you. If you mess up your story, you, I, or both of us could be in trouble. You understand this, don't you?"

"Yes, I understand. And the last thing in the world I would want would be to lose you now, after all I've done to make you mine. It took me so long to make you see that we have always been right for each other."

"Yes, exactly," he said, annoyed. "Now, remember, when the police arrive, say as little as possible. Stick to the story we invented. The less you talk, the better."

She nodded.

"All right, we're ready. Now, go to the phone and call the police. Tell them that your husband has shot himself and you need an officer to come over right away. Don't forget to sound very nervous and upset. You've just lost your husband. You should be in tears when they arrive. In fact, take your lipstick and smear some red around your eyes so it looks like you've been crying."

She nodded. "But you're not going to leave me here alone with the police, are you? I hope you will be here with me when the police come. You will, won't you?" she was shaking.

"Yes, I'll be here beside you. Tell them you were so confused and upset when I arrived that you didn't know what to do. I told you to call the police. That's why it took so long after Rudy died for you to telephone them."

CHAPTER 4

Max was so nervous that he could hardly speak as he and Trudy awaited the arrival of the police officer. But he forced himself to go over the plan with Trudy again so she would be sure to remember what she was supposed to say.

"I'm so worried I will make a mistake," she said. "I'm sweating."

"It's going to be all right. You know exactly what to say. We've gone over it twice. It will be fine. Just follow the plan. I know you can do it."

"Yes, I will do it," she said, but he could hear her teeth chattering.

"Have a drink," he said. "Take a shot of schnapps or whiskey."

She went to Rudy's study and returned with a bottle of schnapps. Then she poured herself and Max a glass each. They both drank it in a single gulp. As they put their glasses down on the coffee table, there was a knock on the door. Trudy jumped. Max nodded at her and gave her a nervous smile. "It's all right. It's only natural that you should be upset. Your husband just died. Now, take a deep breath and open the door."

Trudy unlocked the large bolt on the door and opened it. But then, she forgot her situation momentarily, and a smile came over her face. Max looked at her skeptically. But she smiled at him reassuringly. "I know you," she said to the officer who arrived. Her tone was pleasant. "Won't you please come in, officer?" she said as she opened the door to her home to allow the police officer to enter. She let out a sigh of relief. Her rigid posture became less stilted, and Max could see she had begun to relax. "I remember you. Do you remember me?" she asked. "After all, how could I forget such a handsome young man?" He was blonde, tall, and imposing. He looked at her, confused for a moment. Then she said, "I met you several months ago when you came to our house because you were working on something with Rudy."

He smiled. "I do remember."

She never knew what they were working on but recalled asking this man if he wanted a drink. And the good-looking young officer had winked and smiled at her when Rudy's back was turned. They'd flirted on and off that night whenever she had the opportunity to come into the room and see him. Now, she hoped he would still be attracted to her. If he was flirting with her, this would all be a lot easier.

"So, tell me, Frau Schulze," he said. "What is wrong? What happened? You telephoned the police station and asked that an officer come to your home?" the young police officer asked. Then he said, "In case you forgot, my name is Officer Lucas Heinz."

"Lucas," she said softly, "of course, I remember your name?" She looked into his eyes and recalled how Rudy had treated Lucas as an inferior. Rudy was a superior officer, an *Obersturmführer* at the time, and this man was not his caliber. Rudy had been rude to the young policeman almost to the point of embarrassing him.

Lucas seemed to have forgotten, or maybe he was pretending to have forgotten. But then he studied Trudy's face for a moment; he smiled and said, "You're Trudy Schulze, *Obersturmführer* Schulze's wife. I remember when we met. We were here at this very house."

"Yes," she said, and now that she had his full attention, she put her hands over her face and began to cry crocodile tears.

Max was worried because her tears seemed so fake. He was afraid that the policeman would know that something was amiss.

"I called the police because I didn't know what else to do. Max, my friend over here, told me to call. I called him because Rudy was having an affair with his wife."

"Oh? So, why did you call the police?"

"Oh, it's been just terrible, Lucas. Just terrible," she moaned. "My husband, Rudolf, is dead. He killed himself. He shot himself in our living room, it was over another woman. Max's wife."

"Oh. I see. Rudy is dead?" the young man asked awkwardly.

"Yes, he is. His body is in the living room."

"I'm sorry. But how do you know that he shot himself, and how do you know it was over a woman? Did you see it happen?"

"I didn't see it. But no one else was in the house, just Rudy and me. So, no one else could have shot him. Oh, Lucas, I've known that he was having an affair. He told me. I was so ashamed, so heartbroken. He was in love with Margot, Max's wife. He wanted a divorce because he planned to run away with her. I knew it, but I refused to give him a divorce. I am a good Aryan woman. I wanted to work things out. I think he went crazy when our daughter was murdered by the Jewish nanny he brought home. I think he blamed himself. I was devastated by it, too, but I had hoped that Rudy and I could have more children, beautiful Aryan children, for our *Führer*. We were still young, and we were a perfect Aryan couple. But after our daughter's death, he lost interest in me. He told me that he wanted Margot. I overheard him talking to her on the phone. I heard him say that he had tried to convince me to give him a divorce, but I refused. From what I gathered from their conversation, she must have told him that she'd met someone else and that she was going to be going away, leaving Berlin with the new man, because I heard him on the phone begging her not to go. Then, after he hung up the phone. There was a short silence, and that was when I heard the gunshot. What a horrifying sound. I was scared of what I would find, but I knew I had to see what he had done. So, I went into the living room and found him. I am devastated. Just devastated." She said between sobs.

"Well, that sounds terrible, Trudy," he said, using her first name. And Max was surprised to see how easily she had charmed this young officer. Then Lucas added, "If you'll excuse me. I must go and see the crime scene."

"Yes, of course," Trudy said. "Do you remember where the living room is?"

"I remember," he said.

Trudy and Max followed Lucas as he walked into the living room. Upon seeing Rudy's lifeless body on the floor in a pool of blood, still wearing his officer's uniform, Lucas gasped.

Trudy was afraid he would start asking more detailed questions, so she began to cry again to distract him. "How could a thing like this happen? What did I ever do wrong? I tried to be the perfect Aryan wife. I did whatever he asked. I obeyed his every command, and yet he still wanted another woman. Why was I not enough for him?"

Lucas handed her a handkerchief from his pocket. Then he turned to face Max. "The woman whom Rudy was having an affair with was your wife?" Lucas asked Max.

"Yes."

"Where is your wife now? Do you have any idea?" Lucas asked Max. "Trudy said she has run off with someone else? Do you know where she went and who she went with?"

"I don't know."

"You must know something. Tell me everything you know. You may not think something you have to say is important, but it might be."

"Well," Max said. Then, taking a long breath and choosing his words carefully, he continued, "Before my wife, Margot, left, there was no talking to her. She said she had made a choice, and she was leaving me. I asked her where she was going, and she told me that she was planning to go to France with a man she had recently met. Of course, I was very upset. But I let her go because I didn't want a wife who didn't want to be married to me."

"I see," the officer said. "Go on. When did you find out about Rudy?"

"I knew that Margot and Rudy had been seeing each other. I tried to stop it. But my wife was a strong-willed woman. So, when she told me she was going to France with some man, I asked her if it was Rudy, and she said no. She said she was done with Rudy because he couldn't get a divorce. A few hours later, after my wife left, Trudy called me. She was hysterical. She said she found her husband Rudolf dead, that he had shot himself, and she thought that it had something to do with my wife, Margot. She asked me if I would please come to her home. I was quite shocked to hear that Rudy was dead, and so I came right away. You see, until Margot and Rudy started their affair, Rudy was a good friend of mine. My wife Margot is Trudy's sister. We were family and all very close friends. I came to comfort Trudy so she didn't have to face this alone. But when she asked me if I had any further information about what happened between Rudy and Margot, I admitted that I didn't have anything else to tell her.

"She said it didn't matter anyway because Rudy was gone, and now there was no bringing him back. I agreed. And although Rudy and Margot betrayed me, too, I am sorry that everything ended this way."

"I see," Lucas said. "It sounds like a terrible family disaster."

"Yes," Trudy said, still weeping. "It is."

"Well," Lucas cast a glance at Trudy. She knew Lucas never liked her husband. How could he? Rudy talked down to him and treated him like dirt. "I don't see any foul play here. So, there is no point in having any further investigation. It all seems quite cut and dry."

Trudy nodded. Then she batted her eyelashes at Lucas. He was eyeing her ample breasts. "I don't know what I will do without him," she said. "He was the love of my life. Sadly, he just didn't feel the same way about me."

"Well, I probably shouldn't say this. But he was a fool," Lucas said, his voice a little hoarse with desire.

Max found Lucas to be disgusting, but he was glad that Trudy's feminine wiles had distracted him enough for him to put aside the investigation.

She looked up at Lucas, her eyes glistening with tears. "Do you really think so? Do you really think I am worthy of a man like Rudy?"

"Any man with a woman like you should consider himself lucky."

Max looked away. This whole scene was repulsive to him. And yet, he was glad that Trudy was playing it so well. The police officer seemed to be eating right out of her hand.

"Every woman wants to be loved in a way that makes her feel that her man would never want any other woman." She sighed. "Rudy just didn't feel that way about me."

CHAPTER 5

Lucas used Trudy's phone to place a call to the station. He made arrangements for a car and two officers to come by and collect Rudy's body. Then, while Lucas drank a glass of schnapps that Trudy offered him, Max began to clean up the mess.

Max got down on his hands and knees and scrubbed the blood out of the rug. Then he took a bucket and mopped the remainder of the blood up from the floor. Lucas watched with little interest while Trudy flirted with him subtly. He was responsive to her and didn't seem to notice that she was flirting with him while she should have been prostrating with grief. Instead, he let his hand fall on her breast when she poured him another glass. She giggled and said, "You must come and see me when you have a little time. We can have a drink, perhaps?" He smiled in anticipation of a future meeting that would prove to be a sexually satisfying one.

Max watched Trudy out of the corner of his eye. It amazed him that the officer didn't notice that although she'd claimed to be upset by Rudy's death, she seemed not too concerned at all. She was a natural seductress, and the more she talked, the more she wrapped the young officer around her finger. This would make everything go more smoothly. He let out a deep breath as he continued to clean, but Lucas didn't notice. He was smiling at Trudy, and she was smiling at him.

Max had to admit to himself that he had never liked Rudy. But he had never thought he would be capable of killing him. Max had never killed anyone before. And the very idea of committing murder made him shudder. *Trudy is so calm. How could a woman have lived with a man for years and had a child with him and yet not care at all that he had come to a terrible end? How can she tell me she loves me, then flirt with a young officer while Rudy's body is still warm? She's definitely one of them, a Nazi.*

But things worked out well because when Lucas left, he had forgotten about the case and was entranced by the promise of a future meeting with Trudy. And, as soon as he was gone, Trudy confidently promised Max that she was quite sure that there would be no further investigation. "Of course, I will probably have to see Lucas again. I will have to fulfill my unspoken promise to him. But it means nothing to me. It will ensure that we will be safe. Max, you must know that you are the only man I want," she said.

"I know." Max nodded. "I understand."

"You won't think any less of me for doing this, darling?"

"No, I won't, of course not," Max said. *I couldn't think any less of you than I already do.*

Trudy poured Max a glass of schnapps, and he gulped it down. It had been a terrible day for him. He wished he could just go home and that he would find Margot waiting there for him. But he knew that it was not the case. Margot had run away, and he didn't know where she'd gone. But he was fairly sure she would not have gone back to their apartment. She would have to have hidden somewhere.

"Come, follow me," Trudy said, taking Max's hand and leading him to her bedroom. He looked at the bed with a white bedspread embroidered around the edges with tiny swastikas and thought. *She made love to Rudy in that bed, and now his body lies in the morgue. I can't do this. I just can't.* "We have both needed this for a long time," she said softly.

"Yes, perhaps you're right. But not tonight, Trudy. Too much has happened today. I need to go home and get some rest. I'm spent," Max said.

"Yes, you're probably right. I am spent, too. I need some time," she lied. He knew she was lying. If he had agreed to it, she would have made love to him in her bed without a single thought of her dead husband. Then she added, "Are you all right alone? Or shall I come home with you and spend the night there? We don't need to make love; we could just lie in each other's arms. It would be soothing."

"No, not tonight. I am still heartsick over Erik and drained from all the rest of what happened today. I am sorry, but I need some time alone. I hope you understand," he said carefully.

"When will I see you again?" There was a slight twinge of irritation in her voice.

"Just give me a little time. I need a couple of days to pull myself together."

"Are you going to search for Margot?"

Be careful what you say. If she even has the slightest inkling that you are still interested in Margot, she'll send the police after her. "No, I am not. It's best that she and I part ways. I told her to run, and I'm sure she's gone far away by now."

"After you pull yourself together, as you say, will you come by and see me?"

"Yes, of course, I will. I'll come by."

"How long will it take before we see each other again, Max? I could be such a comfort to you now during all of this. I hate to see you face it alone. Are you sure you aren't going to try to find Margot?"

"Yes, after you told me that she is Jewish, I don't want to be involved with her. I don't need problems with the law. Besides, Margot and I haven't been getting along very well lately. And now, with Erik gone, there is no reason to continue our marriage. It's against the law for her and me to be together, and that makes it too dangerous to go on the way we were." He lied; he was proud of himself for how convincing he sounded.

"Please stay in touch while you are pulling yourself together. I will be so worried about you. Call me as soon as you want to see me. I'll make sure that I am available. As you know, there is going to be a funeral for Rudy. I will have to explain what happened to my mother and my sister. I'm sure you will have to explain things about Margot to your parents. I am sure you'll agree that when we tell our families what happened, we should keep the same story we told the police. Let's keep the truth between us only. That way, we never have to worry about the law coming down on us. Don't you agree? Unless, of course, you want proof that Margot is a Jew. Then you are going to have to ask my parents."

"I believe you. I don't need proof," he said. "And I agree with you that we should keep everything to ourselves. It's best that way." *I don't need to ask Adelaide if Margot is Jewish because I don't care if Margot is Jewish. It doesn't matter at all. But I think Trudy's right. We should keep Rudy's murder to ourselves. The less that people know about what happened here today, the better.*

"You will have to tell our parents about Erik, though," Trudy said. "He was their grandchild."

"I know. They will be heartbroken."

"Don't tell them the truth. It won't help anyone to know that he was euthanized. I think it's best that you just tell them what the letter said, that he died of pneumonia at the hospital. It would only hurt them if they knew the truth, and they couldn't do anything about it anyway."

"Yes, you're right," he agreed. *It is better this way.* The fewer the people who knew, the better he and Margot would be when he found her.

"I'm going to go home now," Max said.

"I'll see you soon?" Trudy's voice was hopeful.

"Yes, soon," he said. Then he turned and left the bedroom. As he walked through the living room, he took another look at the place where Rudy's body had lain just a few hours ago. Then he walked out the door and into the cold, dark night. As Max headed to the bus stop, he thought of Rudy. Rudy would have killed Margot, and it wouldn't have bothered him at all. He was a Nazi through and through. He was guilty of knowing that his fellow party members were planning a program to murder sick children, and it didn't faze him. *What kind of human being can live with such a thing? Rudy could have stopped*

Erik's murder if he had wanted to. In fact, Trudy could have stopped it, too. Or at least she could have tried. If she had told us what was in store for our son, we might have found a way to save Erik before it was too late. But even with all that had happened, even with all that Rudy had done, Max still felt horrible about killing him. *A man is dead. He wasn't a good person by any means. But he was a human being, and I killed him. I took the life of another person today. I am not the same man I was.*

Max walked into his apartment building, half hoping that Margot was waiting for him in their apartment. He ran up the stairs, taking them two at a time. His hand trembled as he turned the key in the lock. The door opened to a dark, quiet room, and Max knew he was alone. He wanted to fall to his knees, to cry out in agony for all that had been stolen from him. Instead, he said quietly into the darkness, "Margot, where are you?"

CHAPTER 6

The room was dark except for the moonlight that filtered under the shade that covered the small window. A musty odor of old things filled the air. Margot's eyes felt dry and itchy, like sandpaper, as she opened them slowly.

"Am I dead?" Margot asked in a broken voice as she looked up to see Ben's soft, dark eyes watching her closely.

"No," he smiled a little. "Thank God you're not."

"Ben? Is that you? The last thing I can remember was that I was in Frau Feiner's house, and she was with me. A tea kettle whistled, and then I woke up here."

"Yes, it's me, it's Ben. I know everything that happened. Frau Feiner was with you when they brought you here, and she told me everything."

"Who brought me?"

"Some of the boys from the neighborhood. Frau Feiner got in contact with them. They are Jewish boys. Old friends of mine. They are hiding, but not like this. They are in the resistance."

"Where am I? Where are we?" she was disoriented.

"You're safe. You're in hiding with me. In an attic," he said, touching her forehead, feeling for a fever. "Don't be afraid. I'm here with you, and you'll be all right."

"The baby? What happened to the baby?"

"I'm sorry," he said softly. Then he gently touched her cheek.

She could see the pain in his eyes and knew the answer to her question before she even asked it. And yet she knew she must ask. "I lost the baby, didn't I?"

He nodded. "You almost died. You've lost a lot of blood. I am still worried about you. But I believe that with the proper care, you'll regain your strength."

"Oh, dear God. Why? Why? I lost my Erik, and now this baby, too." She put her hand on her stomach and rubbed softly. Tears stung her eyes as they trickled down her cheeks.

"Please, Margot. Don't cry. You have to be strong if you're going to get better. There will be more babies. But only if you get better. I know it's hard. I know it's easier to just give up. But please don't. You must try to live. Promise me you won't give up." There was a long silence. Then he said, "Please. Please, Margot. If you don't have the will to live, you will surely die very soon."

She nodded. "I will try. I promise I will."

"That's a good girl." He ran his hand over her forehead, pushing the tiny hairs that had fallen into her eyes away from her face.

She reached up and pushed on the jacket that he used as a pillow for her to fluff it up. Then she noticed she was covered in blankets, old coats, and sweaters. He saw her take notice of all the things covering her. "You were cold, shivering from the loss of blood."

"Where did you get all of these blankets and coats?"

"I got some of these things from Frau Feiner. Others were mine."

"I am so confused. Is this Frau Feiner's attic where you are hiding? Are we alone, or are there others here too? Please tell me everything, Ben. I don't remember anything except being in Frau Feiner's house."

"I know. I know you don't remember anything. But don't worry, I'm going to tell you everything. Then you are going to have to tell me what happened to you. I want to know what caused your miscarriage. And where is Max?" he said.

"Yes, of course. I'll tell you."

"So, I'll tell you what I know…" He nodded. "You passed out at Frau Feiner's house. She knew you were bleeding badly. She was afraid to bring you here. She didn't know if she could trust you. But she also couldn't let you die on her living room floor. The old woman is many things that I don't like, but like I've said before, she does have a good heart. And so, when you passed out and were bleeding, she went down the street where she buys food from some fellows on the black market and asked one of the boys to help her to bring you here to me. It was a great risk for her, the boy, and you. But she said she didn't know what else to do. She told me you had gone to my house looking for me."

"I did. I needed a doctor. And, even more so, I needed a friend."

"So, this is not Frau Feiner's house?"

"No. It's not."

"Whose house is it?"

"I'll get to that," he said, shaking his head. "It makes me tremble when I think of the terrible risk Frau Feiner took. I didn't even realize that she knew where I was hiding. And I am surprised that she told a boy in the neighborhood. But I am glad she did it. I'm glad you're here."

"I never wanted to bring danger to you, Ben, but I know that my being here has done just that." She started to cry again. "Oh, Ben, I'm sorry. I know I had no right to go looking for you, but I didn't know where else to turn."

"Shhh, I'm glad you found me. Now, don't start crying again," he whispered gently. "It's all right. Like I said, I'm glad you're here. Besides, the boy who brought you to me isn't the type to say anything to anyone. In fact, he is a real tough boy. A fighter. I've known him for years. Now, he works selling things on the black market. He's the type that would rather die than give the Nazis even a tiny bit of information. So, I don't think, even if he were arrested, that he would ever say a word about where we are hiding."

"I hope not. What about Frau Feiner? Can you trust her?" Margot asked. "She thinks I am a *shiksa*, so I don't know what that means to her. Would she turn us in because of it?"

"She won't tell anyone where we are. I trust her. She is a tough old lady. Tougher than she appears. Besides, she's dying. She knows she has a terminal disease. I was treating her. So, there's no need to worry. She would not sell us out to the Nazis in exchange for her own life," he said.

Margot winced. "I didn't know she was dying," she said as she tried to sit up.

"Of course, you didn't know. It's all right. But don't try to sit up yet. Lie still for a while."

"I know you said we are hiding in an attic, but where are we? Whose attic is this?"

Since it was dark and the only light was a sliver of moonlight, she could only determine they were in a small room. There was no bed. The floor was made of slats of wood, and on one wall was a small window with a shade over it.

"We are in the home of one of my patients," Ben said. "She is a Christian woman, an older woman. Her name is Frau Danner. You'll meet her soon. She is kind, very kind, with a big heart."

"How did you ever meet her? Jewish doctors are forbidden to treat non-Jewish patients. Did she come to you?"

"Yes, she did, actually. When she came to see me, she was in a desperate situation. Her daughter, Elsa, had gotten pregnant by a Jewish fellow. Although the police didn't know she was pregnant, when they found out that she was dating a Jewish man, they arrested him. Although Elsa loved the man, she and her mother decided it was too dangerous for her to have the baby. She wanted to get rid of it. But because of the laws about abortion concerning Aryan women, she couldn't go to one of her own doctors. So, her mother, who was desperate for help, came to me. I hate to terminate a pregnancy. But when she told me her story and said she was afraid that because the baby's father was Jewish, and the Nazis might torture it, I did what I had to do. I helped her terminate the pregnancy. I thought that was the end of it. Then later, things got bad, and the Nazis began to arrest everyone in our neighborhood. That was when Frau Danner came to see me, and she offered to hide me in her attic. "

"I can't imagine any woman not wanting to have her baby. I would give anything for a child." Margot touched her belly.

"Yes, I know that. But this girl was afraid that the Nazis would take her baby and torture it because the father was a Jew. I understood. I've seen them do it. I've seen them throw tiny infants against a wall or tear them in half while the mother was forced to watch. So, I knew what she was going through and did what I could for her."

"Is the woman's daughter living here, too?"

"No, after the abortion, Elsa left Berlin. Everyone in town knew about her relationship with the Jewish fellow. Her mother was afraid that if she stayed, she might be arrested for having had a Jewish boyfriend. Her mother wanted her to make a new start in a new city. So she left. Frau Danner thinks her daughter went to Nuremberg. She thinks Elsa would be safe there because no one knows anything about her past."

"So, it's just you and Frau Danner here in this house?"

"Yes. You're going to like her. She is a good person. She does what she can for me. She brings me whatever food she can get her hands on. I am grateful to her."

"So, I am assuming that as soon as I feel better, I will have to leave?" Margot asked.

"No, she knows you're here. She's agreed to let you stay as long as you'd like. However, you have papers that say you are an Aryan. I think you should stay until you feel better, then I think you should leave Berlin. Maybe even leave Germany. I have a little money. I will give it to you."

"Oh, Ben, I don't want to go back out on those streets. Can I just stay here with you?"

"If that's what you want. Yes, of course you can."

"But how will Frau Danner ever get enough food for all three of us?"

"We'll manage," he said softly.

Margot nodded. There was a long silence. Then she said, "Ben, I found out that I might be Jewish."

"What?"

"I found out from my sister. If she is not lying, then I am Jewish."

"I don't understand."

"I know it's complicated, but…" Margot took a deep breath and told Ben everything that had happened. She told him what Trudy had said about her being adopted. She told him that Rudy had threatened her, causing her to lose her baby, and Max, seeing Rudy terrorizing her, had shot him. And then she told Ben how the Nazis had murdered her son, Erik. "I blame myself," she said, tears streaming down her face. "I trusted them. They lied to me, and I believed them. I sent him away to the special hospital with that nurse. I had a terrible feeling in my stomach when I watched them from the window as they got into the automobile. Something didn't feel right. I should have listened to my intuition. But I didn't. I wanted to believe that they were going to cure him. I was so hopeful, Ben. I wanted them to cure Erik more than anything in the world. But now, I would happily have him back, just as he was. I would love him just as he was. But it doesn't matter because he's dead, and I won't ever see him again. They took him away, and they murdered him. Oh God, Ben, my little boy is dead." She was sobbing.

He didn't say a word. He just lifted her up and took her into his arms. Then he held her close to his chest, rocking her gently. "I loved him too."

"I know you did. And Erik loved you. He trusted you. He knew. He was just a child, and he knew better than I did who he could and couldn't trust…"

He nodded. There was another long silence. Then he said, "Don't blame yourself. You did what you thought was best for him."

"Erik did not just die in their care. Oh no. It wasn't like that at all, Ben. I could forgive that. But not this. The Nazis murdered him intentionally. They have an entire program designed for the murder of anyone they think is unfit to live."

"That doesn't surprise me," He said sadly as he shook his head.

"This is how diabolical they are. One day, a doctor came to my house. He seemed knowledgeable about Erik and his condition. He was a quiet man. He seemed to be gentle and kind. Well, anyway, he told me that he knew a lot about Erik's struggle with epilepsy and that he had good news. He said the government had built a special hospital for people with epilepsy. And that they had made some ground-breaking discoveries. He said they could now cure Erik's condition. I believed him. I signed the papers that would allow them to take him. I didn't know it then, but those papers were Erik's death warrant. Later, after Erik was murdered, I found out that it wasn't a hospital that offered a cure for epilepsy. It was a hospital that euthanized anyone who the Nazi Party deemed as physically or mentally damaged."

"The Nazi doctors actually told you all of this after Erik was dead?"

"No, they lied to me. They never told me the truth. They sent me a letter saying that Erik died of pneumonia. But my sister Trudy told me the truth. She took pleasure in telling me the truth. I'm sure you remember her. She was married to Rudy, that horrible SS Officer. Because of his position, she had inside information. And she always hated me. When she told me the truth, I knew it was because she wanted to hurt me. But as soon as she said the words, I knew in my heart that what she told me was true."

"Yes, I know all about Rudy. He came to see me once," Ben groaned.

"What? You never told me anything about his coming to see you."

"Yes, he did. It was right after that terrible night in November of '38 when the Germans went crazy in the streets of the Jewish neighborhoods. They were wild with blood lust. It was horrible. They broke the windows in every storefront, burned our temples, and murdered and arrested a lot of innocent people. But those of us who were left alive needed to eat, and there was no food in our sector. So, I took a risk and went out of the Jewish part of town to buy food at the market. He was there. I don't know how he knew where to find me, but my guess is that he followed me from my home. Anyway, when he saw me, he knocked me around and told me I had better stay away from you and Erik."

"Oh, no. I am so sorry. I never knew."

He shrugged. "Nazis." Then he shook his head. "They certainly are a curse."

"Yes, they are."

There was another long silence.

"My own sister, Trudy, is one of them. She is heartless. I always knew she was selfish, but I never thought she would do the things she did. She knew that the Nazis were going to kill my son, and she let it happen. I know she has always hated me. But I was foolish and thought it was nothing more than a sister's competition. I was so wrong. She would have killed me if she could. I just never knew it. I knew she wanted Max for herself. He never wanted her. So, even if I wasn't his girl, he probably wouldn't have chosen her. But no matter what happened between her and what competition she felt, I still don't understand how she could hate my son. He was just a little boy. He never did anything to her. Trudy could have saved Erik's life. At least she could have tried. If she had told me sooner what they were planning to do at that hospital, Max and I would have gone there. We would have done everything we could to get Erik out before they murdered him. But she didn't care at all that her precious Nazi Party killed my son. In fact, she said it was for Erik's own good that they killed him. She's a heartless, terrible Nazi, just like the rest of them. And if it's true that I am adopted, and she is not my real sister, I am glad for it. I wouldn't want to share bloodlines with someone like her. I hate her, and now I know I can never trust her again."

"It's not your fault. Please don't blame yourself." He said, then he added, "Where is Max? What happened to him? Do you know?"

"Oh," she groaned. "I was there when he shot Rudy. After Rudy fell, Max told me to run. I did what he said to do. But the truth is, I am not sure that Rudy is dead. I think he is, but I didn't stay around to find out. I ran. And now I don't know where Max has gone or what has happened to him. I'm really worried about him, Ben. If he is arrested, he'll be sent away for shooting an SS Officer."

Ben nodded. "I know. But let's not get ahead of ourselves. At least not yet. I am going to see what I can find out about Max."

"How? You are stuck here in this attic, just like me. You don't dare leave here. And I am too weak to leave right now. Besides, I am afraid to go home. What if Trudy has the police looking for me? Or what if she sees me and then calls the police? She would be happy to have me arrested. I have no doubt about that."

"I realize all of this. But we will find a way to find out more about Max. I am not sure how yet, but we will. Don't worry. For now, the most important thing is that you rest. You must get stronger before you can do anything."

"I can't help but worry about Max. He's out there with Trudy, and maybe Rudy is alive. I can just imagine what he is facing. It makes me shiver; it must be like being trapped in a den of wolves. I really hope he's all right."

"Yes, I know."

"The Nazis would kill him if they knew that he shot Rudy, even if Rudy didn't die. Rudy was an SS Officer. It wouldn't matter to them that Max was defending his wife. They wouldn't care what Rudy did to me."

"Margot. It isn't doing you any good to dwell on this. For now, just try to get well."

Margot was weak and tired, but she couldn't sleep. She watched Ben. He moved slowly and quietly. There was something so soothing about him. *It has been so long since I've seen Ben, and it is good to see him again. Somehow, I feel safe when I am with him. Although I don't know how I can. We are in an attic in some woman's house, hiding. If we are discovered, we will both be sent away. Yet, his voice and his manner calm me. I just wish I knew that Max was all right.*

Ben glanced over at Margot. "Can't sleep?" he asked.

"No, I'm too anxious."

He nodded. "It's understandable." Then he smiled. "Let me help you get acquainted with this place. As I said, we are in an attic. The window over there," he pointed, "provides very little light. It is at least semi-dark in here most of the time. However, we must be careful to avoid opening the shade because someone on the street may notice us opening the shade and get suspicious. As you can see, we have a few blankets, and we also have your coat and mine. This will help us once the cold winter sets in."

She nodded.

"Over in the other corner, you will notice that I hung a sheet Frau Danner gave me. Behind the sheet, you will find a bucket. That is our toilet. Frau Danner is very kind; she brings us a clean bucket whenever she brings us food and removes the old one," he said in a matter-of-fact tone. She felt her face grow hot with embarrassment. She thought she saw him smile in the faint light that peaked from under the window shade.

"It's only natural. We are both going to need to use the bucket," he said gently. "I know that our living conditions are far from ideal. But I've done my best to give you as much privacy as possible. In a few days, you will be strong enough to walk around. I will help you."

"All right," she said.

When they were younger, Ben had always seemed to have an uncanny ability to read Margot's thoughts. It seemed that he could always tell what was upsetting her or what was bringing her joy. As he studied her, she saw in his eyes that a plan was forming. She watched him without saying a word. Then, finally, he said, "Let's let everything calm down out there, just in case the police are involved. Then, as soon as we think it's safe, I'll go to your apartment and see if I can find Max."

"I would not want you to be in danger. I really don't think you should leave the attic." She said. "It's not safe. As long as the Nazis are in power, it will never be safe."

"I know. But I can see that you are very upset, and you can't rest. I know you, Margot. I know you won't be able to rest until you are sure Max is all right."

"What if he's not there? What if he is gone and some Nazi family is living there? Like they were at your house? That has been happening everywhere. All of a sudden, people disappear, and families of Nazis are living in their homes."

"Yes, I know, that's true," he said. "But what else can we do? I don't know where else to look for Max. The only place I can think of is your apartment. I could go to his job."

"No," she said firmly. "That's worse. He works for the postal service. There are swarms of party members there." She hesitated, then asked, "Maybe that woman hiding us can help. What did you say her name was?"

"Frau Danner?"

"Yes, Frau Danner, maybe she could go looking for Max. She's a German woman, an Aryan, as they say. No one who saw her walking around the streets would suspect a thing. It wouldn't even be dangerous for her."

Ben contemplated what Margot proposed. "I can't promise that she will be willing to do this. But she will bring us food tomorrow, so I'll ask her for you when she comes."

"I know you hate to ask her," Margot said.

"I do hate it. She's an old woman. And I would feel terrible if something happened to her."

"But what could happen? She is an Aryan. Anyone who sees her knocking on the door to Max's apartment wouldn't think anything. They might think she was just an old friend of the family. No one outside of you, me, Frau Feiner, and the boy who brought me here even knows Frau Danner has anything to do with you or me, do they?"

"I don't think so," Ben said. "But I can't be sure what they know. Sometimes it seems to me that the Nazis are everywhere and that they know everything."

CHAPTER 7

Every sound in the house echoed through the attic floor. When it rained, the sound of water dropping on the roof was unsettling. And the wooden floorboards beneath Margot and Ben creaked with even the slightest of movements. It was semi-dark during the day with just a small flicker of light that trickled through the side of the window shade, but it was totally black at night, so dark that one could not even see their own hand in front of them. Sometimes Margot longed to look out the window, to see the world, the sun shining, the children outside walking, the trees blowing in the wind. But she dared not even attempt it. Even the slightest movement of the window shade was forbidden to her because someone might be looking up, and they might just catch a glimpse of the tiny movement. Just this small mistake could mean disclosure. Disclosure would mean certain death, not only for Margot and Ben but also for Frau Danner. Margot and Ben had the utmost respect for the old woman, who risked everything to hide them.

They knew that night had fallen because darkness descended hard and deep in the attic room. Now, not even a sliver of light flickered through the opening on the side of the shade. Margot shivered at the sound of footsteps on the stairs to the attic. "Someone is coming," she said in a hoarse whisper. Then she gasped, reached for Ben's hand in the darkness, and squeezed it.

"It's all right," he whispered. "I am sure it's just Frau Danner. You'll get used to the sound of her feet on the stairs. She waits until after dark to come up here to bring us food and water."

"Are you sure it's her?"

"I'm sure. It sounds like her; besides, she always comes around this time. Don't be afraid."

Margot's heart was beating hard and fast as she waited for the door to open. *Ben is probably right.* She still held tightly to his hand. *It's probably just Frau Danner. But what if it isn't? What if Ben's wrong and someone told the Nazis that I'm here? They might have come here because they are looking for me.*

The small attic door creaked open. Margot's heart felt as if it might burst out of her chest. Then, in the darkness, she saw a flicker of light from the candle that Frau Danner carried. "It's all right," Frau Danner whispered softly. Her white hair illuminated like a halo in the candlelight. "It's just me. You're safe."

"See, I told you," Ben whispered softly to Margot. He squeezed her hand. "Everything is fine."

She nodded, even though he couldn't see her nod in the darkness.

Frau Danner put the candle down first, then put the basket she carried on the ground. Quietly, she turned and closed the door to the attic. "I brought as much food as I could get. I went to the black market," she said, "and I have some good news. I brought a surprise too. I brought a pastry for the two of you. My neighbor baked pastries for me. She knows I am old and alone. She feels sorry for me because Elsa left. So, when she was baking for her grandbabies, she brought a few of the pastries over to my house as a little gift for me. It's raisin and vinegar strudel. I must admit that it's not the best strudel I've ever had. I'm sure that's because she had a hard time getting sugar and raisins. But even so, it's better than nothing."

"Thank you," Ben said. "I'm sure we will enjoy it. It was very kind of you to think of us."

"Of course," Frau Danner said.

"Yes, thank you for everything," Margot muttered.

"Elsa is Frau Danner's daughter. Elsa was the young girl who I told you about. She was my patient," Ben explained to Margot.

"Yes, my dear sweet girl, my Elsa." Frau Danner sighed. "I miss her terribly."

"Have you heard anything at all from her?" Ben asked.

"No, but I don't expect to. After all, she knows it's safer if she doesn't contact me. I just have to hope for the best. It's all I can do. It's all any of us can do."

"Yes, that's true." Ben hesitated for a moment, and then he added, "But I'm sure she's fine. And when this government falls, and it must fall, it's too corrupt to continue this way, then the two of you will be reunited again."

"That's if it ends in time. I'm old and tired. And besides, all I can do is hope we will all survive. Every day is a challenge when there are people who want to kill you. Yes, every night, I pray that we are one day closer to the end of this," Frau Danner said. Then she let out a long, deep sigh in the darkness.

Margot shivered. There was a long silence. No one spoke.

Finally, Frau Danner broke the silence, "But for now, I have a purpose. I have a reason to get up in the morning. And that's a gift for an old woman like me. I have the two of you to care for. It's a reason for me to go on living."

"Yes, you must go on living. You must never think about death," Ben said. "We need you, and Elsa needs you too, even though she's not here right now. And please know that Margot and I appreciate everything you are doing for us."

"Yes, we do," Margot echoed softly. She had to say something but was at a loss for words. She didn't know this woman who she owed her life to. And she didn't know how to speak to her. In fact, she couldn't even see Frau Danner's face clearly. If she saw her in the light, she would not even recognize her. It was strange to be indebted to someone she didn't know and whose face couldn't see clearly. But this sweet old woman had risked her own life to protect Ben, and now to protect her too. Margot wished that she had some way to thank her.

"Like I was saying," Frau Danner said, "my neighbor brought me two pastries. I ate one, and I saved one for the two of you to share. It was nice of her to bring these for me. But even as nice as it was, I hate to admit that I don't like my neighbor dropping by unexpectedly. It's too dangerous with the two of you up here. I mean, don't get me wrong. She's a good person. But they are giving rewards to people who turn in Jews and… well… everyone is very poor. I don't think she would turn us in, but I can't take the chance. So, you must be very quiet even when it seems no one is in the house but me. But you must be especially quiet if you hear the front door opening. Anyway, enough of that. I brought the pastry for the two of you, and I hope you'll enjoy it."

"It was very kind of you to think of us," Margot said.

"It was nothing. Ben saved my daughter's life in more ways than I can ever tell you. Because of Ben, my Elsa has a chance of a new beginning. You see, my husband died young, and so it has been Elsa and me for years. She is everything to me. My daughter is my whole life. And now that I am an old woman, I don't care much about myself anymore. But when my Elsa was in trouble, and I had nowhere to turn, I was distraught. The pastor at my church recommended Ben. He said he knew about Ben and that Ben would help Elsa and me. I went to see Ben. I was afraid he would refuse or ask me a lot of personal questions. But he didn't. He didn't ask me many questions. He listened to my problem and agreed to help, even though he knew neither Elsa nor I had the money to pay him." She was quiet for a moment. Outside, a night bird cawed. Then she went on, "Ben didn't care that we couldn't pay him. He saw that we were in a bad situation and helped us anyway. I will be indebted to him for the rest of my days. Besides that, I brought the pastry because the doctor says I shouldn't eat all that sugar. It's not good for me." She laughed.

"Too much sugar isn't good for anyone," Ben said. "But I doubt you can even get your hands on enough sugar these days for it to matter very much."

"I know. Ben is a wonderful doctor," Margot said. "I have known him for many years, and he would never turn away a patient who is in need. He did a lot for my son, who was very sick." She stopped talking because she felt herself getting choked up.

"Stop it, you two," Ben said, and Margot thought she detected a smile on what little she could see of his face in the candlelight. "You're making me blush."

Margot patted Ben's hand. "It's true. If this miserable government had only permitted you to be Erik's doctor, I know he would be alive today." There was a long moment of silence. Their eyes met by the light of the single candle, and despite all the time that had passed, Margot knew that although she dared not say the words, she still loved him.

CHAPTER 8

Ben and Margot were again left in the darkness after Frau Danner left the attic, taking her single candle. "Would you like a bite of this pastry?" he asked.

"I would."

He broke off a piece and handed it to her. She took a tiny bite and closed her eyes, savoring the dough as it melted in her mouth. "It's delicious. I know Frau Danner said that it didn't have enough sugar. But it's been a long time since I've had anything to eat. And to me, it's the most scrumptious thing I've ever had," she said.

He took a small bite. "It is very good. Especially when you're starving." They both laughed a little. Then Ben put the rest of the strudel back into the basket. "Margot, why didn't you ask Frau Danner if she would go to check on Max?"

"I thought you said that you would ask her. I felt uncomfortable. I hardly know her. And she had done so much for us."

"Yes, that's true. I understand how you feel," he said. "I should have asked her. I just wasn't sure how to approach it. After all, this was the first time you met her. But if you would like, I'll ask her the next time she comes?"

"Yes, would you?"

"Of course. You're right. Going to your apartment shouldn't be dangerous for her. She is a German woman. She is not Jewish. She can move freely about the city. And anyone who saw her would think nothing of it. She could be dropping by to ask Max anything."

"What shall we tell her to say if anyone stops her and asks where she is going?"

He thought for a moment. "We'll tell her that if anyone stops her, she can tell them she is collecting food or money for her church. And if anyone sees her go to your apartment to talk to Max, she can say that is why she went. In fact, if she is willing, she can go to a few of the other apartments in your building. She can ask your neighbors for a donation. That will help divert suspicion of any kind. I'm sure the neighbors will refuse. No one has enough for themselves these days. But if she does this, her behavior won't be suspicious."

"Yes, I think that's a good idea. But do you think she'll be willing to do it? I know we are asking a great deal of an old woman like her."

"Yes, Frau Danner might be old, but she has surprised me many times. You see, she's a strong lady. I think she'll be able to do it."

CHAPTER 9

A week after Rudy's death, Max was transferred from his job at the postal service to a factory that made airplane parts for the war effort. He was assigned to procurement, doing inventory. The factory had an abundance of slave labor, and this was the first time that Max had witnessed anything like this firsthand. It was easy to tell who the unpaid laborers were because they wore gray, stripped uniforms and were treated abominably by the staff. When Max asked a fellow employee about these laborers, he was told that they were prisoners of the Reich. These common criminals had committed heinous crimes. They were handled by a set of special employees who told them what to do.

Any contact with them by other employees, like Max, was forbidden. He would have liked to ask them questions, especially the women in the office. He knew they had returned to a prison camp at night, and although he was terrified of their answer, he wanted to know if they had seen Margot there. He didn't trust Trudy entirely and wasn't sure what Rudy had said to his superiors before he died. Either of them could have already alerted the authorities about Margot's being Jewish. He had no way of knowing because he had no idea where she might have gone. And a constant nagging fear that she might have been arrested was always in the back of his mind. Max wasn't happy about his transfer. Between his current job at the factory and his old job at the postal service, he preferred the postal service. At least at the postal service, he was just delivering mail. He would have preferred to go back to working with his father as a carpenter. Still, here he was, helping Hitler, a man whose philosophy he hated, to win a war that he believed never should have begun.

There were times when he sat back and remembered fondly the days when he had been a carpenter apprenticing alongside his father in a small wood shop at the end of a busy street in town. He loved working with wood, probably because when he was just a child, his mother told him that Jesus had been a carpenter. Max had often thought about that when he was learning to carve intricate designs into the legs of wooden tables. He had marveled as he watched beautiful and practical pieces form from hunks of wood. Carpentry was relaxing for him. He loved the smell of wood, the smooth feeling of it in his hands after he'd sanded and worked it until it was perfect. But he had agreed to join the nazi Party, hoping that they would give his son the medical care he needed. And now, he couldn't see any way out.

As soon as his boss heard about Rudy's death, Max knew he would come directly to him and want to know what happened. And so, it was on a bright sunny morning when the sky was crystal blue. With his heart aching for his dead son and longing for his missing wife, Max opened the door to the large factory and walked inside. He didn't speak to anyone. He went to the large file cabinet in the back of the warehouse, where he began by pulling the files to do inventory on sheets of steel. There were several sizes that must always be available to the workers. If he was late with his order, it would slow down production, which would anger his boss. With the file in hand, he walked to the first pile of steel sheets and began to count. Then, just as Max had predicted, his boss was at his heels. "Come into my office," he said.

Max nodded, not surprised. He knew that word of Rudy's death was circulating. He wished he could avoid this conversation. But He followed the boss to his office.

"Close the door," his boss said.

Max obliged.

"Sit down."

Max sat.

"What happened to your brother-in-law? I heard that the *Obersturmführer* died."

"Yes," Max said.

"Tell me what happened. How did he die?"

Max proceeded to tell him the story that Max and Trudy had agreed upon. His boss listened quietly. When he finished the story, Max asked, "Can I please take off from work to go to the funeral? The funeral is tomorrow."

"Yes, of course. Why don't you take a couple of days? I know how close you and your brother-in-law were. This must all have come as a shock, and I am sure it's been very hard on you."

"It did. I lost my son, my wife, and my brother-in-law all in one day," Max said.

"Yes, take a few days off. Come back on Monday. Why don't you head home now? I'm sure you have arrangements to make."

Max nodded. "Yes, I do. And thank you." He wouldn't have cared if his boss let him go. He would have been happy to go back to working with his father. But he had to admit that he was relieved that his boss had not doubted his story, and this meeting had gone far better than he had anticipated.

Max left the building after meeting with his boss and headed home. He didn't have any food in his apartment, and he knew he should stop and buy some. But he wanted to get home. He needed time to think. Having some time off allowed him to look for Margot. *Where would Margot have gone? Where should I begin to look for her?*

He dreaded calling Margot's parents; he didn't want to discuss what had happened. But he knew Trudy would have told them already. And that he would see them at the funeral tomorrow. But he wanted to speak to Adelaide, Margot's mother, alone. He didn't want to talk about Rudy or even about the terrible thing that happened to Erik. He had to ask Adelaide if she had seen or heard from Margot. And this was what motivated him to make the call. From their conversation, he could tell that Trudy had told her mother the same story she and Max had told the police.

"I'm glad you called Max. I was going to call you. But Trudy said that it was best if I left you alone at least until after the funeral." Adelaide said. "Trudy told me that Margot has gone away, and little Erik died of pneumonia. And, of course, she told me about Rudy's suicide."

"Yes, I'm devastated," Max admitted. He'd known Adelaide since he was a very young child, and because their families had always been so close, he could talk to her like a mother.

"Oh, Max, I am so sorry. I am heartbroken as well. Unfortunately, Leo has not been feeling good these days, and I am worried about him. He is taking this so hard."

"I'm sorry to hear that," he said, his voice filled with desperation. "Listen, I have to ask you. Have you seen or heard anything at all from Margot?"

"Not a word. I can't imagine where she might have gone. I can't blame her for being heartbroken. She lost her little boy. But I wish she would contact me," Adelaide said. Then she added, "Do you have any ideas about where Margot might have gone?"

"No, I am going to try to call Mattie," he said. "She's the only one left, but I don't think Margot would have gone there."

"Let me call her for you. I'll ask her if she's heard from Margot. Meanwhile, would you like me to come over and bring you some food?" Adelaide asked.

"How did you know I didn't have any food?"

"I just guessed," she said. "I can drop by with something for you if you'd like."

"I don't think you should leave Leo alone."

"I won't be long. I can't stay. But I will drop over."

"No, Addie. It's not necessary. I'll be all right," he said. Then curiosity got the better of him, and he asked, "I don't know how to ask you this. But Trudy told me something, and I wondered if it was true. Let me say first and foremost that it won't change anything, especially not my feelings for Margot. But I would like to know if it's true."

"What is it, Max? You're talking in circles."

"Trudy said that when she was a child, she overheard you and Leo talking. She says that she thought she heard you say that you adopted Margot and that Margot's birth mother was Jewish."

There was a long silence. Max thought that Adelaide had hung up the phone. "Addie?" he said. "It's all right if you don't want to talk about this. You don't have to tell me. It doesn't really matter, anyway."

"Do you love her, Max?"

"I love Margot with all my heart."

"Then why do you want to know? It could change things between you two."

"Nothing will ever change things between Margot and me. But I need to know so that I can protect Margot from Trudy if the situation ever calls for protection. Do you know what I mean?"

"Trudy is Margot's sister. I know they have always been in competition, but I don't believe she would ever go that far to hurt Margot."

"Well, just in case. Can you please just tell me?" he said.

"All right," Adelaide said, then she sighed. "Leo and I tried to keep it a secret. But it's true. Margot is the daughter of Alex, Leo's brother, and a young Jewish woman." She hesitated. "I wish Trudy hadn't found out. Of all my children, she is the only one with a streak of cruelty. I don't want to believe that she would hand her sister over to the Nazis. But just to be cautious, you must find Margot and do everything you can to protect her from Trudy."

"I will," he said, realizing that Adelaide didn't want to admit that she knew Trudy was capable of terrible things. Since her girls were little, Adelaide had always tried to believe they were good girls. And it was true of Margot and Mattie. But Trudy was different. She had always been different. Selfish, cruel, and materialistic.

"You just try to relax. I'll call Mattie and see if she knows anything. If I find out anything, I'll call you back. Otherwise, I'll see you tomorrow at the funeral."

"Yes, thank you for making the call for me," he said. Then he hung up the telephone.

CHAPTER 10

As it turned out, Mattie had not heard anything from Margot. Max was at a loss. The only person he could think of who might have information about Margot was Ben. But he couldn't believe that Margot would go to the Jewish sector after learning that she might be Jewish. *It would have been such a dangerous choice for her.* Still, he had no other ideas, so he had to go to the Jewish sector and see if Ben knew anything. Max knew where Ben lived. He'd gone there, nervous and shivering on many terrible evenings when Erik was at home having seizures. Ben had always come back with Max to treat Erik. No matter what time of day or night they needed him, Ben always did whatever he could to help the child. Max considered him a friend, knowing that even though the law had forbidden him and Margot from associating with Ben, they would always be friends.

Max was glad to be wearing civilian clothes, not his uniform, as he boarded the bus to the Jewish sector early the following morning. He had to be back in a few hours for the funeral. But even so, he needed to see Ben. At least wearing civilian clothes, he could take a seat and ride along inconspicuously without everyone staring at him with fear in their eyes. Once he arrived in the Jewish sector, he got off the bus and walked for several streets until he came to the one where Ben lived. It was a lovely street, with well-kept homes and nicely manicured lawns. It was hard to believe that Margot wasn't with him on such a beautiful day and that he had lost his son, too. How could it be such a lovely spring day when he felt terribly sad? He climbed the stairs and used the brass knocker to knock on the cherrywood door of Ben's home. It wasn't long before the door opened. A young woman with straight blonde hair in a messy braid and a child in her arms looked at him skeptically. "Can I help you?" she asked.

"Yes, there was a family who was living here. The Weisman family. Do you know them?"

"I'm sorry, but I don't," she said.

"They used to live here. I am looking for them."

"I don't know anything about them."

"Who are you?" he asked.

She shook her head. "That's none of your business," she snapped.

"But, please, I need…"

The woman slammed the door. Max stood there with the warm spring breeze blowing across his face. Ben and his family must have been arrested. *Dear God, what a terrible time this is to be alive.*

Max had nowhere else to turn. As he walked away and headed back towards the bus stop, he heard the loud boom of a gunshot. He whirled around to see two Gestapo agents walking out of a house that was across the street from Ben's house. The Gestapo men climbed into their black automobile and drove away.

Max shivered. He wondered who had been shot in that house. But he knew better than to get involved.

CHAPTER 11

When the Gestapo threatened to break down the door of Frau Feiner's home, she sat down on the sofa in her living room and waited. The tumor in her belly had grown large and hard. She imagined having a large belly might have felt like the pregnancy she had never been blessed to experience. Sometimes, she pretended that she was a young woman, still married to her now-dead husband and that she was going to have a baby. But of course, she knew that what was growing inside of her body was no child. It was a demon that was determined to suck the life out of her.

There were several kicks to the door. Then the springs gave way, and the door flew open.

"Edith Feiner," the Gestapo agent declared as he entered the house.

"Yes, that's me," she said casually.

"Get up, you lazy swine. You have ten minutes to pack a bag, then you are leaving. I suggest you pack your most valuable possessions. Because whatever you leave behind will be confiscated."

She laughed.

"How dare you?!" the agent shouted. "Get up and do as I say!" He looked at her as if he couldn't believe she was defying him.

"I am not going anywhere. I am going to die right here in my own home," she said. "This is how I planned it."

"You're crazy, you old witch."

"Ahhh, and are you sure I am not a witch?" she said, laughing again. "What would you do if I put a curse on you and your family?"

"Shut up. Shut up right now."

"Or what? Or you'll shoot me?" Then she got an idea. "You see my belly. Would an old woman my age be with child if she were not a witch?"

"Let's get out of here," one of the agents said to the other. "I don't want a curse on me. Let's just leave her here."

"We can't. They are scheduled to take the house tomorrow."

"Go ahead and shoot me," Frau Feiner said. "And after I am dead, you will see the results of what you have done. A curse will fall on you that will make the rest of your lives a living hell."

The more frightened the Nazi was of her, the more Frau Feiner bated him. She was not afraid to die. Everyone she'd ever loved was gone, and besides, she was already dying. If this arrogant Nazi killed her, it would only serve to end her pain and suffering. But she had decided long ago, when the Nazis first began arresting her friends, that when they came for her, she was not going to go. Instead, she would leave them terrified if she could.

"I say we just leave her here. We can tell the officers at headquarters that she wasn't home. Let's let someone else do it. I don't want to. I don't want the curse on me."

"I don't believe in curses," the other one said.

"I've seen the results of a curse. When I was a boy, I lived in the country, and an old witch put a curse on one of the men in town. He died in a fire a week later." The Gestapo agent trembled. "Let's just get out of here."

"Yes, go get out. Run away." Frau Feiner laughed. "You'd better hurry."

"It was a coincidence, not a curse." The other agent said to his coworker, then he turned to Frau Feiner. "Now, get up and get packed."

"I told you; I'm not going. You're going to have to kill me here. I am going to die here in my own home."

The agent, the braver of the two, looked directly at the old woman, but only for a second. She was sure she saw a glimmer of fear in his eyes. *I have achieved what I wanted to achieve. For the rest of his life, this young man will worry that he has been cursed by a witch. Every time something goes wrong in his life, he will be certain that he is cursed. He will never be at peace.*

He pulled his gun. "Don't do it," the other Gestapo agent warned. "Just don't do it."

Pointing the gun directly at Frau Feiner, the young agent gritted his teeth and steeled his jaw. Then he pulled the trigger. Frau Feiner was an old, sick woman. For the past several years, she'd lived in pain. And now, with one shot, life flowed out of her, and her spirit rose above the two Gestapo agents who stood in her living room.

"You shouldn't have done that. She was a witch. I know it. I could tell. She was laughing when you were pointing the gun at her. She is probably consorting with the devil even now when she's dead."

"You're a weak child. You should be ashamed of yourself," the Gestapo agent said.

"You'll see what happens to you now out of fear. Maybe I wasn't a witch, but you'll never know for sure, will you?" Frau Feiner glared at the Gestapo agents. She knew they couldn't hear her because she was dead. But then she turned to see her husband's spirit walk up beside her.

"Edith," he said. "I've missed you. It's been such a long time."

"I've missed you too. I'm glad to be going home."

"Will you make me your chicken soup?" he asked. "It was the best soup I've ever had."

"Of course, Yankel. I'll make it for you tonight."

He took her hand, and together, their spirits flew into the light.

CHAPTER 12

As the Gestapo agents headed back towards the Gestapo headquarters, which was several streets away, they argued with raised voices. The strange old woman had dropped a pebble of uncertainty into their lives, and now they were battling.

"She had to be a witch. She was laughing," the wary one repeated. He was driving the auto while the other one was quickly scanning the list of homes where they were planning to arrest Jews the following day.

"I don't care what she was. We had a job to do, and we did it. We followed our orders. She's dead now," he said, brushing the hair off his sweaty forehead with his fingers.

"But she cursed us," the driver said as he slammed the steering wheel with his fist.

"I don't believe in curses." He put the papers with the list into a neat pile and then slid them inside a brown envelope.

"I'm glad you don't. But I do."

"Like I said, you are a weak and silly child. You should be ashamed of yourself. If anyone at headquarters saw you now, they would laugh at you."

"Shut up. Don't taunt me."

"We're the superior race. No one can hurt us."

"Even the *Führer* and the *Reichsführer* know that the occult exists. I heard that the *Führer* went to see a fortune teller before he came to power. I heard that the man was a Jew and that he told Hitler that he would be a great power someday."

"Yes, I heard that story, too. But I also heard that the great clairvoyant whom Hitler went to see was not really a real psychic. There are no real psychics. That man was little more than a tricky Jew."

"Are you saying he was clever enough to trick our *Führer*?"

"I did not say that. Don't you dare say that I said that!"

"Well, that's what it sounded like to me."

"You are nothing more than a sniveling child, terrified of your own shadow. The Jews will have your balls in a noose if they get their hands on you."

"Perhaps Hitler's psychic was indeed a Jew. However, if you consider his prediction, he was right. Our *Führer* is going to conquer the world. I know you must agree with that."

"Of course, I agree with that. But anyone who met our *Führer* would have been able to see the greatness in him."

"Of course. But this woman who you just killed was a Jew, and she admitted she was a witch. Mark my words. There is going to be trouble."

"Stop it already. Forget about it. We had a job to do; we had to have that old bat out of that house. That was our order, and we followed it. Now, let's put that in the past and get on with our work. Shall we? We must head over to headquarters so we can send someone to pick up the old woman's body and clear out the house."

The other Gestapo agent was silent. But the conversation with his coworker had done little to silence the fear growing inside him. He couldn't concentrate. He was too frightened of what the future might hold. As he turned the corner to the street where the headquarters was located, he didn't see the other automobile turning right toward him. When he did see it, he slammed on his brakes, but it was too late. The other auto smashed into his car head-on. The last thing he heard was the old woman's voice. Then he felt his head smash against the steering wheel, and all the noise stopped. Both Gestapo agents were killed almost instantly upon impact.

CHAPTER 13

Max never learned what happened in the house across the street from Ben's home. He only knew that there had been a gunshot, followed by two Gestapo agents in their long leather coats leaving the house.

He knew that whatever happened there was not good for the residents. As he walked slowly back towards the bus stop, he thought about how dangerous Berlin had become, and it broke his heart. *I am so lost and helpless. I can't protect my wife if I can't find her. And I don't know where else to look for Margot. Where would she have gone?* He sat on the bench at the bus stop. He inwardly pounded his brain, considering every possible scenario until he was so exhausted that he could hardly think. The bus arrived ten minutes late; Max boarded it, paid his fare, and returned home. As he entered the little apartment he'd shared with his wife, he hoped against all odds that he would open the door and Margot would be there waiting for him by some miracle. But she wasn't. *What if she is dead?* He shivered at the thought as he hung his coat on the rack. He grabbed a bottle of whiskey from the shelf and took a long swig. Then, still wearing his clothes, he fell into a deep, fitful sleep on the sofa. He missed Rudy's funeral that afternoon.

He might have slept through until morning had there not been a knock on the door. *Is it Margot?* He bolted upright. *But it can't be Margot. She would have a key.* His stomach hurt. He couldn't remember the last time he ate. A pang of fear shot through him. Then there was another knock. *That could be the police at the door. They might have gone back to Rudy's house and interrogated Trudy. I know she wouldn't intentionally turn me in, but she was so frightened. If they intimidated her badly enough, she could have told them the truth.* Max sat up and rubbed his temples. There was another knock on the door. He stood up and stretched. His body ached, but he walked over to the door and opened it.

Trudy stood on the other side of the door, with her hair curled and her makeup perfectly applied, wearing a cream-colored wool dress.

"Come in," he said, perplexed, as he noticed the suitcase in her hand.

"The Gestapo came by today and told me that I must relocate. They're taking back the house." She said. "Damn them. I knew they would do this."

He nodded. "That was rather fast, don't you think so?"

"Yes," she agreed, her voice soft but hopeful. "I know you said to give you a couple of weeks to get back on your feet before I came by, but I didn't know where else to go." She hesitated. "I suppose I could have gone to my parent's apartment. But, with all that's happened, I didn't want to be there. I didn't want them to have the opportunity to question me. And you know they would have."

He wished she had gone to her parents' home, but he knew she was right. Adelaide and Leo would have wanted every single detail of what happened. However, he was more concerned with Margot. If she showed up, and he was praying that she would, the last thing he needed was for Trudy to be there. But he knew he couldn't tell Trudy this. The most important thing right now was to make Trudy feel wanted and cared for. He knew how angry she could get, and if she thought she was being put aside for her sister, she would probably go to the police and tell them the truth. "No, of course, it's all right that you came to me. I'm glad you came here. Is that all you have?" he asked, indicating the suitcase in her hand.

"No, it's all I brought with me today. It's just some personal items. I was hoping you might come with me later this afternoon or early evening and help me collect the rest of my things."

"I'd love to, but I can't. I am expected to do some paperwork and bring it to the factory later today. If I don't, I'll be behind on my work when I return," Max said. "How long have they given you before you must be out?"

"A week."

"All right, I have the day off tomorrow. I'll go back to your house with you and help you then." He hesitated. "Why don't you sit down?"

She did.

"I must remind you that this apartment where I live is very small, and I don't have room for all your furniture. I hope that's all right."

"Oh." She laughed bitterly. "It's not mine, at least not most of it. Most of it belongs to the Reich. There are a few pieces that Rudy and I bought when we were traveling, but if there's no room, I won't bring them. I'll give them to Mattie. I just need to collect my clothes."

"The closets here are very small. And you have a lot of clothes."

"I do. But I'll figure out a way to store them. Don't worry."

He nodded.

"Shall I make us some tea or coffee?" she asked.

"Yes, some coffee would be nice. I was asleep when you knocked. And I'm still a little groggy."

"Well, I would have waited to come if I had known. I'm sorry I woke you."

"It's all right. I was so tired when I got home that I fell asleep on the sofa. It's been a hard couple of days," he said.

"Where were you that you got so tired?" she asked.

He couldn't tell her that he'd been to the Jewish sector. "I went for a long walk. I had a lot of things to sort out in my mind."

"Of course. I understand. This is very hard for both of us." She smiled at him, and he felt the hair on the back of his neck bristle.

"Let me make the coffee," he said, heading into the kitchen. "You don't know where to find everything. It will be easier if I just do it."

"But I'll learn. You'll see. I'll be the best hausfrau that you could ever have wished for. The perfect Aryan hausfrau."

He smiled wryly.

Then she asked, "Do you think Margot will ever return? I would hate to have to call the police and have her arrested."

He glared at Trudy for a moment, forgetting to hide his real feelings. Then he said, "You have me. I am yours. Even if Margot returns, I will belong to you. We will live together exactly the way you always wanted it to be. I don't know what will happen to Margot. I don't know if she will come back. It won't make any difference to our relationship if she does return here. I will still stay with you. But I insist that you do not have her arrested. You must promise. If she returns, I am going to do what I can to help her find a way out of Berlin."

She looked into his eyes.

"However," he warned, and his face took on a sinister quality that was rare for him, "if you ever do anything, and I mean anything, to hurt Margot, I swear that no matter what you say or do, I will never speak to you again. Do you understand me? Your little secret about her being Jewish stays right here. You must never tell another person. And as long as you don't cause trouble, you and I will be happy together."

"I understand," she said. There was a long silence, and then, in a small voice, she said, "But why do you care? If you are done with her, why does it make any difference if they take her away like the rest of the Jews?"

"Because she was the mother of my son. And she is pregnant with another one of my children. If you endanger Margot, you will endanger my unborn child. I could never forgive you for that. Let her go, and she will be gone from our lives. But if you cause her problems, I will turn my back on you forever."

"I swear to you, Margot's secret is safe with me."

He nodded. "Good. That's what I needed to hear." Then he went into the kitchen and put a pot of water on the stove to boil for coffee.

Max's head ached as he sipped the hot liquid. Trudy was quiet. It seemed that now that she had him where she wanted him, she was awkward and at a loss for words. He knew that soon, probably tonight, he would have to take her to his bed, the bed he'd shared with his beloved wife. He would have to make love to Trudy or at least somehow manage to have intercourse with her. The very idea was repugnant to him. Yet he knew that it must be done if he was going to keep Margot safe.

CHAPTER 14

Later on that evening, they realized there wasn't anything to eat in the house. "Today at the funeral, my mother said she would come by and bring you some food," Trudy said. "But I told her not to. I told her that I was going to bring you some food and she needn't bother. I should have done so. I'm sorry I forgot."

"It's all right," he said. "I'm glad Adelaide didn't come. I didn't want to have to explain anything."

"I know," Trudy said. "That's why I told her not to."

"How was the funeral? I suppose I should ask," he said.

"It was a funeral. My sister Mattie was crying. I think she always had a crush on Rudy."

Carefully, he asked, "Any trace of Margot?"

"No, not at all," she said.

"Did anyone ask about me? I know I should have come, but I couldn't."

"They didn't ask because they assumed you were not there because of the story we invented about Rudy and Margot's affair."

"Good. I'll let all of this quiet down before I see my family or yours again."

"My mother did mention Erik. She was upset about him. I guess she told Leo, and he was devastated.

"My parents were upset about it, too. I am sure everyone had a rough day," he said.

"I felt bad," she said.

He looked at her and knew that she was a liar. "Of course you did," he said, then added. "I'll go and get us something to eat." He went out to a local restaurant, purchased two sausages on rolls, and then brought them back to the apartment. He could hardly eat. Too much had happened, and his stomach was in knots. But Trudy had no problem eating. She was hungry, and she hardly noticed Max's anxiety. After dinner, Trudy took a hot shower and dressed in her most provocative lingerie. She glimpsed herself in the mirror and thought she looked very seductive, like one of the sexy forbidden pictures she had seen of girls during the Weimar. She wore a red corset with red panties and black stockings held by garters. *He won't be able to resist me.* She thought as she carefully applied the blood-red lipstick to her lips. *I look like the kind of woman every man secretly dreams about. And after tonight, he'll forget all about Margot forever because I will give him the time of his life. He's never had a lover like me.* A soft giggle escaped her lips. Then she sprayed the expensive perfume Rudy had given her on her throat and behind her ears. After a moment, she glanced down at her breasts and then added a spray.

When Trudy walked into the room, Max was sitting quietly in his chair by the window, reading the Nazi propaganda newspaper and frowning at something. It was the only paper that the government permitted to be distributed. He glanced up from his reading, and she smiled. Then, without saying a word, she took his hand and led him to the bed. Slowly, she undressed him. He didn't protest. He just sat there staring out into space as if he were almost comatose. "Shall I leave the light on?" she asked.

"No," he said, "please turn it off."

"Are you shy?" she asked flirtatiously.

"Yes. I've never been with anyone but Margot." It wasn't a lie. She'd been the only woman he'd ever made love to. But that wasn't the reason he needed the lights off. He needed to use his imagination to try to get through this.

"Well, all right. Since this is our first time together, I'll turn off the lights. But in the future, once you are more comfortable with me, we can leave them on."

"Yes, that's a good idea," he said wryly.

CHAPTER 15

Max had never had a problem maintaining an erection before. He was young and strong and very healthy. But he couldn't sustain his erection that night with Trudy. Try as he might. He would force himself to concentrate on Margot and make love to her. And for a moment, he would be ready. Then, his worry about Margot's safety would consume him, and his male parts would lie limp and soft. Trudy tried every trick she'd learned from quiet conversations, giggling with her friends, and things she had done, which always satisfied Rudy. But nothing was effective with Max. He couldn't maintain an erection, so he was unable to have sexual intercourse with her. After all the years she'd planned this seduction, after all the times she'd played it out in her mind, it turned out to be nothing but a miserable and frustrating experience. Finally, after two hours, she gave up and sat up in bed. "Is it me?" she asked. "Is there something you want me to do that I'm not doing?"

"No, it's not you. You're very beautiful, and you're also very good in bed. It's just that with all that we have been through these last few days, I can't concentrate." Max knew Trudy had no feelings for Margot. But he wondered how she could put Rudy's death out of her mind so easily. They had been married for years. They had lived together and had a child together. And now it was as if she had forgotten him completely, almost like he'd never existed. But this was Trudy. Max knew that. And that was one of the things he'd found abhorrent about her. When her young daughter died in an accident, Trudy was upset, but only for a very short time. Both Max and Margot were surprised and shocked that Trudy was able to get over the death of her daughter very quickly. Within a few weeks, Trudy returned to her busy social life. She was having lunch with her friends, who were the wives of other Nazi officers, and going to cooking classes. She resumed her endless shopping. It was as if her child had been an unimportant part of Trudy's life.

Trudy nodded at Max. "It's understandable. It will be better next time," she said, and then she fell asleep quickly, but Max couldn't rest. A sick feeling came over him when he looked at Trudy asleep on the side of the bed where Margot had slept. He tried to close his eyes, but when his eyes were closed, he imagined Margot dead. He remembered Rudy's face as he terrorized Margot. This was what made Max go crazy and shoot to kill. *The way he upset Margot and her being pregnant might have caused her to lose the baby. If she did, she could have bled to death.* He thought. *If she's dead, I have no reason to go on. Without Margot and my son, what's the point of all of this? I couldn't imagine spending the rest of my life with Trudy. She's despicable. She always has been. But it turns out she's worse than I ever thought she could be.*

Trudy stirred in her sleep and reached for Max. She put her arms around him and he recoiled.

CHAPTER 16

Trudy didn't know how to excite Max. He was not at all like Rudy. And from their attempts at intercourse, she knew he wasn't as sexually attracted to her as she thought he would be. But she refused to believe that he wouldn't change over time, and she attributed his lack of interest in sex to all that had happened. Trudy told herself that if she continued to act as if everything in their world was normal, he would eventually come around. The wounds he'd experienced on that terrible day would grow dimmer in his mind.

The morning after their failed lovemaking session, Trudy woke early and showered. She had gone to bed the previous night without pin-curling her hair, and now it was straight and stringy. She sighed as she wrapped her hair into a twist at the nape of her neck. *I should have brought my pearl hair comb, the one Rudy brought me back from Poland. How did I forget to pack that? Well, I'll get it when Max and I pick up the rest of my things.* She thought as she took out her tube of candy apple red lipstick and carefully applied it to her lips. When she was done, Trudy looked in the mirror. *I don't look my best, but I still look better than Margot.*

Although Trudy had never been much of a cook, she was determined to prove that she would do everything she could to be an excellent German hausfrau. So, she decided to prepare breakfast for Max. As she took out a loaf of bread and the only two eggs she could find, she realized that she hadn't prepared a meal since before her daughter was born. The Jewish maid that Rudy had brought to serve them, a young girl who was now dead, had done all the cooking. There was a small bowl of some sort of fat in the cupboard. She took a hunk of the solidified fat out with a spoon and put it into a pan. Then she turned on the stove. Trudy was shocked to see how little food there was in Max's kitchen.

Because Rudy had been an important man in the Party, she had never really done without. Her cupboard had always been full. While others were struggling to find the money to buy enough nutritious food on the black market, she'd had plenty of eggs, ham, bread, and preserves. *My parents were poor when I was growing up. I didn't always have everything I wanted. But I suppose I've gotten used to having the best of everything with Rudy. It's going to be difficult to get used to living like this. But Max is worth it.* A thought that turned to worry came over her. *What if we don't go back to my house to get my things before the Party cleans out the place and takes everything? They will surely take my shoes. And, of course, Rudy's boots, which I would love to give to Max. He could use them if they would even fit. Max is so much taller than Rudy. However, giving Max Rudy's clothing and boots is less important than getting my own things before they're gone. Once the police see how many pairs of shoes and sweaters I have, they will take them all. I find it annoying that this country claims it must now confiscate everything we have for the war effort. I'm tired of this war.*

CHAPTER 17

With Ben's constant nurturing, Margot drank water, ate, and finally recovered from the loss of blood. But Ben could see that she was still weak. He gently encouraged her to stand up and walk around the attic each day. At first, she held on to his arm, but as she grew stronger, she was able to walk on her own.

Time was a circle. It was impossible to follow. Days drifted into night, and night blossomed into day, and because of the lack of light in the attic room, it was difficult to tell how much time passed. But they did know that the food had run out, and Frau Danner had not yet returned to bring more.

"Do you think she's been arrested?" Margot asked Ben.

"For what? You mean for hiding us?"

"I don't know. For that maybe, or maybe for something else."

"She could have been. Anything can happen out there in the city. We know that. But if someone turned Frau Danner in and she had been caught hiding Jews, the Gestapo would already be here looking for us. Since they haven't come, I assume we are still safe."

"Maybe the Gestapo have arrested her, and she is refusing to tell them anything. I know that if they think she is doing something wrong, they will torture her until she tells them what they want to know." Margot was worried. "Poor old woman. I hate to think of her suffering. But I must admit that I am terrified she will break under their pressure."

"Margot, Margot…" he cooed softly. "Please, let's not get ahead of ourselves. Frau Danner is probably all right. She might have had something she had to take care of, some personal business. And there is a very good chance that she might not have been arrested at all. And if, God forbid, she was, then she might have been arrested for something other than hiding us. We'll have to wait and see," he said.

"I'm sorry to sound so callous about Frau Danner. I do care about her, but I am more worried about us. I don't mean to be so selfish. As you know, this is not like me. But I am not myself anymore. I find that I am frightened all the time. Every time I hear a sound, I am certain they have found us, and they are coming for us."

"I know. I understand," he said in a gentle voice. "But panicking won't help anything. The best thing to do right now is to try to stay calm."

"You're right. And I do feel bad for Frau Danner. She's an old woman, and she is probably frightened too."

"Yes, I'm sure she is. She is all alone. And she is breaking a very serious law. If she is caught, they won't treat her kindly."

"Dear God. I hate to think about it."

"I know. Their cruelty is unparalleled by anything I've ever seen. But we can't dwell on it, or we'll both go out of our minds."

"So, what are we going to do? We can't live without food and water. If she doesn't come soon, we're going to starve."

"Yes, I know." He sighed. "I have already decided that I'm going to go downstairs after dark tonight and see if I can find out anything about Frau Danner. I'll also bring up any food and water I can find."

"I can't stand the thought of you leaving this room. I'm worried about your safety."

"I know," he said. "But I have no choice."

It began to grow dark, and Margot felt sick in the pit of her stomach. She knew that soon Ben was going to leave the attic, and she would almost have rather starved than put him in danger. He stood up and glanced at the tiny space between the window shades. "It looks like the sun has set," he said. "I'm going to go downstairs now."

"No," she said, grabbing his arm. "Not yet. Wait a little while. Go during the middle of the night. Even if one of the curtains is open, it will be less likely that anyone will see you then."

"All right. I'll wait a few hours."

Neither of them spoke much. She sat beside him with her head on his shoulder. It was getting late, and Ben stood up to go, but before he opened the door to leave the attic, he and Margot heard footsteps on the stairs. They stared at each other wild-eyed because these footsteps were not the soft ones they were familiar with from Frau Danner's shoes. These were hard shoes. They clicked as the heels hit the stairs. Margot gripped Ben's arm. She felt like her heart was going to explode in her chest. With her other hand, she grabbed Ben's hand. He squeezed her hand in return. Then he touched her face. "Margot," he said in a whisper.

"They've found us," she said softly.

"I think so." He nodded.

CHAPTER 18

Trudy was disappointed that she could not bring all her things to Max's apartment. Max gently explained that she would have to siphon through her clothes and decide which ones she loved the best. And take only those. She had a large walk-in closet in the sprawling home she'd shared with Rudy. So, she hadn't realized how little room there would be for her things in Max's apartment. It was as if she'd completely forgotten what it was like to be poor. Max waited patiently while Trudy picked and chose what she would bring. But even after she'd finished and had left a great deal of her things behind, Max could see that she was still taking too much with her. He wanted to tell her she must leave even more behind, but he knew it would start an argument. So, he carried what he could back to his apartment. Then, he made a second trip the same day and picked up the rest. But even though Max had made a tremendous effort to keep Trudy happy, he could see she was losing her desire and admiration for him.

Two weeks had passed since Trudy moved in with Max, and it seemed like a lifetime to him. His ability to perform sexually with Trudy was still lacking, and she was no longer kind to him. She had changed her attitude since that first night they'd been together. Now, she no longer kept quiet when he failed to perform. She would glare at him and say hurtful things to him. He didn't care what she thought of him. But he found her disgusting, and sometimes his anger was so great that it took everything he had not to tell her what he thought of her. But he knew it was best not to retaliate. He was waiting, biding his time. Praying that Margot was still alive. *If only I knew where to begin to look for Margot. I'm at my wit's end. I can't believe she is gone. I'm lost without her.*

He was worried every day, and he prayed Margot hadn't been arrested for any reason. *What if Trudy told the Gestapo about Margot being Jewish, and she is keeping it from me that she turned her sister in? She knows I would throw her out on the street if I found out she did that. So, she'd never admit it to me even if I asked her. I would try to check the arrest records if I could, but I have no way of doing that.* Max could not check arrest records because his job was not important, and consequently, he had no access to such files. And despite the fact that he'd made acquaintances who worked in government offices and police stations, he couldn't ask them to help him. He dared not ask them to let him see the current arrest files. They would ask too many questions. So far, things had been quiet concerning Rudy's death. It seemed that the police had accepted what Trudy had told them. They believed it was suicide, and the case was closed. Max knew that it was very important that there was never a reason for the case to be reopened. The police must never doubt that Rudy had committed suicide or had any reason to search for Margot.

Max was restless. He felt like an animal in a cage trapped by Trudy. There were times when his frustration was so strong that he felt like he could kill her. He did not sleep well. His dreams were fitful. Often, he dreamed of Margot, of finding her and running away from this terrible place. He didn't care where they went. He would be content to live with her on an island somewhere, as long as they were far away from the Nazi death machine. However, other times, his dreams made him shiver. The worst was when he dreamed that Margot was dead, and he would wake up still sobbing with his pillow wet with tears. Other times, he would wake up in sweat-soaked sheets, trembling, after having hideous dreams of strangling Trudy, her eyes bulging as he squeezed the life out of her. These nightmares were so real that he feared someday he might lose control and act on this horrible fantasy. Cruel and vicious thoughts like these were unlike Max. Before Hitler and the Nazis had come to power, Max had been an easy-going person, kind and soft-spoken. Yet, he found that now he was no longer that gentleman. He had been pushed to the limit, and what scared him most was that he hardly knew himself anymore.

CHAPTER 19

Max was right. Trudy was bored with him. She missed going out to parties and flirting with Rudy's friends. And it seemed Max was always working, too tired to go out, or he preferred to save his money. One afternoon, after Trudy had reread all of her movie magazines, she devised a plan. *Maybe I will make Max jealous. That will surely spark his interest.* So, the next afternoon, when Max had come home early from work, she slipped away into a room where Max couldn't hear her, then she picked up the telephone and called the local police station.

"I'd like to speak with Officer Lucas Heinz," she said, thinking of how flattered she'd been by the young man's attentions to her when he had come to her house to report Rudy's death.

"Who is this?" a gruff male voice asked.

"Oh," she cooed in a very sexy voice, "an old friend of his."

"Is this an emergency? Because we don't allow calls during working hours."

"Yes, it is. I really need to speak to him."

There was a moment of silence. "Hold the phone. I'll get him. But don't talk too long. I could get into trouble for this."

"Thank you. I won't keep him long. You have my word."

A few minutes later, Lucas answered the phone. "Allo, this is Officer Heinz."

"Lucas, it's Trudy, Rudolf's wife. You remember me, right?"

"Yes, of course, Trudy. I tried to reach you, but your number was disconnected."

"The SS took the house because Rudy was gone. I've been living with Max." She bit her lip. *I shouldn't have told him that about Max. But he would have found out, anyway.* "Max and I are just friends, nothing more. But I couldn't afford to rent an apartment on my own because I don't have a job yet. So, he was kind enough to let me stay with him."

"I see. Well, I would love to take you out for a beer. Are you free tonight?"

This is exactly what I wanted. Now, let me be loud enough for Max to hear. In a loud, cheerful voice, Trudy responded, "I am, as a matter of fact."

"There's this very friendly, busy *Biergarten* that I go to with the other fellows from work. I'd love it if you joined me tonight."

A little louder, she responded, hoping Max would hear, "I can't wait. Where is it, and what time?"

CHAPTER 20

Later that evening, Trudy came out of the bedroom dressed and ready to go out. "I'm going out. I'll see you later," she said. She was hoping to get a rise out of him.

Max just nodded. He was glad to spend the evening alone.

There was nothing to eat in the apartment because Trudy had not gone shopping. So, Max walked to the main street in town and stopped at a café where he had a sausage and a beer. On his way back to the apartment, he saw Trudy in an open *Biergarten*. She was surrounded by policemen, stumbling, laughing too loudly, and flirting. He watched her for a moment and wondered if he should be worried. *I don't care if she had another man. I hope she doesn't tell them anything that incriminates Margot or me. She always talks too much when she's drunk. I'll have to keep a closer eye on her from now on.*

Trudy didn't see Max as he walked back home.

CHAPTER 21

From that night on, Trudy began to see Lucas twice and often three times a week. They always went to the same *Biergarten*. Sometimes, they had dinner first. Other times, they made love in his small apartment. Dating him wasn't as exciting as being married to Rudy, but it wasn't as boring as being with Max. Lucas and his friends were only policemen. They were not nearly as high-ranking as Rudy and his coworkers had been. But she was having fun for the first time since she'd moved in with Max. She was enjoying the flirting and drinking. It made her feel good to know that these men all found her desirable when she could sense that Max did not.

Trudy never noticed that Max had begun to take long walks at night. She didn't realize that he was following her because she wasn't really paying much attention to him these days. Her focus was on what she was going to wear each night she went out. Over the past three weeks, she'd been invited to two luncheons given by wives of other police officers who worked with Lucas, and she was enjoying being a part of something again.

It was difficult for Trudy to keep her drinking to a minimum. When she drank too much, she had a tendency to talk too much. Max knew this about her. And he also knew that she was coming home drunk. This was a concern because he knew he couldn't trust her to keep quiet.

Meanwhile, Lucas was wild about Trudy. He would sneak calls to her from work just to hear her voice. He bought her small tokens of affection. And she was charmed. It made her head spin to know this man was falling madly in love with her.

"Move out of Max's house and marry me," Lucas said one night when he and Trudy had finished making love.

Trudy was taken with him but not so taken that she was willing to marry him. She had already made the mistake of moving in with Max and saw how life was with a man not rising in the Party. It was true that she had grown tired of Max. But if she were going to marry again, she wanted a husband who was as successful and ambitious as Rudy had been.

"I can't. Not yet. It would be too scandalous. I think I should wait for a while. It's too soon after Rudy's death."

"I have a question for you," he said. "You must tell me the truth."

"Of course."

"Are you and Max really just friends, or are you lovers?"

How does he know this? She thought. *How can he tell?* "We are just old friends. He was married to my sister. She is the one that turned out to be adopted. She was having an affair with Rudy."

"That's terrible."

"Yes, it was very sad for Max. He was heartbroken. But we were always friends, so when I needed a place to stay, he insisted I stay with him."

CHAPTER 22

One evening, Max returned from work exhausted and not feeling well. He went straight to bed and would have fallen asleep had he not overheard Trudy talking to someone on the phone. Trudy was explaining that her sister, Margot, was adopted and that she might have been Jewish. Max felt a shiver run down his spine. *She thinks I am asleep and that I can't hear her. But she must be talking to that man she's been seeing. The policeman. I can't let this get out. They might start searching for Margot. I have to take care of this right away.*

Trudy laughed on the phone and talked for nearly a half hour. Max was trembling in bed, worried about what she might say next.

That evening, Trudy went out. As always, she returned drunk. Max was awake, sitting in the living room, drinking whiskey when she arrived. "I know you are seeing someone. What are you telling him?"

"How dare you accuse me?" she said.

"Trudy." His voice was loud and harsh. "I don't care that you are seeing someone. I want to know if you are telling him things you shouldn't be telling him. Things about Margot, about Rudy's death, about me. What are you telling him, Trudy?"

"Don't you dare sit there and question me? You are not worthy of me. You can't even give me what I need. What did you think was going to happen? Of course, I met someone else."

"I don't care about that. But you are talking too much. You're going to land us both in a prison camp if you don't shut up."

"You're the one who likes Jews, not me."

"Trudy, shut up. I've never hit a woman, and I don't want to hit you. But you're going to make me do it."

"You make me sick," she said. Then she walked out of the room.

The following night, Trudy went out to meet Lucas at the *Biergarten*. As soon as she left, Max followed her. He waited all night until, finally, Lucas walked Trudy back to her apartment. Then Max followed Lucas. He knew Lucas was headed home because he knew where Lucas lived. Max had followed him and Trudy to his apartment before. Lucas was quite drunk. He was ambling along at a slow, leisurely pace. Max ran ahead and waited in an alleyway. When Lucas passed, Max grabbed him from behind. The shock of it paralyzed Lucas for a moment, and that was just enough time for Max to snap the policeman's neck. Before he left, Max checked Lucas for a pulse. He was dead. *Now, he won't be any danger to Margot.* He thought.

CHAPTER 23

L ucas' body was found the following day. One of his friends telephoned Trudy to tell her the news. She was stunned and devastated. Trudy couldn't be sure if Max had done this, but she thought he might have. And now, she was feeling a little afraid of him. If she was correct, he had killed two men. Her husband and her lover. Max was more dangerous than she had initially thought. And somehow, she must get rid of him. But she must also be very careful, or she could be next. Because of this, she did not mention Lucas' death to Max. Instead, she decided to stay quiet until she could find a safe way out.

CHAPTER 24

Margot and Ben held hands tightly as they waited for the attic door to open. "Margot, I don't know if I ever told you, but I must tell you now, just in case I never have another opportunity." He squeezed her hand. She felt tears fall hot on her cheeks. Then he said in a choked voice, I never stopped loving…"

The door swung open. "I'm so sorry," Frau Danner said. She carried a single candle. "My sister was ill. I had to go to her. I was so upset that I forgot to bring you food." She set a basket on the floor and closed the door behind her.

"Is your sister all right?" Ben asked.

By the light of the single candle, Margot saw Frau Danner shake her head. "No, she passed. I just realized that you probably listen to the sound of my shoes on the stairs, and these are different shoes. They were my sisters."

"Oh, I am so sorry about your loss," Margot said.

"Yes, I'm sorry for your loss," Ben echoed.

"There is nothing more I can do for her. At least I know her suffering is over."

"She was sick?" Ben asked.

"She had a hard life. Her husband left her when she was very young. She never remarried. We were very close. A few days ago, she came down with a fever. When she had her neighbor call to tell me that she needed me, that she was dying, I went right away. It wasn't that I forgot about the two of you. I was just so frightened to hear that my sister was so ill. She was older than me, and I was afraid she would die without my having a chance to say goodbye. You know? I just wanted to say goodbye." Frau Danner grew silent. But Margot could see the tears lit up like tiny diamonds on the old woman's face, and she knew Frau Danner was crying.

For a while, no one said a word. It seemed like a long, awkward silence. Then Frau Danner said, "When I first got to my sister's house and saw that she was very sick, I thought about coming back here to ask you, Ben, if you would come with me and examine her. I thought maybe you could do something. But it was too late. By the next morning, she was gone. Besides, it would have been terribly dangerous."

He didn't say a word.

"Anyway," Frau Danner cleared her throat. "I haven't been able to eat. And my sister couldn't eat either. So, the basket I brought you two has more food than usual."

"Thank you," Ben said. "Thank you for everything."

"Yes, thank you," Margot said. "I wish there was something we could do for you."

"Eh, there is nothing. My life is empty. My daughter is gone. My sister is gone now, too. I am alone." She hesitated. "But at least I have the two of you. Yes?" She tried to sound cheerful.

"I'm afraid we're more of a burden than anything else," Ben said.

"No, I'm glad to help you. I have nothing to lose anymore. If the Gestapo should come for me, I have a little something that I can use to help me. It's a pill that I stole from a soldier who came here and spent the night a few months ago."

"What are you talking about?" Margot asked.

"It's a little pill. The soldiers use it to end their lives if they are being interrogated. For me, it would put an end to all of this. If I am captured, then I'll take it. Then, at least, they won't be able to torture me."

"A pill that will kill you?" Margot said, shocked.

"Yes, that's what it is. When the soldier was here, it fell out of his pocket. I picked it up for him. It was in a little vial. When I gave it back to him, I asked him what it was. He told me. Then he put it back into his coat pocket. But when he fell asleep that night, I stole the pill. He didn't notice in the morning, and I have been keeping it just in case."

"Ben, have you ever heard of such a thing?" Margot asked.

"Yes," he nodded. "It's a cyanide pill. The top Nazis all have them, from what I've heard."

She gasped. "Well, please don't use that. We need you, Frau Danner."

"Of course. And I know that. But what I am trying to say is that I have no fear of getting caught. I won't use it unless I have to, which would only be if I were being tortured for information. I would take the pill before I would tell them about you two being here in my attic."

Margot didn't realize it, but she and Ben still held hands. She loosened her grip, and he let his hand go. She thought he must not have realized it, either.

"I hate to impose because you have done so much for us. But there is something very important that I must ask of you," Ben said.

"Go ahead," Frau Danner said. "I'll do what I can for you."

"Margot's husband, Max, is a friend of mine. He is very kind, and he is a gentile man. Right now, he is probably searching desperately for Margot. But because of what happened between Margot and her sister, I am afraid to let Margot go home. I was wondering if you would go to him and tell him where Margot is and that she is safe."

"What happened between Margot and her sister?" Frau Danner asked.

"It's a long story," Margot said.

"I have time. If you want me to do this for you, you must tell me everything. I can't do such a thing without knowing all the details. I don't want any surprises."

Margot shot Ben a quick glance. Ben nodded. "Tell her everything."

"Everything, even about Rudy?"

"Yes, everything," Ben said.

"All right. I'll tell you," Margot said, adding, "but you must keep all of this a secret."

Frau Danner let out a short laugh. "Yes, I know. I have kept the two of you here in my attic a secret. So, I can assure you that I can be trusted to keep this secret, too."

Margot nodded, and then she told the old woman all about how the Nazis had murdered her son, all about her vicious sister Trudy and how Max had shot Rudy, who was an SS Officer.

When Margot finished her story, Frau Danner said, "When I go to the apartment where you lived with your husband, would you like me to tell him that he can come at night and find you here?"

"Yes," Margot said. "Would you do that?"

There was a moment of silence. Then Frau Danner said, "I'll do it tomorrow evening." She stood up and stretched her back. "I'll come by late tomorrow night when it's dark and let you know what happened."

Frau Danner left the attic, taking the single candle with her.

CHAPTER 25

Ben tore a hunk of bread in half and handed half of it to Margot. They both ate without a word for several moments. Then Margot asked, "Do you think she'll actually do it?"

"I think she will," Ben said.

They finished their bread and drank from the same bottle of water that Frau Danner had brought them.

"I have never been so hungry," Margot said.

"Yes, I was hungry too."

"Are you afraid for her?"

"Of course. I am afraid for all of us," Ben said. "I wish we knew what was going on at your old apartment. I wish I knew if Max was all right. He could be gone; he could have been arrested for shooting Rudy."

"I have been so afraid that Max has been arrested for shooting Rudy. I have been worried about it every minute of every day. But I've been too terrified to put it into words. I was afraid that if I said it, it would be true. I know that's childish, but I can't help it. My poor sweet Max. If he has been arrested for shooting a Nazi officer, they will punish him severely. He's not an important member of the Nazi Party. He just has a small, insignificant job. I'm afraid they will kill him.

They don't care about human life. Oh, dear God, I pray that hasn't happened."

"It's all right. Don't get worked up. We have to stay calm and wait until Frau Danner returns."

"But, Ben, Max might even be dead already." The words caught in her throat, and she began to cough.

"Calm down. This isn't helping Max and certainly isn't doing you any good. Here…" Ben handed Margot the bottle of water, "drink some water."

"But I already had some," she choked out the words between coughs. "We won't have enough."

"It's all right. Just sip a little. Then, once you are calmed down, take deep breaths. I am here with you. I'll be here with you; whatever happens, we'll face it together."

Margot calmed down enough to stop the coughing but couldn't sleep that night. Every possible scenario dashed through her troubled mind. She was worried about the old woman. She was worried about what had become of Max, and she was also worried about Ben and herself. *I am afraid I shouldn't have asked Frau Danner to go find out about Max. If the poor old woman is taken away, she might not turn Ben and me in, but the Nazis will come and confiscate the house. Then what? Where will Ben and I go? At least I have papers saying I am a gentile. If Trudy had not caused her any problems either by blaming me for Rudy's death somehow or by turning me in for being Jewish, I would have been able to leave Berlin. But not Ben. Ben has no papers or a way to survive other than this tiny attic. I could not leave him behind. I would not do that.*

A terrible wave of guilt came over her. She longed to let Max know she was safe, yet she had put two other people in danger to accomplish this. She lay there with her eyes open in the darkness and listened. Ben's breathing grew slow and steady, and she knew he'd fallen asleep. It was difficult for her to sleep because they spent their days without doing much of anything. She tried not to think about the following day. She tried to turn her thoughts to better times when she was still a girl in school, and she and Ben worked on science projects together. But tonight Margot thought of Max. As she lay there, her mind began to drift. She recalled an afternoon when she had gone swimming in the pond with Max before Erik was born. She and Max were young, still newlyweds. They swam and played in the water for hours, then ate the picnic lunch she'd brought. *I am in love with two men. It wouldn't make sense to anyone else. But it's as simple as that. I love them both. I always have.* She turned over on the hard floor and glanced at Ben, who was sleeping soundly. Her heart swelled with affection for him. *No, I can't leave Berlin. I'd rather die than leave him here alone.*

CHAPTER 26

The following day, Margot was nervous and edgy. There was nothing to do in the attic but worry, and although she tried to fight off the feelings of dread consuming her, she couldn't. If something happened to Frau Danner, she would never forgive herself. It would not only be a tragedy for the old woman, but it would endanger Ben and his hiding place. She began to wish she had not asked Frau Danner to go to her apartment. But there was no turning back now. It was far too dangerous to go downstairs and tell the old woman she'd changed her mind. The hours moved slowly. Ben tried his best to comfort her. He rubbed her shoulders and promised everything would be all right. But she wasn't sure that it would. Finally, the tiny bit of light that filtered through the shade was fading, and she knew it was quickly growing dark outside. Her stomach felt queasy as she asked Ben, "Do you think she's gone to my apartment yet?"

"I don't know," Ben said. "It looks like it's early evening outside. So, she's probably on her way there right now."

"This waiting here in this closed-in place, not knowing what is going on outside, is driving me crazy," Margot moaned as she squeezed her temples.

"It's true. You're right. It's driving me crazy as well," Ben said. "You should eat something. You haven't eaten a thing today."

"Would you believe I forgot? It's not like we are busy here. But my mind is elsewhere."

He laughed a little. "I would believe you forgot. I forget sometimes, too. Although we have nothing to do, our minds are always thinking and driving us a little bit mad." He smiled and touched her hand, then in a gentle voice, he coaxed, "Come on, eat a little."

She nodded, although he could only see her shadow in the half-darkened room. He watched her as she took a hunk of bread out of the basket and tore it in half. She handed him his half, then took a bite of the other half.

"It's hard to do nothing all day. I would give anything to have a book and light to read it." She sighed.

"You could light a candle during the day and read by it. Because it's light outside, no one would see it. But I don't know if it would be enough light. You'd have to try it."

"I'd hate to waste the candle. What if we need it later?"

"It's not a waste. It's food for your soul. And that's just as important as your body," he said.

CHAPTER 27

Frau Danner took the bus, getting as close as she could to the address Margot had given her. She knew Berlin very well, so it was not difficult for her to find her way. After she got off the bus, she walked for a while and arrived at the apartment building. No one on the street took notice of the old woman in her well-worn, dark-colored wool coat as she made her way up the stairs and to the door of Max's apartment. She shivered, both from the cold and a little from nerves, as she knocked on the door. It was early evening, but she assumed Max would be home from work.

It didn't take long for a pretty young woman with curly blonde hair and stunning red lipstick to open the door. "Who are you, and what do you want?" the woman said curtly.

"I'm looking for Max Kraus."

"Who are you?"

"An old friend," Frau Danner replied, her lips quivering as she smiled.

"I know all of my husband's friends, and you are not one of them."

"I am the mother of a friend of his from work." Frau Danner said as calmly as she could, remembering the whole story that Margot had told her about Max working for the postal service.

"What is it you want to tell him? I can relay your message to him when he gets home."

Frau Danner felt the hair on the back of her neck bristle. *Who is this woman? Is it possible that this could be Trudy, Margot's sister? Why would she be living here with Max? Why would he allow her to move in with him? Or has he been arrested for Rudy's murder, and now Trudy has taken over his apartment? It could also be possible that this isn't Trudy at all. It could be another woman, someone who had no connection to Margot. But she had referred to Max as her husband. Did he marry someone after Margot disappeared?* Frau Danner had a million questions, but she could see by how this woman treated her that it was best that she proceed very carefully. She'd come all this way, yet now she wasn't feeling as brave as she had the night before. If this was Trudy, she was as cold as Margot described her to be, and chances were good that she would call the police and say that an old woman was bothering her. But even if it wasn't Trudy, this girl was not welcoming and could very well call the police. Frau Danner decided to make up a story and get out of there before the young woman started asking her questions. "All right. I'll give you a quick message to relay," Frau Danner said, smiling just a little. "Please, can you tell him that Frau Meir, Hans Meir's mother, came by and said that Hans is feeling better and will return to work at the postal service tomorrow?"

Trudy looked at the old woman skeptically. "The postal service?" she asked. "Max doesn't work there anymore. He's been transferred. Your son should know that."

"Oh, well, it's been a while since my son was at work. He's been very ill. He had surgery in the hospital and has been gone for a while."

"I see," Trudy said, smiling as if she knew the old woman was lying.

Frau Danner shivered, "All right then, I will go. Please relay the message."

"Oh, but of course I will," Trudy said, closing the door.

Frau Danner was ashamed of her cowardice. She thought of all the things she might have said as she made her way back to the bus stop. *I was afraid of her. I still am. I am certain she knew I was lying. It's funny how the nature of living things is. Even an old woman doesn't want to die.*

CHAPTER 28

Trudy closed the door and sat on the sofa, waiting for Max. *Lying old woman.* She thought. *Who was she, and why was she really here? I am sure it has to do with Margot.* Max had telephoned earlier that day to say that there was a mix-up in the inventory, and because of this, he would be late coming home from work. Trudy got up, poured herself a glass of schnapps from the bottle she'd left on the coffee table, and then lit a cigarette. *Max isn't as wonderful as I thought he would be. For years, I thought he was going to be the man of my dreams, but it turns out he's not. He's still very handsome, but he's a terrible lover. And, I must admit, I miss Rudy. He wasn't perfect by any means, but we had a lot of fun together. Rudy understood me, but Max doesn't understand me at all. When Rudy and I were married, I could shop for whatever I wanted to my heart's content. We traveled. Yes, I always knew he had other women, and I didn't like it. But he never let it interfere with his home life. Max isn't running around. He always comes right home after work. And I think he's over Margot. But he is boring. We don't have enough money for me to buy pretty dresses, and we never go out for dinner. He expects me to cook his meals every night. He looks at me as if I've committed a crime if I don't cook and there's nothing to eat. Then and only then*

will he prepare something for himself. I am sick of him. I miss the fancy restaurants and the parties with important people. Even so, I still hate my sister, and if Margot ever returned, I wouldn't let her have him. I'd have her arrested. She deserves to suffer. It's her fault that Rudy is gone. It's her fault that I became so obsessed with Max. She dangled him in front of me like he was a jewel or something. Everything that is wrong with my life is Margot's fault. Besides that, it's my duty to have her arrested. After all, I know that she's a Jew. And everyone knows that Jews are bad for Germany.

By the time Max returned home, Trudy was fast asleep in bed.

CHAPTER 29

As Frau Danner returned home from her attempt to find Max, she quickly drew the curtains and lit a candle. Then, even before having her evening meal, she went up the stairs to the attic. "It's me," she whispered, turning the key in the lock.

Margot's heart raced. Ben took her hand. They waited. The old woman entered. "Did you see him?" Margot asked, perhaps a little too abruptly.

"No, I'm sorry. But I think I saw your sister, Trudy."

"Trudy? She was at my apartment? Are you sure it was her?"

"I am not sure, but from how you describe her, I think it was her."

"Has Max been arrested?" Margot asked, squeezing Ben's hand.

"I don't think so. The girl who I saw said that Max wasn't home from work yet but that she would give him a message for me. That led me to believe that he has not been arrested but still lives there," Frau Danner answered.

"But of course, you couldn't leave a message," Ben said. "What did you do?"

"Well, I couldn't leave the real message I wanted to give him. But I had to say something, so I told her that I was the mother of one of Max's coworkers and that my son had been ill. He'd had surgery, but he was feeling better and would return to work tomorrow. By the way, she said that Max is no longer working at the postal service. He's been transferred?"

"Where?" Margot asked.

"I don't know. I couldn't ask. She wasn't the easiest person to talk to."

"It was Trudy," Margot agreed.

There was a short silence, and Ben said, "Max is smart. If Trudy gives him this message, he'll know that this has something to do with you, Margot."

"You think so?" Margot asked.

"Well, unless he has a sick coworker who has been out of the office for a while, he will know this is a false message. Besides, if Trudy tells him that his coworker didn't know he was transferred, he'll think something is up."

"I gave her a false name," Frau Danner said.

"But the message doesn't really tell him anything. I mean, I guess if he thinks it is from me, it will give him hope that I am alive," Margot replied.

"Exactly. Think about it. Why else would he receive a strange message from an older woman he doesn't know?"

"I can only hope that this works," Margot said.

"Yes, and me too. I want him to know that you are safe."

"But do you think Trudy will actually give him the message?" Margot leaned against the wall. The futility of the situation was dragging her down. "I doubt it," she answered her own question in a small voice. "Trudy is smarter than that. She'll know it was me."

"Maybe not," he said. "It could have been the mother of one of his coworkers. Try to stay positive if you can."

"Oh, Ben, I'm afraid I will never see Max again."

"I know. I understand." He took her hand in his.

"I've lost my son. I let him go with a stranger, and now he's dead." She began crying. "I was so angry about my little boy that I caused these problems with my sister and her husband. It didn't help me. It only made things worse. Now, I might never see Max again."

"Shhh, don't think that way. It will do you no good. Let's try to think about something else."

"There's nothing else to think about. I may never see my mother or my sister Mattie again, either. All this uncertainty is driving me crazy. Whenever I hear a siren outside, I am sure they have found us. I feel like I am going mad sitting in the dark all day with nothing to do but wait for them to come."

"I know how you feel. But instead of thinking about the Nazis finding us, think about the end of the war when we'll be free," he said softly. "Believe me, I know it's hard. But you must try to keep your mind steady, or you really will go crazy."

"Oh, Ben, I am not strong. I can't bear it. We never see the sunshine or even the light of day. We sit here in the darkness and contemplate all the horrible things that could be happening to our loved ones and eventually to us. What's the point of going on?"

"The point is that we are lucky to be alive. God's greatest gift is life. As long as we are alive, there is hope. And no matter what happens when this is over, we can start our lives again."

"I used to believe that. But I am doubtful now."

Frau Danner stood up. "I am going to leave you two now. I'm tired and hungry. I'll see you in a couple of days." She stood up and left the attic, closing the door slowly behind her.

After the old woman left, there was a long silence, and then Ben said, "I have a story to tell you. Do you want to hear it?"

"Sure, yes, tell me."

He smiled. "When I was a little boy, I used to tell my father that I didn't want to live if I couldn't be good at athletics. I wanted to be popular, to have lots of friends. And to have everyone admire me. But that was not my calling. I wanted it, but I wasn't meant to be an athlete. I was meant to be a doctor, to save lives. And later, when I grew up, I saved the life of a boy I knew when we were both in school. He was an athlete who had become a soldier and was badly wounded."

"So, what's your point?" she said. She found that she was losing patience.

But Ben ignored her loss of patience and said slowly and softly, "My point is that we all have a purpose for being here on earth. God has sent each of us here with a gift. We have a reason for living and can't give up on our destiny. Do you know why?"

"Why?"

"Because every job every person was sent to earth to do is important. Every one of us has the potential to do God's work."

"What about the Nazis? Are they doing God's work?"

"No, of course not. But that is because they are not following their inner guidance. They're too busy following Hitler."

"Hmm…" she groaned. "Is this always true, Ben? Does every person have a destiny?"

"Yes, every single person here on earth has a destiny. It might be something earth-shattering, like saving a life. It might not be a form of fortune or fame, like a movie star or an athlete. But, believe me, God has a purpose for all of us. And I believe that we must honor the gift of life that he has given us so that we can use our lives to fulfill our reason for being on earth."

There was a long silence, and then Margot said, "I think my purpose was to be a mother. And I wasn't a good one. I should have been smarter. I should have known better. Somehow, I should have protected my son."

"You didn't know what these monsters had in mind for Erik. Who would ever think that anyone could be so cruel? It's hard to fathom. You were only doing what you believed was right, and being a mother may well have been one of the reasons God sent you here. But you are still alive, so there is more coming."

"How can you be so sure?"

"I am sure." He said in a comforting tone. Then he took her hand and squeezed it. "I may not know what God has in store. But whatever it is, I know it is our job to see it through."

She took her hand away and said, "Do you want to know what I am really feeling, Ben? I'm angry with God. Why would he let them kill my innocent child? Erik never sinned; he never broke God's laws. So why? Why did he have to die? And then, after I lost my boy, it wasn't enough for God. He had to take my unborn baby, too. Why?" Her voice was louder than usual.

"I don't know why God does what he does. I wish I could tell you,

Margot. I understand your anger, and I have no answers for you. But what I can tell you is that Erik and your unborn child are both free of this world and are with God now. They will not suffer anymore."

She was weeping. "This isn't what I thought my life would be like," she said. "I thought I would have children and raise them. They would marry and have children, and someday, I would be a grandmother."

"This is not the way I thought my life would be either," he said. "But I keep reminding myself that God has a reason. And someday, we'll understand why all of this happened."

Margot couldn't talk anymore. She shook her head, then curled into a fetal position on the cold attic floor and tried to sleep.

As Margot slept, Ben looked at her. He could hear her breathing finally go steady, and in a soft whisper, he said, "Maybe your purpose was to be here with me. The light you have brought into this little attic with me has given purpose to my life. When I hear your little moans in your sleep or when you touch my hand, I feel I am being blessed by God that you are here with me."

CHAPTER 30

Trudy didn't see Max when he arrived home that night, and she was still asleep when he got up for work the following morning. So, she hadn't mentioned the visitor who had left him a strange message. She wanted to see the look on his face when he told her about it. That evening, Max was late getting home from work again. After nine pm, the key turned in the lock, and the door opened. Max was home, and Trudy was annoyed. She'd wanted to go to a *Biergarten* that night. Instead, she knew that if she asked him to go out to eat, he would say it was too late because he had to be up for work in the morning, so they were stuck inside again.

"I'm sorry," he said. "Someone miscounted the steel sheets, and we had to recount them all so that we could get our order right."

"How exciting," Trudy said sarcastically.

"It wasn't. I'll admit that. But we need the money, so I must do whatever they ask so I can keep this job. But I have to tell you, I miss carpentry."

"That doesn't sound very exciting either," she said.

"I loved it. I loved the feeling of working with wood. Of creating something out of nothing."

"Yes, I suppose," she said, then lit a cigarette. "There's nothing for

121

dinner. I didn't go to the store today to buy food because I wanted to go to the *Biergarten* tonight. I thought maybe we could have a beer and a sausage."

"I'm sorry," he said.

"Can we still go? I know it's late, and you have to get up early, but we must have something to eat. Can't we just go for a little while?"

He nodded. "All right. I'm hungry, and so are you. But we can't stay late. I must get up early, as you know."

"Yes, I know." Then she remembered the strange old woman who had come by to leave a message the day before, and she wanted to see Max's face when she told him about it, so she said, "You had a visitor."

"A visitor?" he seemed concerned. "Who, not the police?"

"No, it was an old woman. She knew your name. She said you worked with her son at the postal office."

"Oh? Who is her son?"

"She said his name is Hans Meir. She wanted me to tell you that Hans would be returning to work tomorrow at the postal office. She didn't know you didn't work there anymore."

For a moment, Max was stunned. He didn't know anyone by that name and could not recall anyone by that name at his previous job. Yet this old woman had come to his house and told Trudy this elaborate story. *This must have something to do with Margot.* "Yes, of course, Hans Meir. I remember him," he lied. Then he asked, "Did she say anything else?"

"No, that's all. What else would she say?"

"Oh, I don't know. I just wondered. I suppose her son didn't know I had been transferred." *Be careful. You must not let on that you think this is about Margot. Whoever the old woman is, she might return and deliver more messages from Margot. Maybe the message that her son is feeling well is really a way for her to let me know that Margot is feeling well. I have been worried that she would get sick because of everything that had happened with Rudy.*

CHAPTER 31

M argot couldn't escape her melancholy feelings. She told herself that she should be grateful to be alive. Still, her circumstances overwhelmed her, and sometimes, she was afraid she couldn't endure what the future might hold for her.

As they sat on the floor one afternoon staring at the tiny flicker of light that filtered through the opening in the shade, Margot said, "Ben, I am grateful to be alive. And I am grateful to be here with you. But I find it hard to believe everything that has happened to me, you, and everyone we love."

"I know. Me too," Ben said.

"I am brokenhearted over Trudy. It's not that I didn't know Trudy was jealous of me when we were growing up. She made no secret of the fact that she wanted Max to marry her. And even then, I thought she only wanted him because he wanted me. But I always thought that when things were all sorted out, she was my sister, and there was a bond between us. Never in my wildest imagination would I have believed she could have done the terrible things she did. Allowing my son to be murdered. Forcing me into hiding like this. I have to admit, I never really knew her."

"This government has had a strange effect on lots of people. It has brought out the ugliness they used to be ashamed of."

"Yes, I know that too."

Ben shook his head. "I can't tell you how many horrible things I've seen. And these things were done by my neighbors, who I thought were our friends. My life has changed too, Margot. It has changed in so many terrible ways. My father and mother are both dead. The young girl who lived next door, the one who helped me with my in-home medical practice, was taken away by the Gestapo. There was no reason for it. One day, she was just gone. A young, healthy woman. I don't know if she is even still alive. Her parents, too. I don't want to go into detail about the violence against Jewish souls that I have witnessed on the streets of our small neighborhood. Or about the people who came to me beaten up and bleeding on the day after that riot, the one they call *Kristallnacht*. Some were harmless, unable to fight back, old people and children. It was a sin. I'd rather not tell you anymore because I wouldn't want to make you even sadder than you already are. Let's just say that we have both experienced terrible things. You are not alone. But we are lucky to be alive."

She sighed. "Yes, lucky."

"I'm glad you're here with me," he said with a twinge of hope in his voice. "I would never have wished this on you, Max, and sweet little Erik. But if it had to be this way, I am glad you're here."

She didn't answer. She had to admit that she was glad to be with him. It would have been far worse for her if she had never found him. In fact, she would probably be dead. And, if she were completely honest with herself, she had to admit she had never stopped loving him. But she loved Max too, and it was hard not knowing if he was all right. Her heart ached for her husband and her dead children.

They were both quiet for a long while, perhaps a half hour, maybe a full hour. Time had no meaning in the attic. Then, Margot heard the laughter of young girls coming from the street outside, and she was suddenly overcome with memories of her teenage years when she walked home from school with her sisters. She remembered going out after school to shop at the resale stores with Mattie and Trudy. She recalled the Christmas season when the three of them searched for pinecones to string and hang on their Christmas tree. They had all three been so young then, and she had believed that no matter what happened between them, they would always be sisters and close. Her throat hurt from holding back the tears, and then it ached with thirst, and she thought about the water bottle. There wasn't much water left, and they had to make do until Frau Danner brought more. So she swallowed hard, her tongue feeling like sandpaper. Then, she softly asked, "Do you think it's true?"

"What's true?"

"You know. The things Trudy said about me."

"You mean about you having been adopted and your mother having been Jewish?"

"Yes, that?"

He sighed long and hard. "I don't know. But it could be." He hesitated momentarily, then said, "You know, it really wasn't so bad growing up in a Jewish family."

"Tell me about it, Ben. What was it like?"

"Well, there was a real sense of community in our neighborhood. It seemed that everyone I knew belonged to the same *shul*. We all had the same friends. We had *Shabbat* dinners together sometimes. And if someone was in trouble or needed help of any kind, we helped each other."

"*Shul*? What is that?"

"Synagogue."

"And *Shabbat*?"

"Shabbat is the holiday that falls on every Friday night."

"Oh."

"Yes, Friday nights were special. During the day on Friday, my mother would clean the house and prepare a special dinner for *Shabbat*. When the sun set, we would all gather around the table, and my mother would light two candles and say a blessing over them. After we lit the candles, we would walk to the *shul* for a short service."

"Like a sermon?"

"Yes. Exactly. I guess you could say it was a lot like what going to church on Sunday must have been for you. Then, after the service, we would walk home and have dinner as a family. It was almost like a celebration dinner. I miss those the most. I can still hear my father singing *birkat hamazon*, a prayer similar to grace after a meal."

Margot listened with her eyes closed, smiling.

"The next morning, which, of course, was Saturday, we relaxed. It is a holy day for us. We wake up and go to *Shabbat* services again until lunch, and then we come home and have a wonderful stew my mother makes called Cholent. It's made with meat, beans, potatoes, and barley. Oh, Margot, I can just close my eyes and taste it now."

"My mouth is watering. That sounds so wonderful."

"It really was. After lunch, we would discuss torah or play chess. Sometimes, my father would take a nap. It was a special day with family."

"It reminds me of Christmas, but you did it every week." Margot paused for a moment. "I guess you didn't celebrate Christmas. Of course, you wouldn't have. But I have such memories of Christmas with my sisters and Max."

"We didn't celebrate Christmas, but we had our own holidays." He sighed wistfully. "And I have such beautiful memories of them, my parents, and our friends. There were the high holidays in the autumn: *Rosh Hashana*, the Jewish New Year, and *Yom Kippur*, the day of atonement. I always loved *Sukkot*. On that holiday, we built a sukkah, which is like a little outside dwelling. Then there were Passover and *Hanukah*. All the children loved Hanukah. That was when we said prayers and lit candles for eight days, and each day of the eight days, the children received a present."

"It sounds like you liked growing up Jewish."

"I did. Most of the men in our neighborhood had served in the armed forces in the Great War. They were very proud to be German. But they were also proud to be Jews. So many of them thought that they were German first and Jewish second. I suppose that Hitler made it clear that was not the truth."

"Did your father serve?"

"He did. And he was so proud of being a German. For a long time, he refused to believe that Germany was turning on us. He thought all of this Jew-hatred would pass. He always said that Germany was too civilized to have a pogrom against the Jews. He loved his fellow countrymen. He'd always tell people that the Germans were brilliant people. They were the most brilliant of any country, he'd proclaim, in science and in the arts. That was, of course, until he had no other recourse but to finally accept that we had better get out of his beloved homeland because, as Jews, we just weren't safe here anymore."

She took his hand and held it in both of hers. "I'm so sorry."

He paused for a moment. "He died trying to get visas for the three of us to get us out. It was hard to get them. Many steps had to be taken and in a certain order, too. The Nazis sure didn't make it easy for us to get out. But my father wasn't a rule breaker and didn't want to try to run away. He believed that no matter what, one must follow the laws. So, he went to the police station to get them to sign off on one of the papers we needed to obtain the visas. And, you know what happened? The policeman shot him." Ben let out a bitter laugh. "My father, the German war hero who never broke the law in his life, was shot just for being a Jew."

"How horrible." She paused and squeezed his hand. "Do you wish that you had been born a gentile?"

"Never. I'm proud to be Jewish. My people have suffered for thousands of years because they were Jews. I would never deny their suffering."

"If we had known about me being Jewish, things might have been different for us. Maybe we would have gotten married," she said.

"I would have married you in a minute, whether you were Jewish or not. I loved you, Margot." He sighed. "I still do. And I always will." There was a long silence. Then he heard her crying. "Margot, what is it? I'm sorry if I said something that hurt or offended you."

"It's not you, Ben. It's just that I'm so sad," Margot said. "I don't mean to be ungrateful. I know that I am lucky to be alive, and I am lucky to be here with you, my best friend." She hesitated. "But I can't help it. I am sad. I miss Erik. I can't believe he's dead. He was so young. Sometimes, I have dreams about him. I remember his first step, his first word, and the way he laughed. I hope it didn't hurt him. Oh, Ben. He was such a good little boy. He didn't deserve to die like that."

"I know," he said. "He didn't. He was a sweet child. And I am sorry for what happened to him and to you."

She was weeping loudly now. Ben knew he should try to calm her in case someone was downstairs. But he also knew she had to let her grief out, and so he stifled his need to quiet her and let her cry. He put his hand on hers. She squeezed his hand. Then she said softly, "Sometimes I think I am going mad from all the uncertainty. I don't know if Max is even alive. And I know we are safe for the moment, but I don't know how long we will be safe. I have no idea how long we will be alive. Any time we could be discovered. Tortured, murdered. For no reason, none at all. Ben, why are they doing this to us? Why?" She scratched her arm. Then she said, "I don't feel well. My skin is hot, and it itches all the time. I know it's from nerves, and I should try to control myself. But I can't; I am always uneasy. Always on edge."

"I have an idea. Do you trust me?"

"I trust you."

He stood up and reached out his hand to her. "Let's dance," he said cheerfully.

"What?" she said, shocked that he would suggest something so crazy. "Are you crazy?"

"No." He smiled at her.

She was silent for a moment. "But we have no music."

"I'll sing," he said. "I have a decent voice. You'll see." Then he grabbed her hand and pulled her up.

"All right. All right. I used to love to dance," she said.

"I know. That's why I suggested it." He began to sing. His voice was a deep, sweet baritone, comforting and warm. He took her in his arms and slowly guided her across the dirty attic floor. Then he stopped singing for a moment and said, "Close your eyes." She did as he asked. He went on. "Imagine that we are in a ballroom. There are crystal chandeliers, and the light they shine on you makes you look even more radiant than you are. You are the most beautiful woman in the room." He began to dance with her again. She kept her eyes closed, and he continued, "You are wearing a sky-blue gown made of the finest silk. Your diamond earrings and necklace glitter as they catch the light. I look my best in a black tuxedo. I'm not a handsome man, but I look distinguished."

She laughed. "You are handsome."

"You really think so, huh?"

"Yes. I do."

"Can you see my vision in your mind?"

"I can," she said. "I really can."

"Good, keep it in your mind," he whispered, then began to sing again as he whirled her across the floor. Her eyes were closed, and in her mind, the room transformed from a dirty attic to a magnificent ballroom with marble floors.

He stopped singing for a moment and said, "All the men in the room are looking at you. Do you know why?"

"No," she said softly.

"Because you are the most magnificent-looking girl at this dance." He began to sing again.

"I am the only girl here." She laughed.

"You aren't. Do you know who is here?"

"No."

"Princesses and princes. Dignitaries from all over the world. The president and the first lady from America are here, too. Look, they are sitting at the table right over there at the head of the room. Do you see them?"

"Yes," she giggled, and she could see all of it in her mind's eye. Ben started to sing again, and Margot began to feel better. They danced for fifteen solid minutes until Margot, who was still not fully recovered from her miscarriage, grew tired. "Let's sit down for a while," she said, but she felt better.

They sat down on the floor. Ben, with his back against the wall, Margot across from him.

"Close your eyes again. Because now, waiters with white gloves are bringing in our dinner. Do you know what we are having?"

"Oh, tell me," she said hopefully.

"Roast beef. Potatoes, and a fresh green salad. There are huge baskets of bread on the table, and we can eat to our heart's content."

"You're making me hungry," she admitted. "But I must say that I am enjoying every minute of this."

He broke off a piece of stale bread from the hunk of bread that

Frau Danner had brought. "Keep your eyes closed," he said. "Now open your mouth."

Margot did as Ben asked. He slowly put the bread into her mouth. "Taste this. It was freshly baked last night for this very ball."

The bread tastes so different. She thought. "How is it that this bread tastes so delicious?"

"The human mind is very powerful," Ben said. "You can use your mind to help you whenever you are in a bad situation. You can change your situation by using your imagination. Just like we just did."

She hugged him. "Thank you, Ben. I feel so much better. I know that my problems are not gone, but I feel lighter somehow. And I am grateful to you for helping me to feel this way."

"Did you know that when a person is very sick, their mind plays a big part in whether they will live or die? Not always, but sometimes."

"I never knew that."

"Yes, your mind is your greatest asset. It can be your best friend or your worst enemy. It's all in how you use it."

"Oh, Ben, you are so wise."

He laughed. "Not really. I just understand people. It's only because I studied medicine for so long. I read every book I could get my hands on. I always thought that my purpose in life was to help people. I have wanted to be a doctor for as long as I can remember. I wanted to be a healer. And, because I love you, I want, more than anything, to do whatever I can to make you feel better."

Then, outside, the screaming sound of a siren ripped through the silence in the attic. "Bombs." Margot jumped as she gripped him tightly. "We're being bombed. And we can't leave here and get anywhere safe. We're stuck. If they hit this house, we're done for."

"Yes. I know." He held her close. "Shhh, just close your eyes, and I'll sing to you."

He crooned a love song he'd once heard by an American singer. Softly, he sang into her ear while the siren roared over them, drowning him out. Then, deafening and terrible explosions followed. He held her tightly and continued to sing. She wept softly and prayed for Ben, herself, and Max, wherever he might be. Another bomb exploded; this time, it was even closer. Margot let out a cry and began weeping hard. "We are going to die here," she said with certainty.

"Maybe, maybe not. But if we do, it will be fast, and we will be in each other's arms when it happens."

She needed him. She pulled him tighter. How she needed his warmth and the comfort of his arms. Without another word, she laid her head on his chest. His heartbeat was soft in her ear. Then she kissed him on the lips. He let out a sigh, a sigh of longing, a sigh of years of suppressed love, a sigh of yearning. "I love you," he whispered, his voice hoarse in the darkness. "If this is the last chance I have to tell you, I want you to know it. I want you to know that I have always loved you. I have never stopped. Not for a single moment."

She looked at him. "Ben, I love you too."

They kissed again. The loneliness and heartbreak of the past years fell away. He held her close to him, and slowly and lovingly, he made love to her. It was as natural as breathing. For Margot, it felt like she was finally coming home. After it was over, she lay in his arms and still weeping softly. "I'm afraid. I'm a coward, Ben. I don't know what it feels like to die. And I don't know what happens after you die."

"Don't be afraid. Put your trust in me. I'll hold you, and I'll keep you safe. And if we die, we will die together, and wherever we go after death, we'll go there together."

"Do you think it will hurt?"

Another bomb exploded outside. Someone who sounded like a young child was wailing loud enough that they could hear him in the attic.

"No. I don't think it will hurt at all," Ben whispered, running his hand over her hair. "You are safe. I'm here with you, and you are safe. No pain will come to you, my love."

Her entire body was trembling with fear. Chills ran down her back, and sweat beaded on her brow. But they stayed like that with her head on his chest until morning when the sunlight flickered through the window shade, and the bombing finally ceased.

"Are you all right?" he asked finally. "We made it."

"Yes," she said. "Thank you for comforting me last night."

"You don't need to thank me. I meant what I said, Margot. I really do love you."

"Yes, and I meant what I said, too. I've always loved you, too, Ben. Not that I didn't love Max. I did, and I do. But I love you too."

"I know, and I am happy to have whatever love you can give me," he said.

"I feel so guilty about us because of Max. I love you both. They say it's not possible to love two people in this way at the same time, but I do. My heart belongs to both of you."

He held her tightly. "It's all right. You need comfort right now, and so do I. I know you love Max, and if you are ever reunited with him, I would understand and expect nothing of you. I am just glad to have been able to spend this time with you. I guess you could say that I am glad to have any time with you that you can give me." Then, there was a long silence. Ben let out a soft sigh. Then he said, "Margot, I have been thinking, and this is important."

"What is it?"

"I think it's best that if you and Max are reunited, Max should never know what happened here last night between us. It would hurt him terribly, and there is no need for him to know. I know that you and Max will be together again as soon as possible. But your marriage would never be the same if he knew we were lovers. So, you must keep this a secret. Do you understand me? I am always looking out for you. I only want what is best for you because I love you."

She squeezed his hand. "I hate secrets. I've never kept any secret from Max or from you. Now I will have a secret. Margot's secret," she said sarcastically.

"It's best that you keep this secret. I am telling you it is. I know Max. He would not be able to stand it if he knew."

She nodded. "You're probably right." Then she kissed his hand. "Oh, Ben, I suppose we should be happy for what we have. We can't predict the future. I pray that Max is all right. But I don't know if he is. It scares me to think of what could happen to him, but again, I have no way of knowing and no way of helping him. All I can do is give you all the love in my heart and hope it will sustain you. At least for now."

Neither of them moved for a long time. It seemed like hours. Ben told Margot a fairy tale he remembered from his childhood. And the hours passed.

The light from the window shade faded, and they knew it was night. A little while later, Frau Danner arrived with food and water.

CHAPTER 32

"I have a wonderful surprise today. You'll never guess what it is."

"Oh, do tell us?" Ben said.

"I brought some cheese." Frau Danner said. "I was able to get an extra block through the black market."

"That is a wonderful surprise. Thank you," Ben said. "But what about you?"

"I don't need it. I'm all right. At my age, my appetite is not as strong as it was when I was young. A little bread and some hot tea are enough for me."

"This is very kind of you," Margot said. "I wish there was something we could do for you."

"Just survive. That's all I ask," Frau Danner said. Her voice was soft.

"Have you heard anything from your daughter?" Margot asked.

"Not a word. I wish I could see her again. But who knows if that will ever happen? I miss her terribly."

"I am sure you do. It's hard to separate from family like that."

"Would you like me to go to your apartment again? I could try to wait outside your building and see if I can get in touch with Max that way?" Frau Danner asked.

"No," Margot said. "You don't know what he looks like, so you would be taking a big risk. You'd have to speak to other people coming and going from the building to find him. Who knows what their agendas might be? It's just too dangerous."

"I agree with Margot," Ben said. "We'll have to come up with another solution to finding Max."

"Well, I'll let the two of you work on it. I must admit that I am very tired tonight. I am going to go downstairs and get to bed. I'll return with more food in a couple of days." Frau Danner said, groaning a little in pain as she stretched out her legs to stand up. But before she could get up, she fell over and lay silent on the floor.

The tiny candle still flickered. Margot stared at Ben. He returned her nervous gaze. Then he put his fingers on Frau Danner's neck to see if she was still alive.

CHAPTER 33

Max was both excited and worried about the message he'd received from the strange old woman. He was certain that the message came from Margot because he'd never heard of a man named Hans Meir. He spent hours that night lying in bed and staring at the ceiling, trying to decipher the meaning behind the message. *Hans Meir was no longer sick. He was going to be returning to work.* Max wondered if that meant that Margot was all right and that she would soon be returning. Or maybe being back at work meant that she was still pregnant and the situation with Rudy had not hurt her or the baby. He hoped that this was the message the old woman had come to deliver. It was so difficult to try to figure out a code when he really did not have any way of knowing if he was correct or not. And he found that the more he had to pretend to care for Trudy, the deeper his hatred for her became. In her eyes, he saw the depths of her cruelty. Until Erik's murder and Rudy's death, he'd always chosen to believe that Trudy was not as bad as she appeared to be. He made excuses for her because he'd known Trudy, Mattie, and Margot since they were all very young. He'd always known that Trudy was jealous of Margot, but he attributed it to siblings competing. He never thought Trudy was capable of really hurting her sister. He knew Trudy was lying when she said she had no idea of what the Nazis had in store for Erik. He was also aware that she might not have been able to stop it, but the least she could have done was tell her sister or Max the truth about what she knew. This might not have changed the outcome, but at least it would have allowed Max and Margot to try to save their child. No matter how hard Max tried to put this act of betrayal on Trudy's part out of his mind when he had sex with Trudy, it always surfaced. No matter how hard he tried, his body would not cooperate. It was becoming obvious that she was losing interest in him, and he also knew that she could be dangerous. If she stopped caring about him, she might report Margot or tell the truth about what happened that day with Rudy. He wouldn't put it past her to tell the police that he had killed Rudy. There would be no reason for her to if she no longer wanted him, but he couldn't trust that she wouldn't. Sometimes, it seemed that Trudy did cruel things for no reason other than to be malicious. *I must find a way to win her affection back, no matter what it takes. I must keep her in love with me so she feels she must protect me. This will keep her quiet about Margot and about my killing Rudy. I'll get her a bouquet of fresh flowers on my way home from work tomorrow. We don't really have the means to waste money on such frivolities, but I know that receiving flowers will warm her heart. Then, I will have to find a way to make love to her as if I were in love with her. If my manhood does not cooperate, I will do something else. Something that will make her believe that I am hers. Meanwhile, I'll wait to hear more from that mysterious old woman about Margot.*

The following day, after work, Max stopped at a flower shop. He purchased a small bouquet and then took the bus and headed home. When he opened the door, Trudy was sitting on the sofa reading a movie magazine. She was smoking a cigarette when she looked up to see Max had come in. At first, she seemed annoyed when she saw him. But then her eyes fell upon the flowers, and a big smile came over her face. "For me?" she asked coquettishly.

"Of course, who else? You're my girl, aren't you?"

It hadn't taken much to win Trudy's affections back. She was smiling and beaming as she took the flowers from him. He followed her into the kitchen, where she took a vase from the shelf and filled it with water. Then, she carefully placed each flower in the vase. When she was done, she asked Max, "What's the occasion?"

"You."

"Me?"

"You're the occasion," he said, trying to sound as romantic and sincere as possible. "I must apologize to you. I have been so distracted lately by all that has happened. I forgot to let you know how important you are to me." He hesitated for a moment. Then he said, "You are, you know. You are very important to me."

She looked into his eyes. He saw tears welling up in the corners of her eyes, and he tried to feel sorry for her. But he couldn't even evoke pity.

"I was losing faith in us," she said softly. "I didn't think you cared. I must admit, I thought you were still thinking about Margot all the time."

"Nonsense. That's over. I do care. I care very much," he said in the sexiest whisper he could conjure. "Let me show you how much I care." He lifted her up into his arms. Max was very strong, and so she felt light to him. Pressing her head into his chest, he carried her like a baby to the bedroom. Max kissed her, then moved down to her breasts and then further down until he removed her panties. He stifled the desire to gag. Then he spread her legs and pressed his tongue and lips against her womanhood. She moaned with delight. He gagged a little, but she didn't notice. He continued and tried to force himself to pretend she was Margot.

"That was wonderful. No one has ever done that to me before," Trudy said.

Max smiled. "I want you to feel loved. I don't know what's been wrong with me lately. I think it's just all this nervous tension we are under."

"I understand. And now it's my turn," she said. She did the same thing to him. And he tried to picture Margot, but he couldn't. Whenever he thought of Margot, he felt sick and guilty. *Damn, I wish I had a way to hide my feelings.* He thought. But he gently lifted Trudy up to where their faces were only inches apart. Then he said, "Give me time. I'll be all right. But for now, just please know that I love you."

"Oh, Max. I am so happy," she whispered into his ear.

He breathed a sigh of relief.

CHAPTER 34

t was difficult to examine Frau Danner by the light of a single candle. But Ben did the best he could. "Is she alive?" Margot asked nervously.

"Yes, she's alive."

"What do you think is wrong?" Margot asked.

"I can't really tell. I don't have any equipment. But I am hoping it's nothing more than exhaustion."

The old woman stirred. Her eyes fluttered open. "Where am I?" she asked.

"It's Ben," he said gently. "You're in the attic with Margot and I."

"Oh…." she said.

"Yes," he smiled. "You're all right. But can I ask you when the last time was that you ate?"

"I can't remember," she admitted.

"You fainted," Margot said. "Did you eat today?"

"I don't think I did. I think I forgot," Frau Danner said, sounding confused.

Ben glanced at Margot. "Have you been bringing us all your food, Frau Danner?" he asked.

"I am rarely hungry," she said.

"But you must eat," Ben said.

"Yes, I must," she said, still sounding bewildered.

Ben ripped a piece of bread off the hunk that Frau Danner had brought for him and Margot. "Eat this," he said.

"Yes, of course," she answered.

He helped her up to a sitting position, and she began to nibble on the bread. When she finished, he gave her the water bottle. "You must drink too. Every day. You must have water each day, Frau Danner. It's very important."

"You're right. Of course, you are."

She sipped the water.

An hour later, Frau Danner left the attic and went downstairs to her bedroom. After she had gone, Margot asked Ben, "Do you think there is anything else wrong? Or do you think she's not eating because she feeds us?"

"Anything is possible," Ben said. "Poor old woman." He shook his head.

Margot was quiet. But she was thinking that if something happened to Frau Danner, they would not be able to get any food. And even worse, as soon as someone realized the old woman was dead, the house would be confiscated by the Nazi Party. *Where would she and Ben go? What would they do? They'd have to leave there right away.*

It was as if Ben heard Margot's thoughts. "If Frau Danner doesn't return in a couple of days, I'll go down and check on her to make sure she's all right," he said.

"That's a good idea. But what will we do if something happens to her?"

"We'll have to leave here. We'll have to find another place to hide."

"But where? How?"

"I don't know. We'll have to address it if the situation arises."

There was a long silence. Then she said, "My mother and father would probably be willing to help us. But their apartment is so small, and there is nowhere to hide, no attic, no basement. If we went there, it would just be a matter of time before Trudy came over to see my parents, and then she would see us. I can't believe that my own sister has become my worst enemy. I am terrified of what she might do."

"Yes, I know. Jealousy is a terrible thing. It turns people into monsters. And your sister is completely committed to this Nazi doctrine. I'm sorry to say that I agree with you. If she saw us, she would turn you in in a minute."

"The only thing that might stop her is my parents. If she thought she would endanger them, she might not do it. But I can't be sure. I can't trust her at all. She's not the person I thought she was."

"And we can't take that risk. I've heard of Nazis turning in their own parents because they didn't follow the rules," he said. There was a moment of silence, and then he sighed. "I was thinking I could leave the attic, go out, and see if I could find Max. He might have a solution for us. I know he will help us if he can."

"Yes, he would help us. That's for sure. He always liked you, Ben. You know that he only joined the Nazi Party because he thought he was helping Erik. He'd never have done it otherwise."

"I know that. I've always liked him, too. It's kind of funny. When you first told me that you were getting married, I was consumed with jealousy. Without ever meeting Max, I hated him. But then, when I did meet him, and he turned out to be such a nice fellow and a good husband, I found I couldn't help but like him. Then, after Erik was born, he was a good father too, and I admired him for it."

"You weren't jealous anymore?"

"I can't say that. Of course, I wished that you were married to me. But if you had to marry someone else, I couldn't have chosen a better man."

"I love you both," she said. "I know that's strange, but I do. Circumstances have made it so that you and I could never marry legally. At least we couldn't in the past when we thought I was a gentile. Perhaps we could marry, but we might not live long enough for you to break the glass." She laughed bitterly.

"How did you know about breaking a glass at a Jewish wedding?" he asked.

"Oh, when we were young, still in school, I used to dream of marrying you. So, I read all about Jewish weddings. And I used to imagine us having this big elaborate Jewish ceremony."

"That's very sweet," he said. "I wish I had known about it."

"I couldn't tell you. But I hoped you would ask me. Then, they passed the laws forbidding it, and I realized it could never come true. That's when I accepted Max's proposal."

"Yep, I could see our beautiful wedding. You are looking stunning in your gown, me in a suit. A chuppah filled with flowers. You know what a *chuppah* is, don't you?"

"Of course, it's a canopy. Jewish couples get married under a canopy, right?"

"Yes, you're right."

"Well, of course, if I weren't already married, we would have a lovely wedding. That's if the Nazis didn't find out. I guess we'd have to get married in hiding. Do you think our guests would attend?" She let out a sad laugh.

Then he laughed, too.

"I'll tell you something about my people," Ben said. "Jews like to laugh. We even make jokes and laugh at our own misery. It's the Jewish way. We are good people, Margot. Be proud to be one of us. I guess our people have suffered so much through the ages that we have learned to laugh at it."

"Oh, Ben, I am trying hard to see the bright side. I really am. I keep reminding myself that we have so much to be thankful for. And we have each other. Even if it is only for a short time, we have loved each other. Our dream of being together finally came true. We have truly loved."

"Yes, we have. And I know we are living under constant fear and in terrible conditions. Yet, I am happy to have had this time with you. You can't imagine how many times, in the past, I dreamed of holding you in my arms. It's like my prayers have been answered," he said.

"And mine." She sighed. "I am grateful for that. Truly grateful. But I feel guilty, too. I am worried about Max; do you think he's all right?"

"I hope so," he said. "I know if we survive this, you will return to him. I realize this. You and I will be just friends again. And I won't stand in the way of your marriage. But I want you to know that no matter what happens, I will always treasure the time I had with you."

"Yes," she said softly, "if we survive and this does end, you and I will not be able to continue like this. I will go back to Max and be the wife he deserves."

"And I will understand," Ben said softly. He reached up and touched her hair. "Now, as I suggested to you before. I will go out and see if I can find Max."

"I don't want you to go," she said, then hesitated. "But Max might be able to help us. His parents have a house. It's a big old house with an attic and a basement. When my father was away at war, my mother took my sisters and me, and we stayed there. I spent a lot of time there when I was growing up. Not only does the house have an attic and basement, but it is full of small rooms, strange hallways, and lots of places to hide. It would be a good place for us to go. And I am sure Max would do all he could to bring us enough food. There is only one problem that's worrying me. It's Artur, Max's father. He has strong Nazi tendencies. If he found out that I was Jewish and you were my Jewish friend. He might turn us both in. Even though I am his daughter-in-law, I don't know if we can trust him."

"And then, of course, there is always Trudy," Ben said. "We would have to be sure she didn't find out we were staying there."

"Yes, Trudy. I don't know what Max has told his family about my disappearance. Or even what he's told my parents, or Mattie, for that matter," she said.

"Well, if Frau Danner is right, Max is living with Trudy. I wonder how that happened," he contemplated.

"I don't know. But I do know that no matter what, we can trust Max absolutely. Whatever he has done, it is to protect me. And he would never hurt you intentionally."

"So, I think the best thing for me to do is to go out and see if I can find him."

She leaned against the wall. "You look Jewish," she said. "I don't mean that as an insult. I find you terribly handsome. But you have very dark hair and eyes. And I am afraid that a Nazi will spot you on the street and, God forbid, hurt you." She reached over and ran her fingers across his cheek and down his chin.

"Well, all right," he said. "We don't have to do anything yet. As long as Frau Danner is taking care of us, we can continue the way we are. I will keep an eye on her health the best I can. I'll go downstairs and check on her every few nights."

"Yes, that's a good idea."

CHAPTER 35

Over a month had passed, and Max had still not heard a single word from the mysterious woman who had come to his apartment and left a message with Trudy that night. He was doing what he could to keep Trudy happy and to maintain her interest in him. Once a week, he took her out for dinner. It wasn't as nice as the expensive dinners she was used to with Rudy, but she seemed to look forward to it. He knew she was often frustrated because she couldn't afford to shop for dresses the way she had when she was married to a high-ranking officer. However, Max did what he could to keep her satisfied in bed. He also complimented her often and tried to give her plenty of attention. All the while, he was waiting and watching for the old woman.

It was on a Sunday afternoon. Max was off work and in the living room, carving a wooden statue. He loved to whittle wood. Trudy walked in and asked him what he was making.

"A horse," he said.

"But why?"

"No reason. I just like the feel of wood in my hands. There's an honest feeling to it if you know what I mean?"

She shook her head. "It's messy. I really don't feel like cleaning up those wood chips. I wish you would do that outside.

"Yes, you're probably right. I should. But don't worry. I'll sweep all of this up. You won't see a single wood chip."

"Good. I got a splinter the other day trying to clean up one of your messes."

"I cleaned it up," he said.

"Not good enough," she grumbled.

Trudy had been nagging Max almost every day to consider asking if he could take time off from work to take a vacation. She longed to go to Munich. She was bored, she told Max, and she needed a vacation. "I want to talk to you about Munich," she said.

"Again, Trudy?"

"Yes, I keep telling you I want to go, and you just ignore me."

"I have told you a thousand times that I can't get away from work."

"But I am so bored. Rudy could always get away. I want to do something fun. It's been so terrible since Luzie and Erik died. I've been so depressed. I need something to lift my spirits."

He thought for a moment and then said, "Perhaps you and your sister Mattie could go."

"Oh, Max, really? You would allow me to go with Mattie?"

"Yes, of course," he said, smiling.

She ran to where he was sitting and threw her arms around his neck. He dropped the wooden horse he was carving. She kissed him softly. "That would be just lovely. I would love to go. I hate to ask this, but can we afford it?"

It would be difficult for him to find enough money. Max was a small-time employee in a less-than-important job. It was a good, steady job. The pay was enough to live on, but he didn't earn a large salary nor receive free travel through the Party. The cost of this trip would be his responsibility. However, Mattie's husband, Ebert, was doing well in his position. He might be able to get the women a few free hotel nights through the Party. Trudy had remained on good terms with Mattie.

"I'll see Mattie at dinner tonight at *Mutti's* house. I'll talk to her about it then," Trudy said.

"Good idea."

Trudy and Max had plans to have dinner at Adelaide and Leo's apartment that evening. This had become a Sunday night family tradition, and everyone in the family, except Margot, was there, including Mattie, her husband, and Max's parents. No one asked Trudy anything about what happened to Rudy or Margot. She had told everyone the same story that she and Max had told the police about Rudy's death and Margot's disappearance. But when they were alone, Adelaide and Leo questioned the story. And later that night, Adelaide had found a way to get Max alone. She tried to press him for more information about Margot. But Max stood firm with his story. He felt that the less anyone knew, the better.

There was a long silence. Then Adelaide said, "I think it was Erik's death that drove her crazy. That's why she ran away."

"Yes, that could be," Max said.

"I know you still love her."

"Yes," he whispered. "I'll always love her."

"And I am sure she still loves you."

"Perhaps," he said, not wanting to reveal any more of the secrets he held in his heart.

"She's going to return to you, Max. Then what will you do about Trudy?"

He wanted to explain everything, to unburden himself with the truth. Instead, he said, "I don't know."

Adelaide nodded, and Max thought she might know more than she was revealing. Or at least, she suspected. But she didn't ask him anything else.

Trudy entered the room without knocking, and the mood instantly changed.

"What are you two talking about?" Trudy asked.

"Oh, nothing. We were just chatting." He smiled. Then, he changed the subject as Adelaide left the room. "I was just thinking about what a lovely time you and Mattie will have in Munich."

"Are you sure you wouldn't want to join us?" she asked.

"Of course, I would," Max lied. He was looking forward to being alone. He hoped the mysterious woman had been watching him and waiting for such an opportunity. "But I can't get off work. You know that I can't just take time off. Still, it will make me happy to know you are enjoying yourself."

"Oh, Max, you are so good to me," she said.

He nodded and smiled. "I try." *I don't know where I will get the money for this. But it's important that she goes away for a while. It might just be what the old woman is waiting for. A time when I am alone so she can talk to me.*

CHAPTER 36

The next day, Trudy was awake when Max got ready for work.

Mattie was as excited as Trudy to be going to Munich. As it turned out, Ebert could not take time off work, so Trudy and Mattie would go alone. "I wish I could purchase some new dresses for the trip," Trudy said.

"I'm sorry. We just don't have the money," Max answered her. "The trip is costing us money we don't have. I have dipped into the little we have saved."

"I know." She pouted. "I just wish you earned more than you do. I don't know why you're not more ambitious. You could rise in the Party if you were. You are a good-looking Aryan man. You have everything going for you. Except that you're lazy."

Her words stung. But he didn't want to start a fight. *I am not lazy. I just hate your Nazi Party, and I wish more than anything I could go back to work at my father's carpentry shop. I miss it.* "You have plenty of nice dresses," he said.

"They're old-fashioned. I need something new, a new style."

"Trudy, please stop pushing me. I am doing my best."

She huffed. Then she walked into the bedroom and closed the door.

CHAPTER 37

After Max left for work, Trudy lay on her bed with a wet rag on her forehead. Her eyes burned with unshed tears. She thought about Rudy, and although she had never truly loved him, she realized he was a good match for her. *I know he was never faithful. I hated it when we went to parties, and women would smile at him with that special smile that women save for men they are sleeping with. They would think I didn't see, but I did. Even so, I never had to do without. I could shop for pretty things whenever I wanted to. And there was always enough money to buy meat. Now we eat cabbage and potatoes.*

She sighed out loud. "But Rudy is dead," she whispered to herself.

I know Max has been trying to make me happy. I believe he loves me. But I can't seem to regain the excitement I had about being with him when he was with Margot. He's handsome, there is no doubt about that. However, he can hardly afford to give me the things I want. He's gotten better in bed, but his lovemaking hardly makes me see stars. I am bored with him. Not that I would ever want to see him back with my sister. I hate Margot. And I would still like to see her arrested. She's an imposter, even though she never knew it. Well, at least I will get away for a few days with Mattie. It will give me time to think.

Max came home from work late that night. Trudy was already in bed when he arrived. Trudy would have waited for him in eager anticipation when they first started living together. But now she didn't care that he was late. She didn't even want to see him. Instead, she just took off her makeup and went to sleep.

Trudy got up late the following morning. It had been a while since she'd bothered to prepare Max's breakfast. In fact, she didn't really even want to see him. She no longer rushed to apply her lipstick and rouge in the morning before Max saw her. She listened for the front door to close, letting her know that he had already left for work before she crawled out of bed. Trudy had grown tired of listening to Max when he tried to explain that he couldn't afford the things she wanted. And she dreaded the lecture he would give her about spending money when she was in Munich on her trip. She thought of him as petty and penny-pinching. His attempts to save money annoyed her. So, instead of talking to him when he was at home, she took long walks so she could be alone and unburdened by his troubles. It was during these times that she could allow herself to enjoy the excitement of thinking about her upcoming travels.

CHAPTER 38

Ben left the attic every other evening and went downstairs to check on Frau Danner. He reported to Margot that the old woman seemed to be doing better. "I think she was just tired and had forgotten to eat. She's getting old, Margot. It would be ideal if we could live downstairs and take care of her. But the circumstances don't permit it. So, we must do what we can."

Each time Frau Danner came upstairs, Ben checked her pulse and did his best to examine her by the light of the single candle. She always claimed to be fine when he asked her how she felt. The old woman returned to the attic every few days with food and water throughout the summer. She seemed to be in good spirits, but she was thin and growing thinner. Whenever she left the attic, Ben would say, "Don't forget to eat something and drink some water every day."

The closeness between Margot and Ben grew stronger. They were completely dependent on each other for the company. Sometimes, they argued for no reason other than they were bored and unable to leave the small room. When that happened, Margot would go to the other side of the room, and for a little while, they would not speak. But soon, they were talking and laughing again. Margot found that she truly adored Ben. They were lovers and friends, but most of all, they were each other's lifeline. They shared everything from feelings to food and water. And although this was a terrible position to be in, never to bask in the sun's light or to count the stars, if she had to be in prison, she was glad he was with her. Sometimes, they talked for hours, reminiscing about better times. Other times, they discussed books, or Ben told Margot stories he'd read. And somehow, the time passed. Even so, the attic was dark and musty, and there were times when Margot terribly missed Max and her old life outside the attic. She knew making love with Ben would be considered a sin, but it was her only bit of happiness, and she couldn't let it go. Even so, she prayed for Max's safety every night, hoping God would forgive her and understand why she had broken her marriage vows to be faithful.

The weather was beautiful outside, but Margot and Ben never knew it. They never felt the warm wind on their faces. In the attic, it was hot and humid. It was difficult to sleep, as they lay on the floor sweating each night. Then, finally, autumn came, and although it brought some welcome relief from the heat, both Margot and Ben knew that it was just a short time before winter would arrive. The cold would be worse than the heat of summer.

Margot ate very little because she wanted to be sure that Ben would think there was enough for them both and that he would eat, too. She had seen him refuse to eat, thinking there wasn't enough for them. She never complained but was always hungry, and she assumed he was too.

Her menstruation had always been regular. It always came on time. But lately, it was not consistent. Some months it was late. In other months, it did not come at all. The hardest part of being a woman in hiding in the attic was the difficulty she was having washing her menstruation rags. She tried to hide them from Ben, but it was almost impossible. "It's all right," he said, assuring her he was not disgusted by the stained rags. "It's natural, love."

She hated feeling dirty and often dreamed of bathing and cleaning herself thoroughly. Finally, when she could no longer bear the feeling of being unclean, she asked Frau Danner if she could take the risk of leaving the attic for an hour or so one night to go downstairs to take a bath. Frau Danner agreed, but Ben was nervous about it. He feared she might be careless and walk by an uncovered window. Even so, she felt she must bathe. One evening, after it had grown dark, Frau Danner assured Ben and Margot that she had checked to ensure all the drapes were closed and that no one could see inside the house. "All right, but be careful," Ben insisted.

Margot followed Frau Danner out of the attic and down the dimly lit stairs into the bathroom. When Margot turned on the light in the bathroom, she had to cover her eyes. The blinding brightness was painful; it took several minutes before her eyes adjusted. Frau Danner had already prepared a bath for her. It wasn't much water, but she welcomed it. The soap burned her tender skin, but she ignored the burning and scrubbed until her skin was red but clean. When she got out of the tub, she felt strangely renewed. Then Frau Danner gave her an old dress to wear, and the feeling of clean clothes on her newly washed body was delightful.

"I'm sorry, but it's time for you to go back upstairs," Frau Danner said. "Every minute you are down here is dangerous for both of us."

"I know," Margot said. Then she followed the old woman back up the hidden staircase into the attic.

That month, Margot did not get her period. "Do you think I could have missed my period because of taking a bath?" she asked Ben in a worried voice.

"No," he said. He was worried, too. A pregnancy in this attic would have been far from ideal.

"Do you think I am pregnant?"

"It's very possible," he said softly.

"Oh, Ben. I do so much want another baby."

"Yes, of course you do. And so do I. But not here, not like this."

"I know. You're right. You're so right. What are we going to do? My arms are so empty without Erik. And my miscarriage nearly broke me." She began to cry. He took her in his arms.

"Please understand me," he said gently. "I want more than anything to have a child with you. But we can't take care of a baby here in this attic. Our own lives are so uncertain. Babies cry. They make noise. It would be too dangerous."

"Are you asking me to get rid of it? Are you asking that of me?"

There was a long silence. Then he said, "No, I couldn't ask you to do that. I don't want that any more than you do."

"So, we'll have the baby."

"If there is one, yes, I suppose we will have it and let it be in God's hands."

"What do you mean by that?" she was defensive.

"Only that you may not be pregnant. The loss of your monthly period could be due to a lack of food. You hardly eat, Margot."

"There's hardly anything to eat," she admitted.

"Well, you should eat more than you do."

She shook her head. "I can't," she said, tears ran down her cheeks. But it was too dark for him to see her tears.

CHAPTER 39

Trudy was packed three days before she and Mattie were scheduled to leave. She was filled with excitement but still complained about not having anything new to wear on her trip. Max ignored her complaints; he was eager for her to go. He refused to give up hope that Margot was still alive. And he was praying that, somehow, Margot would get in touch with him once Trudy was gone. Trudy visited the hairdresser to get her hair cut for her trip. Max was annoyed that she spent the money, but he said nothing. He was surprised at how thoughtlessly Trudy could waste the small amount of money that he earned. Margot had understood that Max was not wealthy, and so she had been thrifty. She had always cut her own hair, but not Trudy. Trudy was used to the finest of everything. After her haircut, she also went to get a professional manicure. Max wished she would get a job of some kind so there would be enough money for all the luxuries she seemed to need, at least for now. He sighed. It amazed him that Trudy and Margot had been raised in the same household, yet they were so different. *Well, it doesn't matter. All that matters is finding Margot again and getting out of Berlin with her.*

157

CHAPTER 40

The night before Trudy was to leave for Munich, she carefully set her hair in finger waves and pin curls. It had been a long time since she'd bothered to style her hair. There was little reason to make a fuss over herself these days. Even when Max took her to the *Biergarten* for dinner, it was not one of the better ones. It was a less expensive neighborhood place. The men who ate there were working men like Max, and she didn't even care to bother flirting with any of them. Trudy was unimpressed, and it showed in her appearance.

The following day, Trudy and Mattie were scheduled to meet at the train station at nine in the morning. Trudy hated getting up early, but she did want to get to Munich as soon as possible, so they decided to take an early train. She forced herself to get out of bed and kiss Max goodbye when he left for work. She did this because she needed to ask him for money. He gave her what he had in his pocket and left. After Max was gone, Trudy quickly but carefully applied her makeup. Then she combed out her hair and put on her dress. She looked in the mirror and was satisfied with her appearance. As she walked to the bus stop, she silently cursed Max because she had to carry her suitcase. Trudy remembered traveling in luxury with Rudy.

I miss the automobile Rudy and I had. Now, I have to take the bus everywhere. And I miss having a maid. I can't stand being forced to clean and wash clothes. It's degrading. She thought as she sat down on the bench at the bus stop. A little boy and his mother sat down beside her on the bench. It had rained the night before, and there was mud on the ground. The child was kicking his feet and playing in the mud. His mother was ignoring him. Then, a glob of wet dirt flew off the boy's shoe and landed on the hem of Trudy's dress. She gasped, then she turned to the boy and slapped the child hard across the face. The boy burst into tears, then she turned to the mother and said, "Can't you control your child? He's a monster. It seems to me that you didn't raise him properly. Just look what he did to my dress?"

The young mother stood up and eyed the dirt on the hem of Trudy's dress. "I'm so sorry. I'm so sorry," she said, picking up her son to quiet him. The boy's mother was almost in tears. "It should come right out with water. It's only dirt."

"How dare you? Don't tell me what you think I should do to clean my dress. Instead of telling me what you think, you should pay more attention to your brat's behavior."

The young woman got up from the bench. She put her son down on the ground, away from the pile of mud. He sat, and she stood over him until the bus arrived.

During the entire ride to the train station, Trudy continually glanced at the dirt on her dress. It had ruined her perfect traveling outfit, an outfit she had planned for weeks. She was so devastated that she secretly fantasized about choking the little boy. As the bus made its way down the street, she shot looks of hatred towards the child. The mother noticed it. She took her son's hand and got off the bus. Trudy wondered if the stop where they had gotten off was actually their stop or if she had driven them away. She hoped it was the latter.

Mattie was at the train station when Trudy arrived. "You look beautiful as always," Mattie said to Trudy with the same admiration she'd always shown to her older sister.

"Thanks," Trudy said sourly.

"What's wrong?"

"Look at my dress?" Trudy said, her shoulders slumping. "My dress is ruined."

Mattie looked down at the mud stain. "It's just a little dirt. I didn't even notice it. But don't worry. We'll get it out when we get to the hotel," she promised reassuringly.

The train arrived, and they boarded. "I'm so excited to be going on this trip," Mattie said. "However, I do wish Ebert and Max had been able to join us."

"I don't. Max is a bore. You and I will have more fun alone," Trudy said.

"Do you ever miss Margot?" Mattie asked wistfully.

"Never."

"I must admit, I do, sometimes. I hope she's all right," Mattie said. Trudy was silent. Then, a few minutes later, Mattie said, "You said Max is boring. Are you happy with Max? At all? You've always had such a crush on him. Now you are finally together."

"Maybe I did have a crush on him. But I was young. And I have discovered he's not everything I thought he would be."

"I don't understand," Mattie said. "We've known him since we were all very young. I would think you would have known exactly what he was like."

"Yes, well, never mind. It doesn't matter. I don't want to talk about it."

CHAPTER 41

The train arrived in Munich. With suitcases in hand, Trudy and Mattie began walking towards the main area of town where they would search for a reasonably priced hotel they could afford. Trudy was silently angry with herself for packing so heavily. This was a lot different from trips she'd gone on when Rudy's driver had taken care of the luggage. Then, she had never thought about the weight of her bags. She had been able to pack whatever she wished. But now, there was no one to carry her belongings but her, and she was already getting tired.

When they arrived at a busy street near the famous clock in the city, Trudy walked directly to a sign that said hotel. She entered the building. It was not as fancy as the hotel where she, her sisters, Max, Ebert, and Rudy had stayed when they had attended *Oktoberfest*. But it was clean. Trudy walked up to the desk and asked for two rooms.

"I'm sorry, but we have nothing available. This is our busiest time of year." The hotel clerk was apologetic.

"Do you know of any other hotels in the area that might have a vacancy?"

"There's one right down the street. When you walk outside the building, turn to your right and keep going. You'll see it."

It seemed to Trudy that her suitcase grew heavier as she and Mattie walked back outside. Her arm was beginning to ache as they followed the directions that the hotel clerk had given them. A magnificent building stood at the end of the road. Trudy felt a pang of excitement. *This is more like what I am used to.* She thought as they walked inside.

"Do you have two rooms available?" Trudy asked a young woman who was at the desk.

"I do," the young girl said. She was a petite and energetic girl with her golden hair braided and twisted across the back of her head.

"We'd like to take them, please."

Mattie was standing beside Trudy. She shook her head. Then she turned to the hotel clerk and asked how much the rooms would cost. When the pretty blonde answered with a smile, Mattie froze. Then she turned to Trudy. "We can't afford to stay here," she said, shaking her head. "We'll have to keep looking."

Trudy's face had fallen. "I realize that," she said bitterly. Then, without another word to the desk clerk, Trudy walked out of the hotel with Mattie at her heels.

"Don't feel so bad. It will be all right. We'll find something."

"Yes, I am sure we will. But this suitcase is getting heavier, and I guess I am frustrated. I don't want to stay in some low-priced, miserable place. Damn Max for his lack of ambition. He's doomed to be poor for the rest of his miserable life."

"Stop it, please. Be happy, or at least try to. We are on holiday," Mattie said, smiling. Then she took Trudy's suitcase. "It is rather heavy," she said. "But I'll carry it. Does that make you feel better?"

Trudy nodded.

The streets were crowded with people. Most of them drank beer. Trudy's throat felt dry. She would have liked to stop and have a beer and something to eat, but before they stopped, they needed to find a place to sleep before nightfall, and it was already getting late in the afternoon.

They walked another two streets until Mattie saw a sign that said hotel. When they approached the door, a sign in the window said, "No vacancy."

"This is terrible," Trudy said. There was panic in her voice.

"It will be all right." Mattie tried to assure her sister. She was sweating from carrying Trudy's heavy suitcase. But she didn't complain.

After walking for another twenty minutes, Mattie saw a hotel that looked as if it would be in their price range. They entered the lobby, and Trudy's heart sank. This place was a far cry from the elegant hotels where she'd stayed with Rudy. The lobby was clean, but it was plain. There was a worn brown fabric sofa and a small desk where a registrar, an old gray-haired woman, sat.

"Do you have any rooms available?" Mattie asked.

The old woman smiled. "Yes, I have one left. You're in luck."

This hotel would probably not have been busy at any other time of year, but because they'd come during a busy period, there was only one single room left vacant, and the price was higher than it would have been at any other time, "Do you want to see it?"

"Yes, please," Mattie said.

Trudy and Mattie followed the woman as she showed them their room. It was simple. There were no paintings on the walls, no intricately made furniture. The bed was small. Beside it was a door to a tiny closet and a single two-drawer dresser. The bathroom was located at the end of a long hallway. It had a shower that needed to be cleaned, two sinks, and two toilets.

"It's not very nice," Trudy said. "But I guess it will have to do."

"We'll take it," Mattie said.

"Good," the old woman said, handing them a key.

Once they were alone, Trudy groaned. "I hate this hotel," she said.

"Don't think about the hotel. Let's go out and have a beer. What do you say?"

"I could use a beer. But let me freshen up first. I want to change this dress," Trudy scoffed as she looked at the dirt on the hem of her dress. "Oh, Mattie, this trip isn't turning out how I thought it would."

"Nonsense. It's just the beginning. We are going to have a wonderful time. Now, let me get that spot out for you while you freshen up. All right?"

"Yes, all right," Trudy agreed.

Mattie took the dress down the hall to the bathroom to scrub out the stain. Trudy watched her go, then changed her dress and reapplied her lipstick. When Mattie returned, Trudy was waiting.

"Did the dirt come out?"

"Yes, it's all clean. I will hang it to dry in this little closet, and it should be good as new in the morning."

"I feel so much better," Trudy admitted. "I was upset by that obnoxious child. He almost ruined my entire trip."

"Well, don't worry about it. It's all fixed. Let's go find a place to have a beer and something to eat. Are you hungry?"

"Actually, yes. I am."

"Good, me too."

They left their suitcases in the room and went to the street to join the festivities.

It wasn't difficult to find a busy *Biergarten* that looked like fun. There was one right in the corner. It had a small group of German folk dancers and three musicians.

When Trudy had gone to *Oktoberfest* a few years before with Rudy in his Nazi officer uniform, their entire group had been treated like royalty by the staff wherever they went. But now, they didn't have Rudy's pull behind them. They were just two unescorted women, and consequently, they were treated like unimportant guests. The hostess at the *Biergarten*, a young woman with a serious expression, put them at the bottom of her list of guests waiting for an open table. But most people who were seated were not leaving. They drank large pitchers of dark beer, ate pretzels, and watched the entertainment. It was dusk, and Trudy was growing angry. She and Mattie still had not been seated. "Damn this little hostess," Trudy said quietly to her sister. "I haven't eaten since early this morning, and I'm getting a headache." Then she looked forlorn. "Oh, Mattie," she moaned. "I'm miserable without Rudy."

"Of course you are. I can understand how terrible it must be for you. Even though you said you never loved him, I always knew you did. After all, he was your husband," Mattie said.

"You're right, and I didn't appreciate what he did for me at the time. I thought my life would always be the way it was when I was with Rudy."

"Yes, I know. I tried to tell you. But you would never listen to me. You were too busy worrying about Margot and Max to realize that Rudy was the right man for you."

"We did have a lot in common," Trudy said nostalgically. "Not that we had any kind of great love affair. I mean, there were things that he did that hurt me. But he was a good provider. And would you just look at me now? Look what's become of me. I'm as poor as I was when we were growing up. I am back to living life the way we used to. Can you believe it?" She hung her head, and tears began to fill her eyes. Closing them, she put her hands over her face. But when she opened her eyes, she saw a pair of shiny black boots standing before her.

"Allo," a male voice said.

Trudy looked up. The man who wore the boots was far from handsome. He was very short and at least ten years older than Trudy. His heavy-set body seemed to be muscle-bound. She studied him for a moment. *At least he is wearing a nice suit, so he probably has some money.* "I'm Klaus." He said, smiling at her.

"Trudy." She returned his smile. "This is my sister, Mattie."

"Nice to meet you," Mattie said.

"I have seen you both waiting here for several hours. You must be parched and probably hungry, too."

"We are," Trudy admitted.

"Well, it seems there are no tables to be had, so why don't you girls come over and join my friends and me at our table," Klaus said, indicating a table where two other older, well-dressed men, one of them wearing a Nazi uniform sat watching them and waiting to see what would happen.

"We'd love to join you. Wouldn't we, Mattie?"

Mattie looked at Trudy nervously. "I don't know," Mattie said. "I'm married. I am not looking for a date."

Klaus laughed. "So am I, but that hasn't stopped me from having fun. Come on over and eat. You don't need to do anything but have a good time. No one will expect anything else from you. How does that sound?"

Mattie nodded in agreement.

They followed Klaus over to the table. Immediately, someone from the wait staff added additional chairs and brought out additional glasses of beer. "I know good food. And this place is one of the best in Munich," Klaus bragged. "Do you know how I know?"

Trudy shook her head.

Klaus's friend, the one wearing the uniform, smiled. "Klaus is pretty famous where we are from. He owns one of the most successful restaurants in Frankfurt. All the SS frequent his dining establishment whenever we're in town. It's the place to go, not only for food but for whatever you need. He always has the prettiest girls working for him and the finest beer. I must admit, he's quite an impressive fellow.."

Trudy smiled. *I was right about this old man. He does have plenty of money.*

CHAPTER 42

Max was glad to have Trudy gone when he finished work that night. On his way back to his apartment, he had stopped at a little restaurant where he had a *bratwurst* and a beer. When he sat down at the restaurant, he looked around. He hoped the old woman who had left the message with Trudy was following him. But of course, that would have meant that she had been watching his apartment every minute of every day and now knew that Trudy was gone. Max sighed. He was sad to think that this was nothing but wishful thinking. But the strange message from the old woman was all he had to go on. It was his only hope, and so he clung to it. There had been no other signs that Margot might be trying to reach him. For a single moment, a stab of fear shot through his heart. *Margot might be dead. She was pregnant. Women are vulnerable when they are with child. And that bastard really upset her. Who knows what the consequences of that turned out to be? I don't know because I can't find her. Oh dear God, Haven't I suffered enough? You've taken everything from me, and I still love you. I still believe in you. But I beg you, please don't take Margot. Please, not Margot.*

No one spoke to Max as he sat in the restaurant, eating slowly and looking around. He stayed for a full hour, still hoping that someone would approach him and give him some kind of message. But when it didn't happen, he finally returned to his apartment.

It had taken most of Max's savings to send Trudy to Munich, and he found that he resented her even more for spending the money he worked so hard for in such a frivolous way. *I am not as forgiving as I was when I was happy when Margot and I were together. Then I was a carefree man. Money meant nothing to me, even though I never had an abundance. I never seemed to need more. Margot and I were happy with the little we had. But Trudy has no respect for my hard work. And although I have never felt such terrible feelings of hatred before, I find that every day, my hatred for her grows. Yet, I don't dare say a word to her. I don't dare chastise her for her behavior. I am forced to succumb to her every whim. For now, I must try to keep her happy.* He could taste the bitterness in his throat. *If I could only get rid of her. If I could only find my wife. IF…If…If. My entire life is full of ifs. But none of them are possible. I am trapped by this woman I hate. I am working at a job I hate. My life has turned into a dark hole of misery.* His stomach burned with acid.

That night, Max didn't feel well. He had allowed himself to think too much that day, and his thoughts had caused him a pounding, aching headache. So, he took a hot bath and a sleeping pill and lay down to rest. He was exhausted. His job was taxing. And so he fell asleep within minutes of closing his eyes. Max dreamed of a warm Sunday afternoon long ago when he and Margot had sat on the living room floor in their apartment playing with Erik. He could hear Erik's laughter. He could feel Margot's hand on his shoulder. In his dream, the sun shined brightly through the living room window. It was so real that he didn't realize he was asleep until he awakened to find his face and pillow covered in tears.

CHAPTER 43

Trudy was delighted to have met Klaus. He ordered plenty of food: sausages, pretzels, *sauerbraten*, *spaetzle*, and potato salad. On the table were large pitchers of dark beer to wash it all down. Most importantly, Trudy could sense she didn't have to worry about paying for anything. Mattie was obviously unhappy sitting at this table with these men she didn't know. She was aloof and cold to everyone, especially her sister. Several times, she announced to everyone at the table that she was married and not one to have affairs. "So, you want to be the perfect hausfrau?" one of the men at the table said, nodding his head. "I must admit, I think that's commendable."

"That's exactly what I want to do. I just want to do the right things. I've always been one to follow the rules," Mattie explained.

"Yes, my sister is like that. A real stickler for rules. Not like me." Trudy smiled at Klaus, her candy apple red lipstick shining by the candlelight. "Now, I am different. Very different from Mattie…" Trudy laughed, and Klaus laughed too. "In fact, you could say that I am just the opposite. I love a good adventure."

"Me too," said Klaus.

Klaus was pleasant and jovial, and for the first time in a long time, Trudy found she was enjoying herself. They drank until they were comfortable singing along with the band apologetically for being off-tune. It didn't matter to Trudy that Klaus was much older than she or that he was married. He was fun. And she had been craving a good time for a long time. He told jokes and complimented Trudy on her lovely dress. She smiled, but when she looked down at her dress, she felt self-conscious because it was last year's fashion. And she was sure he knew it and was only being polite.

"Your eyes are as blue as an Iris," Klaus said. "What a beautiful woman you are."

Trudy blushed. "And you are a handsome man," Trudy said to Klaus. She was lying. He was anything but handsome. But she didn't care. She was having a good time, and that was all that mattered. She noticed that Mattie would not look directly at her. In fact, she was looking away, and she seemed ashamed that Trudy was flirting shamelessly.

The food and beer filled the entire table. Not since Rudy's death had Trudy enjoyed such abundance. Mattie couldn't resist the food, even though Trudy could see that she was eating reluctantly. But Trudy wasn't reluctant at all. She ate until she was full. Then, just when she thought she couldn't consume another bite, Klaus ordered dessert, strudel, cake, and real coffee. Trudy took a piece of strudel but was too full to eat it. All she could do was pick at it and wish she could wrap it in her napkin and take it back to the hotel to eat for breakfast. But she was too ashamed to do that in front of Klaus. It was several hours later when Klaus stood up and went to take care of the bill. When he returned, he told Trudy, "Let's you and I go back to my hotel room and have a glass of schnapps."

"I can't. I can't leave my sister," Trudy said.

"Sure you can. Mattie is a big girl. You can get back to your room alone, can't you, Mattie?"

"I'd prefer Trudy to come back with me," Mattie said. There was nervousness in her voice.

Like an abrupt change of weather, from a bright sunny day to a tornado, a dark cloud crept over Klaus' face. "But you will do as I say. You will go back to your room alone," he said firmly to Mattie. Then he turned to Trudy and said, "And you will come with me to my room, where we will have a glass of schnapps."

Trudy looked at him. Something about the look on his face made the hair on the back of her neck stand up. She felt a chill run through her. She was about to say, "No, I have to go with my sister." But then he smiled warmly, and the dark clouds in his eyes were instantly gone. In fact, they had disappeared so fast that Trudy wondered if she hadn't imagined them.

"Please," he said sweetly. "Won't you come to my room and have a drink with me, Trudy? I promise you; it will only be one drink. And I will be a perfect gentleman."

His smile was so reassuring that Trudy agreed. Without a glance at her sister, Trudy stood up and took Klaus' hand. Then they turned and walked back to Klaus's hotel room down the street. Trudy was nervous, but she didn't want to lose him. He would be a wonderful companion for her and Mattie during this trip. She wouldn't have to worry about paying for good meals if he liked her. As she walked back to his room, she made a plan. She would solidify his interest in her by kissing and teasing him that night.

A shiver ran through Mattie at the table as she watched her sister walk away beside this strange older man. She wished Trudy would change her mind. She even waited for several minutes, hoping that Trudy would return. But Trudy continued to walk in the other direction. She never turned to look at Mattie, who finally got up and walked back to her hotel room alone.

CHAPTER 44

The small task of bathing seemed to lift Margot's spirits tremendously. Although she never outwardly complained about their living conditions, Ben knew how difficult living in the attic had been for her. So, that evening, when Frau Danner came into the attic, Ben thanked her for her kindness. "You have been so wonderful to us," He said. "I appreciate everything you've done. And I really appreciate your allowing Margot to go downstairs and bathe. It made her feel better."

"I have only done what any decent person would," Frau Danner said.

"I hate to ask this of you, knowing how much you have done already."

"Ben, what is it?" the old woman asked. "What do you need?"

"It's not for me. It's for Margot."

Margot hadn't expected this. She looked up at him by the light of the candle, and even in the darkness, he could see that she was surprised and curious. "For me? What is it?" then she said to Frau Danner. "I don't know what he's talking about."

"I haven't discussed it with you," Ben said, taking Margot's hand. Then he turned back to Frau Danner. "If it would be too much trouble, I will understand. But, if it's at all possible, maybe you could allow Margot to come downstairs and take a bath once a week. It really did lift her spirits."

The old woman sighed. "It's risky," she said softly. There was a long silence. Then she added, "But what the hell? I know it's important that you both try to stay as upbeat as you can. It's hard living up here in this little room. And a bath can make a woman feel better. I know this, too. So, my answer is yes. I will arrange for Margot to bathe once a week. I will arrange for you to bathe as well, Ben. I can imagine how hard it is for both of you to be stuck up here in this tiny room, day in and day out. We will just have to be very careful, that's all. We'll have to make sure that the shades are completely closed and that there is no possible way anyone can see inside. You won't be able to use too much water. I don't want to alert the authorities by suddenly using an excessive amount."

"Of course. We are more than happy to do all of those things."

"Then we'll plan for it. Margot had the first bath. So, it's your turn tomorrow, Ben."

He looked over at Margot. "You can have my turn if you'd like."

She smiled. "I would, but I can wait until next week. Take your turn. It's wonderful to feel clean."

"You won't have to wait that long, Margot. You can come downstairs with me the following night," Frau Danner said.

CHAPTER 45

The weekly baths changed their lives in many ways. It was something both Margot and Ben looked forward to. They knew it was risky and dangerous to leave the tiny attic. But it was also nurturing for the soul. Margot looked forward to the days when she could leave the tiny room and enter the light bathroom, where she could remove her clothing and feel the water caress her skin. She loved to wash her hair. The harsh soap dried her hair out, but it didn't matter. She finally felt human again. However, when Ben left the attic and went downstairs for his weekly bath, Margot felt a tremendous sense of nervousness. Her constant fear was even stronger when she was alone. But she would never tell him this because she knew he would not go downstairs if he was aware of it, and she knew it was good for him. When she was alone, Margot had nothing to do but lose herself in her thoughts, and there was far too much horror outside the little room for her mind not to dwell upon it. Her mind would go on a terrifying roller coaster ride. She thought of Max but was also worried about her parents. There was no telling what kind of havoc Trudy had created outside in the world. Staying all day and night in a dark room was taking a toll on them both. So, one afternoon, Ben took a huge risk. He stood up and cracked the side of the window shade open just a bit more so that some additional light could flow into the room during the day. Then, staying far away from the window, he walked over to where Margot was sitting on the floor, pulled a small wad of bills out of his pants pocket, and showed them to her. "I have some money," he said. "I've been holding on to it for an emergency," he said. "In case we need it."

She was surprised. Until that moment, she didn't know he had anything of value. Then he pulled out a handkerchief that was bunched up out of his pocket and unwrapped it. Inside was a beautiful diamond ring and a gold band. "This was my mother's engagement ring and her wedding band." He said, handing them to Margot so she could get a closer look. "I planned to use them as bargaining tools if we got into trouble. But now, with the circumstances being what they are between you and me, I thought that perhaps you might wear them one day."

"Don't say that," she had said to him. A sick feeling came over her.

"I didn't mean to upset you."

"I know. But the only way I would ever wear them would be if Max was dead."

"I don't want that. Of course, I don't. I would never want to see anything like that happen to Max. He was my friend, after all. But we don't know what has happened out there in the world, and I would be lying if I said I didn't want to marry you someday."

Her heart was conflicted, so conflicted that she was unable to answer. All she could do was turn away from him and let the tears roll down her cheeks.

CHAPTER 46

Klaus poured two glasses of schnapps. He handed one to Trudy and placed the other on a coffee table in front of the sofa in his suite. "Did you enjoy your dinner?" he asked.

"I did. Thank you. It was lovely," she said.

He reached up and curled one of her blonde curls around his finger. Then he kissed her. She allowed him to kiss her again, more passionately this time. He took his glass and, in a single gulp, swallowed his schnapps, then he began kissing her neck and took her breast into one of his hands. His other hand found its way up her skirt. She had decided she would allow him to do whatever he liked short of intercourse. To keep his interest, she would save that for another time. But he began to pinch her nipples, and his hands on her womanhood became rough. "You're hurting me," she said, trying to push away. But he would not let her go, and his sexual exploration of her body became more painful. "Stop," she said. "That's enough."

He slapped her hard across the face. It scared her. She got up and tried to run to the door. Klaus followed her. He grabbed her. He was incredibly strong. Then he pulled her by her hair and pushed her onto the bed. When she entered his room, she hadn't noticed the handcuffs already attached to the top of the bed frame. On the bottom, there were thick ropes. Trudy struggled to get away, but he grabbed her hands one at a time and cuffed them to the bed. She tried to kick and get away, but he was stronger than he looked. Trudy let out a cry of protest, but he slapped her hard across the face again, and the fear silenced her. Then he took her feet one by one, even though she was still kicking, and tied them with the rope. She was now spread eagle on his bed and at his mercy.

"We are going to have a little fun," he said. "Plain, regular sex doesn't excite me anymore. I like it rough. Once I'm through with you, you will too."

Trudy was crying. Her heart was pounding, and she was terrified.

He ripped her dress open and pulled the skirt up over her hips. "I love power," he said in a hoarse voice. "I've killed people. And I've had intercourse with dead bodies. You can't imagine the feeling of power when you kill someone, then you can do whatever you please with their body. It's quite exhilarating, I assure you."

"Are you going to kill me?" she asked in a small, frightened voice. "Please, I beg you. Don't hurt me, don't kill me. Just let me go."

He laughed. "I don't need to kill you. I have plenty of young Jewish women to kill whenever the mood suits me. And since they are nothing but *Untermenschen* swine, not even human, it doesn't matter to anyone." He let out a maniacal laugh. "Do you know what I enjoy most about the Jews?"

She shook her head. "Please, just let me go."

"Not yet, my lovely blonde Aryan goddess," he laughed. "We are having too much fun for me to let you go."

"I want to leave. I made a mistake coming here. I don't know you."

"Well, that's why you're here. You're getting to know me. And it's fun, isn't it?" he said sarcastically.

"No, it's not."

He laughed again. "You interrupted me when I was telling you about the Jews. Say you're sorry."

"I'm sorry," Trudy whimpered. "Please let me go." Her limbs were shaking. She was cold and freezing, although it was not cold in the room.

"I like to torture them; the Jews, I mean. I can do as I please with them, and no one tries to stop me." He cleared his throat. Then he stood up and got something out of the dresser drawer. He clamped it on her nipple. Trudy let out a scream of pain. This time, he hit her in the face with his fist. Her nose spurted blood. "Scream again, and I will kill you. I don't want the hotel staff to come up here. Do you understand, my little *Fräulein*?"

"I am married. I am not a *Fräulein*, I am a Frau. My husband is at home waiting for me. He is a party member." She tried to convince him. "Please, I shouldn't be here. I don't know what I was thinking. I want to go back to my hotel room with my sister. Please, Klaus, let me go."

"You weren't so very married a few hours ago. You thought nothing of eating my food and coming back to my room. You're not the good little Aryan hausfrau you would have your poor husband believe you to be. You are a dirty, sinful creature. You know it as well as I do. And you deserve to be punished."

He began to sing and hum a German folk song. Her eyes watched him wide with terror. Then he stopped singing and laughed. "When I was a young boy, my father brought home a dog. I hated that dog because I was certain my father liked it better than he liked me. I wanted my father to love me. So, do you know what I did?"

She shook her head. *I am going to die here tonight.*

"I killed that mangy mutt. I knew how to make my *vater* suffer. He loved that beast. Oh, I knew he wouldn't care if I did something to myself. So, I cut him where he would bleed the most profusely. I killed his precious dog and left its mutilated body for him to find." Klaus hesitated for a moment. He closed his eyes, and then a smile came over his face. When he opened his eyes, he took a cigar out of the breast pocket of his jacket and lit it. "Ahh, my father was a good-for-nothing louse. He hit my mother. Not that she didn't deserve it. She was a miserable excuse for a mother. We never had enough to eat. My clothes were tattered and dirty because we were poor, and she was too lazy to wash and mend them. It's not that my father didn't earn a living. He did. Not a great living, but enough. However, he didn't care about us. He spent his money drinking and gambling. And on whores like you."

Her teeth were chattering so hard she was afraid she might break a tooth.

"But let me tell you something, for as bad as he was, and he was, it made me sick when I saw that he was capable of love. There was no doubt he loved that stinking mutt. When he found the dog, my father wept like a broken child. Then he came looking for me. He was furious. He knew I did it and beat me with his belt buckle. I didn't cry. In fact, I never said a single word. I just smiled at him. He beat me so badly that I had to go to the hospital. After that day, I no longer wanted his love. I knew that I hated him, and I would spend the rest of my days on earth shaming him and punishing him for his treatment of me."

She moaned.

"Anyway…" He took a long puff on his cigar. "It was years later, but I got my revenge. I made him suffer. Do you know how I did it?" he didn't wait for her to answer. His face was red now and turned redder as he spoke. "When our teacher at school told us that children should turn their parents in if they found out that they were breaking Hitler's laws. I knew I was no longer the powerless little boy that my *vater* could kick and punch until I was bloody. No, I was older now, and that teacher had given me the power I longed for. I knew just what to do with it. I turned my father into the Gestapo. I went to my school administrator and told him that my father was helping Jews. And do you know what?"

Trudy's eyes were closed. She was having trouble catching her breath.

"Did you hear me? Don't you dare die on me? I'm not done with you yet. I am in the middle of a story. Now, you had better answer me. Or I'll wake you up all right. I'll wake you up with such pain you won't be able to bear it."

"What? I am awake. Please. Please let me go," she said.

"That's better." He sighed. "I'll continue my story now. As far as my father was concerned, it turned out that I was lying. My father wasn't helping Jews. He didn't care about Jews at all, or anyone else for that matter. But I knew that helping Jews was a huge offense, and he would be severely punished." He put the cigar down in the ashtray. Then he nodded his head. "So, do you know what happened?"

"No, I don't know. Please let me go. I want to go to my hotel with my sister."

"Hush." He hissed. "The day after I reported him, my father was arrested. They sent him to a work camp, and he died there. I'm sure he suffered, but it was good. So, I got my revenge. And it all worked out just fine. Just fine, I tell you."

His fists were balled up. His eyes glowed with wild madness. But most frightening of all was the maniacal smile on his crimson face.

Trudy didn't answer. She just nodded. Her body was shaking violently. Her heart was pounding in her ears. She couldn't think of anything that she could possibly say to bring him back to sanity. *He's an insane monster. And he's going to kill me.*

Klaus reached into the drawer of the hotel dresser and took out a hunting knife with a long blade. *He's going to carve me up like that dog he killed. Oh, dear God. No, please. No.*

Then he took the knife and cut long but very thin and extremely shallow slices from her breasts all the way down to her womanhood. It hurt as thin lines of blood formed on her body. She cried out, but he slapped her again.

It was almost dawn when Klaus finally finished playing his painful and terrible games with Trudy. Then he mounted her and finished. His eyes were gleaming. *This is it. This is the end. The pain will be over, but my life will be over, too.*

"I'll be right back," he said, and there was that maniacal smile again. She shivered.

Klaus was gone for a moment, and then she heard the water running in the bathroom. Trudy struggled with all her strength to free herself from the tight handcuffs that were cutting into her wrists. She tried to kick her feet, but he'd tied them very tightly, and the rope was very thick. Still, she knew she must continue to try. The muscles in her neck protruded. Her eyes bulged. Her body was tense and ridged. Tears covered her cheeks. Her heart raced so hard that she thought it might burst.

And then Klaus returned. He was showered and dressed in a clean shirt, tie, and dark suit. His hair was neatly combed. "We had a nice evening, didn't we, *Fräulein*?" he said in a calm, almost normal-sounding voice.

She didn't correct him. She just lay there watching him, praying that he would not kill her, but waiting to see what he would do next.

"Let me untie these ropes and remove these cuffs so you can freshen up before you leave." He said in a sweet voice. She studied him as he removed the ropes and the cuffs. Klaus's face was no longer red. His eyes were steady and even. He looked the same as he had during dinner. *The madness seems to have disappeared. Was it ever really there? Of course, it was there.* "I hope I didn't scare you." He smiled gently. "I just like to play rough. It excites my passion. If you know what I mean. But I would never really hurt you. Not really. Although I am sorry about all this blood."

She nodded. Her hands and feet were free. Now she must hurry and find a way to get out of this hotel room before his personality changes again.

"Did you have fun?" he asked.

Are you serious? She thought. *Fun? No, I didn't have fun. You hurt and terrified me.*

When Trudy didn't answer, Klaus' eyes narrowed, and she could see he was getting angry. "Of course, it was fun. Just different from anything I've ever done before," she stammered, lying to pacify him.

"Yes, but you'll learn to like it. You'll see." He smiled. "Now, run along. I have some business to attend to before I can get to bed. But we can have dinner later tonight. I can meet you at your hotel. Where are you staying?"

"Not tonight. My husband is coming to Munich. He's on his way right now," she lied. She wanted him to disappear. "We will be changing hotels, so I don't know where I'll stay. Either way, he'll be here in Munich for the rest of my trip, so I am sorry, but I can't meet you." She cleared her throat, hoping he would believe her and just go away.

"But I want to see you again," he said, sounding like a spoiled child.

"Of course, of course," she said. "Don't worry, I know where you are staying. Drop by your hotel when he leaves later in the week. I have an extra day here after he is gone. So, we could get together then. Would that be all right?" She was talking fast. She knew she sounded nervous. But she hoped this promise would be enough for him to let her go.

"Of course." He smiled. "I'll drop by the hotel anytime you are free. If I am not here, just leave me a message at the desk with the name of your hotel and your room number. I'll get in touch with you as soon as I return."

She nodded, "Yes, yes, of course I will."

"I'm looking forward to seeing you again," he said. His voice was calm. His eyes and smile hid every aspect of his madness. She was stunned by how normal he could appear. But she knew what he was capable of. She'd experienced it last night, and this act of being sane was almost as frightening as his underlying madness.

"Yes, I'm looking forward to seeing you as well." She smiled, trying to keep her lips from quivering. She couldn't move fast enough. Picking up her shoes and holding them in one hand, she gripped her dress closed where he had torn it open to reveal her breasts. He opened the door. And seeing freedom, she ran out of the room. Without looking behind her, Trudy ran all the way back to the hotel where she and Mattie were staying. As she dashed through the streets, shoeless with her torn dress, people turned to stare at her. Her face was stained with blood, the front of her dress was bloody as well, and trickles of dried blood ran down her legs.

When she entered her hotel room, Mattie was looking in the closet for something to wear. Before she looked over at Trudy and saw her condition, she said, "Where have you been? You've been out all night like an alley cat." But then Mattie turned around and gasped when she saw her sister. "What happened to you?" she said, running to Trudy and taking her in her arms.

"He was crazy. Klaus is a monster. My night was a night in hell," Trudy said as she began to weep.

"Sit down," Mattie said, taking Trudy to the bed. They sat together while Trudy told Mattie everything that had happened. "He was violent. He said things that frightened me. He hurt me, too. He sliced me up with a knife. Not deep enough to kill me, just surface cuts. But I am sure I'll have scars all over my body. Oh, Mattie, it was horrible. I know he was out of his mind. He had me tied up to the bed and was talking about murdering Jews and having intercourse with dead bodies." She shivered. "And he had this terrible smile. I can't close my eyes without seeing it. At one point, he said he took a bath in the blood of Jewish women because he read somewhere that some royal person stayed young by doing that. It was beyond terrifying."

"You can't go home with strangers, Trudy. You're lucky to be alive."

"Although Rudy never came out and told me this, I always knew that the Nazis were killing Jews. I'm sure you have heard some things from Ebert, too."

"Yes, but I try not to think about it," Mattie said. "It's better that way."

"I never really gave it much thought, either. I mean, whatever the Party was doing with Jews didn't affect me directly, and I always felt that a world without Jews would be a better world. Have you and Ebert ever discussed this?"

"We have."

"Doesn't he work in some capacity to keep the Jews under control? Isn't that right?"

"Yes, he does. But we don't talk about it. It's a job. It needs to be done, and my husband and I are good Germans. My husband does what he must do for our fatherland."

"Well, Klaus does, too, and he thoroughly enjoys it. I don't know about Ebert."

"I'd rather not discuss this anymore," Mattie said coldly.

"Well, all I know is that I'm done playing around. I swear I am," Trudy declared. "I'm going home to Max, and I will be a good hausfrau, just like you, from now on."

"Does Klaus know which hotel you are staying in?" Mattie asked. "Because if he does, we should move. I don't want him to come looking for you."

"He has no idea. I am sure of it. I never told him. And besides, he thinks that Max is coming into town and that we will change hotels once he arrives. He has no idea where to find me. He expects me to come looking for him when Max leaves Munich. I had to tell him that I would come to him as soon as I could. It was the only way I could make him let me go."

"That's good," Mattie said. "You're safe now. Go and take a shower. Clean yourself up. Then lie down and get some rest. I'm sure you need it."

"I do," Trudy admitted. She was still very nervous as she walked to the bathroom down the hall. When she began to wash the blood from her body, she saw the real damage he'd done. There were long, thin marks down the front of her. Trudy wept as she tried desperately to wash away the horrors of the previous night. And even though she was alone in the bathroom, she continually looked behind her. She was edgy, and although she was alone, she was afraid that she would look up and see Klaus' horrible face watching her.

After Trudy was clean, she put on her robe and went back to her room. When she got there, she slipped into a clean nightdress. Then she lay down.

"I'm going out for a little while," Mattie said. "Just to walk around and see the sights."

"No, no, please, don't leave me. I can't stay here alone. I can't close my eyes to sleep unless you are here with me. I'm afraid I'll wake up, and he'll be here," Trudy said anxiously.

Mattie nodded. "All right. I'll stay. But shall I go and get us something to eat? I could bring it back to the room with me."

"I'm not hungry. Please, Mattie, don't leave me. Stay here with me. I can't bear to be alone right now."

"All right. I won't leave you. I'll wait to eat until you awaken."

Trudy fell into a fitful sleep filled with nightmares. In her dreams, she saw Rudy coming towards her. He was covered in blood and laughing at her. Then she saw Margot. A harsh voice cackled behind her. It said, "Margot is a witch. She's a Jew, and Jewish women are witches. This curse, this man you spent the night with, came from her." In her dream, Trudy turned around to see who was speaking. It was Max. "You know deep down inside that I don't love you. I loved

Margot. You took her away from me, and you killed my little boy. You are being punished. Margot is a witch, and she is punishing you. I am only living with you so that I can help her curse you."

"No, no," Trudy screamed as she tossed herself awake.

Mattie was at her side immediately. "You're all right," she said. "It was just a nightmare."

"Yes, just a nightmare," Trudy said, but she was shaking. "I'm so cold."

Mattie covered Trudy with the blanket from the other bed. "There. Is that better?" Mattie asked.

"Yes," Trudy said. "You've always been such a good sister to me."

There was a long silence. Then, in a soft voice, Mattie said, "Margot was a good sister to you, too. You couldn't accept her kindness because you were always jealous of her. But she never tried to hurt you. She never tried to hurt any of us."

"I wasn't jealous. I knew the truth and couldn't accept her as our sister. Margot is not our real sister. She was adopted. Uncle Alex and some Jewish whore were her real parents."

"That's not true. Where did you hear that?"

"It is true. I heard *Mutti* and *Vater* talking years ago when we were young. They said it."

Mattie gasped. Then she shook her head. "All right, well, what if it's true? Margot isn't a real Jew. She isn't like the other Jews. She grew up with us. It didn't matter where she was born or who her parents were; she was our sister, Trudy. She loved us. I loved her, too. Now, we don't know where she is. And I am worried about her all the time."

Trudy felt guilty. She dared not tell Mattie the truth about what happened that day that Max shot Rudy. So, she just restated the lie. "Margot wasn't the good sister you thought she was. She had an affair with Rudy. You know that. You heard it when I told the police."

"I don't believe it. Margot loved Max. They were happy together. I am not sure what happened or where Margot is, but I never believed that story."

"Mattie? I can't believe you, of all people, would doubt me. I have never lied to you," Trudy said, staring into Mattie's eyes.

Mattie smiled a sad but knowing smile. "You've lied to me plenty,

Trudy. Even so, you're my sister, and I love you. But I also know you. And I know that you can be very mean. I don't know what you did to Margot or what really happened. I know that Margot would never have had an affair with Rudy."

"You insult me, Mattie."

"Yes, I am sure you feel insulted. But I do know you very well. Still, there's no reason to keep talking about this. You need to try to get some rest."

Trudy fell back to sleep quickly. This time, she slept without dreaming for several hours. Occasionally, she would turn over and open her eyes, glancing at the chair beside her bed where Mattie was reading a magazine. The sight of Mattie sitting there quietly reassured Trudy, and she closed her eyes again.

Finally, when night fell, Trudy awakened. "How long did I sleep?"

"All day," Mattie said. "I'm glad you're awake because I didn't want to leave the room while you were asleep in case you woke up. I must go to the bathroom. I've been waiting for hours. Then I want to go downstairs to get something to eat. I'll buy some food and bring it back for both of us."

"No, I told you I can't stay here alone," Trudy said, sitting up. "At least not for that long. You can run to the bathroom, but then please come right back. Don't go out."

"Trudy, I'm famished. I need to get something to eat."

"All right. I suppose you must eat," she grumbled. "Let me get dressed, and I'll go downstairs with you."

"Maybe we can eat at a restaurant or a *Biergarten*? After all, I haven't had a holiday in years. I would like to get out of the hotel room," Mattie admitted.

"Yes, I suppose it would be all right," Trudy said. "Let me freshen up. I'll be ready in a few minutes."

Trudy's entire body ached as she climbed out of bed and walked down the hall to the bathroom with Mattie. She washed her face with cold water that stung the cut near her eye. But when she glanced in the mirror, Trudy gasped in horror. A purple and red bruise surrounded the cut and covered her cheek. "Look at me," she said to Mattie when Mattie came out of the bathroom stall. "Look what he did to my face."

"Yes, I know." Mattie sighed. "I don't know what you're going to tell Max. I hope it's gone by the time we go home."

"I don't know what I am going to tell him, and I don't care about Max right now," Trudy snapped. "I am so angry. That man destroyed my face."

"It's not destroyed. You're just bruised. It will heal. But at least now, you know it's not a good idea to go to hotel rooms with strangers," Mattie said.

"Please don't lecture me after all I've been through."

"I'm trying to help you," Mattie said.

"Yes, well, I don't need that kind of help right now."

Mattie shook her head. "I don't understand you sometimes. You can be so arrogant."

"I'm sorry," Trudy said. "It's just been a terrible trip so far. And I hate to go out looking like this. What will people think?"

"It doesn't matter, does it? We need to eat. So, we will find somewhere where you can feel comfortable. All right?"

"Yes," Trudy nodded.

They returned to the room, where Trudy wore a clean dress. She had to dispose of the one she'd worn the night before, which was her favorite. But it was torn and stained beyond repair. Once Trudy was ready, they left the hotel and walked a few streets until they found a small, intimate café. "This looks quiet and private," Mattie said.

The host was a young man. He was cheerful and pretended that he did not see the bruise on Trudy's face. There were only a couple of tables in the restaurant, and only one other was occupied. From how the host spoke to the waitress, it seemed to Trudy that the waitress was his wife. He seated Mattie and Trudy at a table in the corner, then he turned to the waitress and said, "Helga, get these two ladies water and menus."

The waitress nodded, and in seconds, Mattie and Trudy were reading a small menu.

"It's expensive," Mattie said, grimacing.

"Yes, it is. I suppose they've raised the prices."

"Yes, probably. We'll have to be careful with what we order," Mattie said.

Trudy nodded. "If it weren't for Max being so lazy and unambitious, I would never have had dinner with that terrible man last night. I would have had plenty of money to go out and eat and order whatever I wanted. It's really all Max's fault that happened."

"Don't blame Max for what you did," Mattie said. "You did that because you wanted to."

"I did it because Max didn't have the kind of money I am used to spending, and I just didn't want to have to economize on our holiday."

"I see," Mattie said, there was annoyance in her voice. "Let's order."

They placed an order for a pretzel with spicy mustard and two sausages. "We must have a beer with our dinner. We must order two glasses at least," Trudy insisted.

"All right. Order two beers. But we can't afford to have more. We don't have enough money to be spending it so frivolously. It must last for the whole week."

"Yes, all right," Trudy said, then she ordered two beers.

The beer came before the food. Trudy took a sip. "Oh, this is delicious." She smacked her lips.

"Yes, it is," Mattie agreed.

Just then, two young Nazi officers wearing the black uniforms of the Waffen-SS walked into the café. When Trudy saw them, she gasped. "Look at that blond fellow. He is so handsome. I think he's even better looking than Max."

"Trudy, I thought you'd learned your lesson about strangers," Mattie scolded.

"I did, but you must admit that he is handsome."

"Yes, he's handsome, but you have a husband at home."

"You know, Max and I aren't even married. Technically, he's still married to Margot. We just live together. It's convenient."

"Come on, Trudy, I know you arranged that," Mattie scoffed. "You wanted him. You won him. And now, you're bored with him. Trudy, you have never been satisfied with anything you have. That's a bad trait to overcome. But you really must try. I promise you that you will never be happy this way."

But Trudy wasn't paying attention to what Mattie was saying. She could see that the young Nazi had taken notice of her. He was studying her with admiration, and she was smiling.

The waitress brought their food and, with it, two more beers. "We didn't order these," Mattie said, indicating the beer.

"I know. The officers over there sent the beers to your table," the waitress said.

Trudy was beaming. It was as if she'd forgotten everything that had happened the night before. She was smiling broadly at the most handsome of the two young men. Then she winked at him and lifted her glass, taking a long sip. When she finished, she said, "Thank you."

He stood up and walked over to the table where Trudy and Mattie sat. "May we join you?"

"I don't think that's a good idea," Mattie said.

"Yes, of course, you can join us," Trudy piped up cheerfully. Mattie stared at her sister in disgust.

The Nazi waved to his friend to come over and join them. His friend nodded and got up. Then, both officers sat down at the table with Mattie and Trudy. "I'm Peter, and this is my friend Gunter."

"Nice to meet you both," Trudy said.

The room was dimly lit, and it wasn't until he got closer that Peter saw the bruise on Trudy's face. "Fräulein," he said with what appeared to be genuine shock and concern, "what happened to your lovely face?"

"I got back to the hotel a little drunk last night and walked into the room door. Too much beer, I guess." Trudy laughed nervously. Mattie glared at Trudy.

Gunter tried to talk to Mattie. She was polite but immediately told him she was married and not interested in other men. Meanwhile, Trudy was flirting shamelessly with Peter.

The men ordered a pitcher of beer. Peter seemed lighthearted as he told stories that made Trudy laugh. The four of them drank until the restaurant was about to close. "Would you two ladies like to come to our room for a nightcap?" Peter asked.

Mattie shook her head and shot a look of warning at Trudy. Trudy felt her blood run cold. It was one thing to flirt with a handsome man in the safety of a public place, but quite another thing to go to his room where they were alone, and he could do anything. She had learned that the hard way as she thought of the night before. But she liked Peter and didn't want to lose his interest. So, as coyly as she could, she said, "I think perhaps it's a bit too soon for that."

He laughed. "Yes, perhaps it is. Would you two like to join us tomorrow night for dinner?"

Trudy looked at Mattie, who was shaking her head. Looking away from her sister, Trudy closed her eyes for a moment. *He's very handsome. He's not old and strange like Klaus. Besides, what could it hurt to have dinner in a public place? Mattie and his friend Gunter will be with us. Besides, he really has been such a gentleman so far tonight. Not only is he handsome, but he will pay for the food and beer.* "Yes, we'd love to," Trudy said.

"Then it's settled. We'll go to a nice restaurant that I think you two girls will enjoy. Shall we meet you in your hotel room?"

"Yes, that would be fine," Trudy said.

"No, I don't think that's a good idea. I'm sure you understand. After all, we hardly know you," Mattie interrupted quickly. "So, I don't think you should come to our hotel room. We'll meet you at the restaurant. Give us the name and address of the restaurant and the time you'd like to have dinner, and we'll be there." She gave Trudy an angry look.

When they arrived back at the hotel room, Mattie was enraged. She turned to Trudy. "One of these days, you're going to get yourself killed. And I don't know how to stop you. You can't seem to learn from your mistakes. You should never have started flirting with that man. He's a stranger. You don't know him. Look what happened the night before. That crazy lunatic almost killed you. Do you want to go through that again?"

"Peter is much different from Klaus."

"How do you know that, Trudy? Just because he's nice-looking? That means nothing," Mattie scoffed. "You don't know that he's not just as crazy as Klaus, or maybe even worse. You don't know a thing about him."

"Well, I didn't go back to his room now, did I? We are meeting him at a restaurant for dinner. That should be safe."

"I hope so," Mattie said.

CHAPTER 47

The following night, when Trudy and Mattie met Peter and Gunter for dinner, Trudy was taken in by Peter's good manners. He pulled out the chair for her and ordered for her. Not only was he extremely good-looking in an Aryan way, but he also had a lot of Rudy's good qualities. He had plenty of money, and he was generous. Like Rudy, she was proud to be seen with him in his uniform, which, along with his badges, got him many benefits at the restaurant where they met for dinner. But unlike Rudy, he was attentive to Trudy. While they were at dinner, his eyes weren't roaming the restaurant to see what other women were eyeing him.

But just like Rudy, Peter knew how to dominate a conversation. He seemed to have a never-ending repertoire of jokes and funny stories to amuse everyone at the table. There was no mention of any unpleasant subjects. Not once did Peter mention Jews or the war or anything that would put a damper on the evening. Only one thing worried Trudy. Mattie was cold towards Peter throughout dinner, and when he had asked Trudy if she had a husband or a boyfriend, Mattie had started to tell him about Max, but Trudy quickly interrupted her and changed the subject. Trudy was furious with her sister. She glared at Mattie. There was a tension between them for the rest of the evening.

Once again, like the night before, they drank until the restaurant was ready to close. The terrible events of that night with Klaus were behind Trudy. She refused to think about them. And she had already made up her mind she was going to go back to Peter's room. She would not have sex with him, not yet. She was planning to make him wait. But to her surprise, he didn't ask her to come to his room. Instead, after he paid the check, he just pecked her on the lips. A soft, tender kiss without passion. The kind of kiss one gives to a relative. Then he said goodnight. Trudy and her sister stood on the street for a moment and watched the two men walk away. Peter did not look back. Finally, they turned around a corner and were gone.

"Let's go back to our hotel," Mattie suggested.

Trudy nodded. She was hurt and disappointed.

Trudy and Mattie were a little drunk as they returned to their hotel room. "He didn't ask to see me again. I don't think he likes me anymore," Trudy said. "What did I do wrong?"

"I don't know," Mattie said. "But it doesn't matter. We're going home to Berlin in a few days. Let's just say we had a nice time with these fellows and forget about them."

"I can't. I really saw something in him."

"Oh, Trudy. You always want the men who you can't have. Once you have them, you are done with them. Let this fellow go. He bought us a nice dinner. What more do you want?"

"I want to see him again."

"Well, he might have other commitments."

"You mean like a wife?"

"Yes, or a girlfriend. Who knows why he didn't ask to see you again?"

"Or maybe it's because you saw fit to stick your nose into my business." Trudy turned on her sister, hissing like a snake. "Why did you try to tell him about Max? It wasn't your place to open your mouth and tell him my business. Yet, you tried. And I think you ruined it. I believe this is all your fault. I can't forgive you. Not ever." Trudy didn't say another word.

When they got back to their room, Trudy was exhausted. She got ready for bed and lay down. But she couldn't sleep. She closed her eyes and thought about choking Mattie for ruining her chances with Peter. Trudy imagined Mattie's eyes bulging and her face turning crimson. She was furious, but she couldn't kill Mattie. So, she turned over and cursed her sister under her breath.

The following day, Trudy awakened to find the room empty. Mattie was gone. A wave of panic came over Trudy. *Why do I rely on her so much? She ruined my chances last night. I should be glad she's gone.* But she wasn't glad, she was worried. Her stomach felt sick, and she began to itch all over.

Then, a key turned in the lock on the door, and Mattie walked in, freshly showered. "I was feeling a little under the weather from drinking so much last night, so I took a quick shower. I suggest you do the same."

"You're right. That's a good idea. I will go right now," Trudy said, relieved Mattie had returned. But her tone of voice still had a twinge of anger. "Please stay here. I'll be right back." She said as she picked up her soap, towel, toothbrush, toothpaste, and the last of the shampoo Rudy had given her and left the room.

It was a pleasant and easy day. They walked around Munich and stopped for an inexpensive meal at midday. That night, they splurged. Instead of having dinner, they drank two pitchers of the rich, dark beer they both loved. Wherever they went, Trudy's eyes scanned the area in search of Peter. But she didn't see him. And she was becoming sure that she would never see him again. *It's all Mattie's fault. She should learn to keep her mouth shut.* She thought, but there was no use in arguing. The damage was done. Peter was gone.

After finishing the beer, Mattie and Trudy returned to their hotel room. They were both tired and went to bed.

The next day, Trudy got up late. Mattie was still asleep, but she woke her. They both agreed that they had slight headaches stemming from hangovers. Trudy said she was not hungry, but Mattie insisted they eat something. And since Trudy was too sick to her stomach to argue, she went along. They found a street vendor who sold pretzels. He offered spicy mustard as a condiment, but neither of the women had the stomach for that. They bought two salted pretzels and sat on a bench to eat them.

"Let's find those special gingerbread heart cookies we got when we came here last time with Rudy," Mattie suggested.

"Are you still hungry?" Trudy asked in disbelief. She could hardly swallow the pretzel.

"Not really. But I loved them. They were so charming with their sweet little sayings written in frosting. I would like to buy one and bring it home for Ebert."

"All right. I suppose walking a bit wouldn't hurt. Although I would rather go back to the room and lie down," Trudy admitted.

"Yes, let's walk a bit."

As they ambled through the streets, still nibbling on bits of pretzel, they passed by an outdoor café where a group of teenagers dressed in traditional German dirndl skirts and *lederhosen* were on a small stage singing German folk songs and dancing. "Let's stop and watch for a few minutes," Mattie said.

"I'd love to, but I have such a terrible headache, and this singing doesn't help," Trudy said.

"No, I suppose it doesn't."

"Don't you have a hangover too?"

"Yes, but I don't want to miss all the wonderful sights. You know? It might be many years, if ever, before we can return. Don't you want to enjoy this fantastic experience? I am so excited to be on holiday."

Trudy looked at Mattie. She was still annoyed with her for ruining her chances with Peter. Now, she wanted to disappoint her sister the way she'd been disappointed. "I don't care about standing here and listening to some children sing. I told you I am not feeling well."

"All right, let's go," Mattie said, and there was clear disappointment in her voice.

Trudy looked the other way so Mattie couldn't see that she was smiling.

They began to walk again, and as they passed the famous brewery known as the Hofbräuhaus, a male voice rang out, calling their names, "Trudy! Mattie!"

CHAPTER 48

A shot of fear coursed through Trudy. Without turning around, she knew who the voice belonged to. A quick glance at Mattie told her that Mattie also knew who it was. Trudy grabbed her sister's arm and turned her around. Then, they started walking as quickly as possible in the opposite direction. "Stop, what's the matter with you girls? How can you expect me to keep up with you?" The man to whom the voice belonged grabbed the sleeve of Trudy's dress, and she halted. "Trudy, I suppose your husband is here in Munich because I haven't heard from you. I have been checking my messages at the hotel desk. But you haven't left one. I'll assume he's back in your room. So I am glad I found you two when you were alone. Without him, I mean." Klaus was smiling. It was not the maniacal smile that he kept hidden until he was ready to reveal that other side of himself. But Trudy shivered because she knew what he was hiding just under the surface, and she knew what he was capable of.

"I'm sorry," she stammered. "Like I told you, my husband is in town. It seems he is staying for the rest of our holiday, and then we return home together. So, I'm sorry, but I can't meet with you again."

"Oh, dear. Yes. The husband. Of course. You are such a good and devoted wife. Now, aren't you? You're faithful and loyal as they come.

Isn't that right?" he said sarcastically. Now that maniacal smile was back, and she could see the traces of that monster who had tortured her the other night.

"I have to go. I'm sorry." She was afraid of him.

"Don't be sorry. We can still find time to be together." He nodded. "Look, you are out alone with your sister now. This is a time we could be together. Something quick? What do you think?"

She shook her head. "I am sorry. But I must go. My husband is waiting."

"Not so fast." He squeezed her arm. "My dear, have you forgotten who I am? The SS officers know me by name. I have a lot of influential friends. I could, if I were so inclined, have you arrested."

"For what? I've done nothing wrong." She was terrified as she pulled her arm away from him. He released her sleeve. She wanted to start running, but she was afraid of what he might do. It felt as if her feet were glued to the ground.

"It doesn't matter if you didn't do anything wrong. You do remember the story I told you about my father, don't you? Of course, you must." He smiled. "I know how to have someone arrested. Whether you're guilty or not makes no difference, really. Besides, you must realize that the police will believe me more than you. You can be sure of that." He laughed. "They'll put you in prison. So, if I were you, I would not make me angry by being so eager to run away."

Mattie was shaking. "Please, Klaus. Please let us go. My sister's husband is very jealous. And..." she was stammering. "A handsome man, a powerful man... like you... would have no trouble finding another girl. Any girl would be happy to have you."

"But, Mattie, the truth is, I don't want just any girl," he said.

Just then, Peter walked by, "Trudy." He said warmly when he saw her.

"This is my husband." Trudy said quickly, "Peter, this is Klaus. Klaus, this is Peter."

Peter cocked his head. He didn't quite understand why she had called him her husband. But his lovely blue eyes were sparkling. And it was obvious to Trudy that he could see that there was some kind of game going on, and he was more than willing to play along.

"You are Trudy's husband?" Klaus asked.

"I am. And it's a pleasure to meet you," Peter said. Peter had plenty of bars and medals on his uniform jacket, and Trudy could see that Klaus was intimidated by him.

"Heil Hitler." Klaus saluted.

"Heil Hitler." Peter returned the greeting. Then he turned his attention to Trudy. "I've been looking everywhere for you, dear."

"Mattie and I were taking a walk."

"Well, we have plans to meet with my friend Gunter in an hour. So, if you'll excuse us," Peter said to Klaus.

"But of course," Klaus said. He turned and walked away.

It chilled Trudy to watch how Klaus could change from an easygoing person to a monster in an instant. Once Klaus was out of earshot, Trudy said, "Thank you so much. You don't know how glad I am to see you."

"My goodness, but you are shaken up. What happened?" Peter asked.

"I'd rather not say."

"But you must. If you want me to protect you, I must know what I am protecting you from." He seemed to be taking this entire incident lightly as if there was nothing to fear. "Well, if you don't want to tell me, then you don't have to, I suppose."

"I'm sorry. I can't talk about it right now," Trudy admitted. "I just want you to know I am grateful you were here."

"Ahh, well, I am too. Anyway, I have an idea." Peter smiled. "Have you girls had lunch? Gunter is busy. He has gone off with some friends for the afternoon. Would you two like to join me to have something to eat?"

"Yes," Trudy said, giving Mattie a warning look as if to say, 'Don't you dare try to ruin this again.' "But please, not in that restaurant. Klaus is in there. That's where he came out of when he saw me."

"Really? Are you sure? It's one of the best. It's been around since the 1500s. They have delicious food."

"Yes, I am sure. Please, Peter, I don't want to see him again. Please?"

"All right. On one condition. Tell me why you are so afraid of that man over lunch."

"I'll tell you if you must know. But can I tell you when we get to the restaurant?"

"Sure. I know of another good one. Come on, follow me." Peter smiled.

That afternoon, following a quick lunch. Trudy told Peter everything that happened with Klaus. She was shaking and teary-eyed. "It was horrible," she said.

When she finished her entire story, Peter looked sympathetic but not surprised. "Some people like those kinds of games. He should have made it known to you that he was involved in that sort of thing."

"Are you?" she asked boldly, trembling and afraid as she waited for his answer.

"Me?" He laughed. "No. it's not my style."

"I'm glad," Trudy admitted.

"Don't get me wrong. I am an Aryan man. And that means that I am strong and, of course, fearless. I don't cower at the sight of death, torture, or blood, but it's not a part of my sexual preference. You see, I am proud to be a member of the Waffen-SS. I do what must be done. If it's murder or torture, I do it. Weakness and pity are unacceptable. The worth of an Aryan man is determined by his willingness to do whatever needs to be done to strengthen our Reich. It's the same for a woman, too."

"Yes, I can understand that," she said, and she did. Trudy knew that Rudy had been able to do heartless things when he felt it was necessary. He had been forced to kill the Jewish maid because she had not been competent. She was a lousy babysitter; she should have been watching Luzie better than she was. So, when Rudy shot the maid, Trudy found it easy to support his action. There was no doubt that Rudy, because of his important position, was forced to kill *Untermenschen* all the time. They didn't discuss it, but she knew it had to be done, and her husband had been one of the men who must do it. It was as simple as that. When he told her that the government had lied to Max and Margot and that Erik was not being sent to the hospital to be cured as they had been told, Trudy understood why Margot and

Max must be lied to. She could easily accept that Erik and others like him must be euthanized to purify the race.

After lunch, Peter did not return to his room. Instead, the three of them spent the rest of the evening together, walking and talking. They found a bakery that sold the heart-shaped cookies Mattie wanted, and although they were huge and one was enough for two or three people, Peter bought one each for Trudy and Mattie. Trudy nibbled on hers, and Mattie put hers in her handbag to bring home to Ebert. As they walked through town, they stopped at several breweries and had a beer or two. Then, later in the evening, they met Gunter for dinner at a small café.

There was music, and the beer was very good. It was late by the time they finished, but Peter did not suggest they return to his hotel room. Instead, he asked Trudy in a polite tone of voice, "Can I see you again tomorrow?"

"Yes, I would like that," Trudy said.

"Good. I look forward to it," Peter said, and this time, he asked Trudy where she was staying. Then, he made sure to write down the name and address of the hotel.

CHAPTER 49

Trudy refused to leave the room at her hotel the following morning. She wasn't sure when Peter would drop by and didn't want to miss him. So Mattie, tired of Trudy's flirtations, decided to go for breakfast by herself. When Mattie left, Trudy quickly applied her makeup and got dressed. Then she thumbed through one of her movie magazines and stared out the window, waiting for Peter. She was excited and nervous, so she lit a cigarette. Trudy had never become addicted to tobacco, but she smoked occasionally when she was anxious. She was afraid that Peter might not return. It might have been just a nice day and nothing more as far as he was concerned.

I really hope not. I hope he liked me and meant what he said when he asked me if he could see me today. I think he and I would be a perfect couple. For a moment, her thoughts went to Max. *I would rather be with a fellow like Peter. The honest truth is, I don't love Max. I probably never did. I think I just wanted him because he rejected me for Margot. Now that I have him, I can see him for what he really is. He's handsome, but not nearly as handsome as he was before Erik got sick. That took a lot out of both him and Margot. It aged them. I realize that they were distraught to find out that their child was dead. But, after the initial grief, they should both have thanked me.*

Rudy was right when he said the boy would have grown up to have no life. He had no potential. Erik is better off now. And so is Max. I don't know what happened to Margot. I don't care, really. I'm glad not to have to be around her anymore. She always made me feel foolish and inferior. No matter how much she aged or suffered, everyone always said she was the most beautiful girl they ever saw. More beautiful than me. I never thought so. But I hated to hear it. Now, she's been reduced to running and hiding because she isn't an Aryan. She's taken her rightful place as an inferior. And I am glad that Max knows the truth. But sadly, I have grown tired of him, and if Peter will have me, I'll tell Max I want to break up. If he refuses to leave the apartment, I'll threaten to tell the authorities about the fact that he killed Rudy and that he was married to a Jew. He'll have to give me whatever I want. I'll leave him no choice. But I can't get rid of him until I am sure I have someone else to pay my bills because I will not go out and get a job.

Mattie didn't return to the room until much later that afternoon. By then, Trudy was miserable. "I thought Peter would have come by the hotel by now," she said. "I'm afraid he was just being nice, asking me out for today."

"You aren't going to spend your entire holiday here in this room waiting for him, are you?" Mattie asked.

"I don't know." Trudy pouted. "What if we are alone in the street, and Klaus finds us again?"

"What if he does? You should not have been with him in the first place. And you shouldn't be looking to spend more time with Peter. You have a serious boyfriend at home. You took him away from your sister. Isn't that enough for you?" Mattie was staring directly at Trudy.

"I can't believe you are taking Margot's side against me. I've always been good to you."

"Yes, you have. You've given me your old clothes when you have grown tired of them. You and Rudy used to take Ebert and me out for dinner. I appreciate all of it. But you are a difficult and selfish girl, Trudy. You ruined Margot's and Max's lives, and now you are looking for a new boyfriend. Max bores you because he doesn't have enough money or power to keep you happy. You should have thought of that before. You should be ashamed of yourself."

"Shut up. I don't want to hear these terrible things from you. Margot is not our sister. She's nothing but a Jew. And Max is a failure."

"I'm going back out. I don't want to fight with you. In fact, I'm sorry I came back to the hotel," Mattie said. "I don't care if you sit here alone all day. It makes no difference to me."

Mattie picked up her handbag and left.

Trudy had almost given up on Peter by eight o'clock that evening when there was a knock on the door of her room. Her heart fluttered as she stood up and opened the door. On the other side of the doorway stood Peter, tall and handsome, smiling, in his black SS uniform. "Peter," she said, smiling her sweetest smile, never letting him know that she had been filled with anxiety all day because she was afraid he might be gone forever.

"I'm sorry. I couldn't come earlier. I had some business to attend to."

"Oh, I thought you were on holiday."

"We can't expect to take time for ourselves when we have a very important job of purifying the race. I had a job to do," he said.

"Did you have a meeting?"

He laughed. "No, it was even better than that. I happened to notice someone moving in the attic of a building right here in Munich. I got this feeling that it was Jews hiding. So I contacted the Gestapo and sent them over to investigate."

"Was it Jews?"

"It was. It was a woman and three little children hiding in an attic. Of course, the Gestapo took them away, and with them, they took the owner of the home."

"Who owned the home?"

"An Aryan husband and wife. They should be ashamed of themselves. Hiding Jews. breaking laws." He shook his head. "If every Aryan would just follow the rules, I could actually take a holiday," he said, shaking his head.

"What will happen to them?"

"Oh, don't you worry. They'll be punished. All of them will be punished severely. But right now, why don't you and I discuss how lovely you look?"

"You really think so?" she asked.

"Oh yes, I do. You are a beautiful woman, Trudy. There is no doubt in my mind about that."

She blushed.

"I'm starving," he said. "Are you hungry?"

"Yes," she said, realizing she hadn't eaten all day. "Shall we go for dinner?"

"Yes, but not yet," he said. "I have more important things for us to do."

Peter put his arms around her and pulled her to him. She felt her knees go weak and surrendered to his touch. He pushed her backward onto the bed. Then he pulled her dress up over her hips and removed her undergarments. He entered her slowly and gently. When he had finished, he smiled at her. "Now that we got that out of the way, let's go to dinner," he said as he winked at her. "Will Mattie be joining us?"

"No, she went out on her own today. I don't know when she'll be back."

"Good. So it will be just the two of us. Gunter had to return to Frankfurt. He had a meeting he had to attend."

They left the room and went to a restaurant where a band was playing German folk music along with new music that had recently become popular amongst the Nazis. They were songs about murdering Jews, and everyone in the *Biergarten* seemed to know them because everyone seemed to be singing along.

CHAPTER 50

After dinner, Trudy went back to Peter's hotel room. They had intercourse again, and Trudy spent the night. They got up late, and Trudy left to return to her hotel room to change her clothes. When she arrived, Mattie was waiting, worried again. "I assume Peter finally showed up," she said, her voice dripping with sarcasm.

"Yes, and we spent the night together."

"I can see that. You're a mess."

"Well, thank you," Trudy said cynically.

"Your behavior is despicable."

"I don't want to hear it," Trudy said.

"Well, you are going to hear it. Because it's true, and I am tired of being gentle with you. I've been holding back my true feelings about your behavior, candy-coating it all our lives because I have always been afraid of offending you. But quite frankly, you are out of control."

"Say whatever you like. I don't care. I'm going to take a shower, and then I am going to get dressed. Then Peter and I have plans to meet."

"I see. So, dare I ask, what happens with you and Peter when you get back home? What happens to Max?"

"I don't know. I haven't thought that far ahead. I am having a good time right now, and that's all that matters."

"Hmmm, I see. All that matters is that you have a good time. That's very responsible of you."

"You don't understand anything." Trudy spun around to stare at Mattie. There was hate in her eyes. "Do you know why you are such a good wife? I'll tell you why. It's because men weren't ever chasing after you. You were always the ugly sister. You had to take whatever you could get. That's why you married Ebert. You didn't have any other choice. Ebert was the only man who was ever remotely interested in you." She glared at Mattie. "You know what, Mattie? I think you would have been forced to stoop low enough to marry a Jew if Rudy hadn't found you, the ugliest Aryan man alive who would be willing to be your husband."

"Shut up already. I am sick of you. And, for your information, I would never marry a Jew. I am as Aryan as you are," Mattie said. "My husband is not ugly."

"Oh yeah? I think he is. Everyone else does, too. And they think the same thing of you."

"I'm going home," Mattie said. "Taking this trip with you was a mistake. Ebert and I can hardly afford to live, let alone for me to take a holiday. I only did it because I thought you needed to get away after Luzie and Rudy died. I wanted to be a good sister. But you don't deserve a good sister. I'll pack and be gone when you return tomorrow."

Trudy shook her head. "Do whatever you like. I don't care."

Trudy spent the night with Peter, and the next day, when she and Peter returned to Trudy's hotel room so she could change her clothes, Mattie was gone. "Why don't you check out of your hotel and spend the remaining days of your holiday with me in my room? You're spending the nights there, anyway. So, you don't need to waste money staying at this hotel."

Peter's room was a far nicer room with a private bath. The hotel had a fancy lobby, and it was located closer to all the restaurants, beer halls, and shops. Besides that, Trudy was already smitten with Peter. She found him exciting, sexy, and, most of all, wealthy and ambitious.

"all right. Give me a few minutes to pack. Then I'll check out," she said.

The next four days were like a dream for Trudy. Peter was everything Rudy was, but he was more attentive, better looking, and more interested in her. Besides that, he was wonderfully romantic. They made love and ate heart-shaped cookies in bed. He told her frightening stories about his time serving in the army. She listened in awe of his bravery. By the time her holiday was over, and it was time for her to leave Munich and return home, she was certain that Peter was the love of her life. He hired a driver to take her to the train station, where he stood on the platform beside her. "I had a wonderful time with you," he said.

"Me too." She touched his cheek. "When will I see you again?"

"Give me your number, and I will get in touch with you," he answered.

She had meant to tell him about her relationship with Max, but it never seemed to be the right time. Trudy didn't want to ruin their lovely days together by telling him she had a boyfriend at home. She was afraid he would lose interest if he thought she was tied to someone else. But now that she and Peter were talking about seeing each other once their holiday was over, she knew she had to tell him the truth, or at least some form of it, because Max might answer when Peter telephoned the apartment in the future.

Trudy glanced at the large round clock on the wall and said, "We have a half hour before the train leaves. Let's get a cup of coffee. I have something I have to talk to you about." There was an anguished expression on her face.

"Oh my, what is so serious?" he said mockingly. Then he smiled and said, "Sure, let's go to the café and have a coffee."

They sat in the small restaurant beside the train station and ordered two coffees. "So, what is so serious that you have such a worried expression on your pretty face?" he said, his tone lighthearted and unconcerned.

Trudy's hands were cold. She was shivering. *I don't want to lose him.* "I am afraid you aren't going to like what I am about to tell you."

"Oh dear! What is it that is so pressing?" He put his hands over his mouth in mock distress.

"I'm serious, Peter. This is very important. So, please listen."

"All right. I'm listening. Go on. Tell me what is so terrible."

"I have a boyfriend. He and I have been living together," she said. He nodded. She took a deep breath and continued, "But we are in the process of breaking up. That's why he didn't come here with me. That's the reason I came with my sister."

"I see," he said.

"I don't want to lose you." Her voice sounded more desperate than she had hoped it would.

"Well, it's all right. We all have our little secrets, don't we?" He sighed. "In fact, I have one of my own." He smiled. "I have a wife."

Her face fell. Her mouth opened wide. She was shocked, stunned, and horrified. This was not what she had in mind. She had been envisioning a future with Peter as her husband. Trudy knew the expression on her face was one of horror and disbelief; she tried to hide it, but she couldn't. "Oh," she said, "I guess that really changes things."

"Not really," he said, smiling. "I have been thinking about it and would like to get you an apartment. Which, of course, I would pay for. And I will come to visit you when I have the time. What do you think?"

"An apartment?"

"Yes." He smiled and then took a sip of his coffee. "You see, I like you, Trudy. We had a good time together. I think this would be a good setup for both of us. Of course, it would be your own place. You could decorate it as you like, and I would try to find a way to see you often. It would be like my sanctuary. And I certainly could use the break from my wife and children. Sometimes, it's even good to get a little time away from my important work. You would be like my little Aryan angel." He smiled. "So what do you say?"

She looked down at her coffee cup. This wasn't the fine coffee she'd enjoyed at the better restaurants she'd gone to with Peter or Rudy or at events she'd attended from the Nazi Party. This was the ersatz coffee to which regular people not affiliated with high-ranking officers were subjected. *It's a terrible coffee. It was probably made from acorns.* She thought. Then she slowly stirred the thick, dark liquid with a spoon and thought for a moment about the fact that she was on her way home to Max and the small apartment where they lived. She hated that apartment and the poverty it represented. Looking up at Peter, she caught his eye, and then, in a soft voice, she asked, "What about spending money? I suppose if I am your mistress, you would supply me with the finances that I need?"

"Of course, I would. But just to be sure of what you are asking for. I want to know exactly how much you will need. Money for decent food? Yes, of course. I would supply that and pretty clothing and visits to your hairdresser. However, in return, I would expect your absolute discretion, and I would expect you to be available when I make plans to visit."

"Discretion? You mean you want to keep our affair a secret?"

"Exactly. You see, love, my wife is dear to me. We are no longer madly in love like we were when we married. Life and children can do that to a marriage. Even so, out of respect for her, I like to keep my extramarital activities to myself. I'm sure you can understand this?"

"Yes." She nodded, but she felt hurt. This wasn't the wonderful ending to her holiday with Peter that she'd hoped for, but there were things about it that she found promising. He said he would give her money for the things she had been denied since she had lost Rudy and moved in with Max. She looked down at her coffee cup, and for a moment, she closed her eyes and thought about shopping for pretty dresses the way she had when she and Rudy were married.

Then he broke the spell of her silence and added, "And just to be clear, I will expect you to be available when I tell you that I am planning to visit. However, I will be fair. I will let you know a few days before I come because I hardly believe you will be faithful to me."

"What kind of girl do you think I am?" she asked, trying to hide the hurt in her voice.

"Come on, Trudy. I know what kind of girl you are. You came here to Munich, leaving your serious boyfriend at home. You say you are breaking up. I don't know if that's true. All I know is that, as of right now, you are still together, and you spent the entire week sleeping with me. And you slept with some other man before me. So, let's not talk about your moral character."

She shivered. Her hands were cold, and she felt sick to her stomach.

Then he added, "Don't feel bad. I am not judging you. I said I like you, and I do. And, of course, I don't expect you to be faithful and wait around for me to visit. But when I do, I want you to make me your first priority. If you have another man in your life, get rid of him. Send him away." He took a sip of his coffee and made a face. "This is terrible coffee, don't you agree?"

She didn't answer.

"Trudy, don't sit there brooding, please. Now, I think I am being more than fair," he said.

She swallowed hard. Then she looked up at him, and tears burned the back of her eyes, but she still wanted him. "Yes, you are being fair." She agreed softly. "I just wish I had known you were married."

He let out a laugh. "Don't try to make me feel guilty. Two can play at that." He touched her hand. "You have a live-in boyfriend, and I have a wife. We are both scoundrels." He laughed. "By the way, what are you going to do with him? The boyfriend, I mean."

"I wasn't lying when I told you we are in the middle of a breakup. We need to break up. We are ill-suited for each other," she said, looking down at her coffee cup.

He nodded. "I see. All right." Then he looked at his watch. "The train will leave in a few minutes. So, have you made a decision? Would you like to accept my offer?"

"Yes, my decision is yes. I will accept your offer."

"Good. I'm glad. When you return to Berlin, go out and find an apartment unless you plan to stay in the apartment where you are currently living. That's your choice. Either way, I'll contact you in a week or two."

She took a pencil and paper from her purse and wrote down her phone number. "You can reach me at this number. I won't move because if I do, you won't have any way of getting in contact with me. I'll wait at this phone number until I hear from you. Then I'll find a new place."

"All right. Then it's all settled. Yes?" He smiled as he pulled some money from his pocket and laid it on the table. "That's for you."

She looked at the wad of paper money on the table, and she felt bile rise in her throat. *He thinks of me like I am a prostitute.* She thought. But she took the money and put it in her handbag.

Peter smiled at Trudy, picked up her suitcase, and walked with her to the train.

Trudy climbed the steps to board. Then she got on the train and sat in a window seat where she could still see Peter. He waved to her. She waved back. But she saw little or no emotion in his eyes. *I hope he calls soon.* She thought as the train whistle blew. Her heart ached as the train started to move slowly. She tried to look out and see him on the platform, but he was already gone.

CHAPTER 51

Max was miserable because he knew his time alone was coming to an end. Trudy was on her way back home. It had been nice to come home from work each evening without having to see her sitting on the sofa looking at pictures in movie magazines. It had been a relief not to listen to her complain about his lack of ambition and his inability to prove himself to the Nazi Party. However, he was disappointed. He had hoped to receive news about Margot somehow. That maybe with Trudy gone, whoever had come before would feel more at ease to come again. However, it did not happen. No one had contacted him during Trudy's absence to give him information about Margot. And every day, his brain was like a tornado whirling with questions that had no answers and endless fears of what might have happened to his beloved wife. He'd asked everyone he knew if they had heard from Margot, but no one had, not Adelaide nor Leo, not Max's parents, not Mattie nor Ebert. He had tried to find Ben because he knew how much Margot trusted Ben, and he thought she might have tried to contact him. But Ben was gone. And he was sorry to say that with the sentiment towards Jews in Berlin, the chances were good that Ben had been arrested. He felt sorry for Ben. The man had always been a good friend to him and Margot, even if he was secretly in love with her. *I am at a complete dead end. I don't know what else to do. I can't find Margot. But I have to believe that if she is alive, she will find a way to make contact with me.*

However, this week, with Trudy gone, had taught him that he was at peace without her. And he couldn't bear another night with her lying by his side. Max didn't love her, and he never would. In fact, because of what she had done to Margot and to Erik, he hated her. It would be best, he knew, if they broke up. But Trudy was dangerous. She was vindictive and mean. So, how could he ever tell her the truth about wanting to break up? He was afraid to ask her to leave. Max was fairly certain that Trudy had no idea where to find Margot, so for now, Margot was safe from her. But he wasn't safe from Trudy. He never would be, not as long as she was alive. She knew far too many things about him that could cost him his life: Rudy's murder and his marriage to a Jewish woman. And probably other things that she remained silent about, like his hate for the Nazi Party. Regardless of how much he hated her, he knew he must keep quiet, at least for now.

CHAPTER 52

Through the crack in the window shade late one afternoon, Margot saw a blanket of colorful leaves covering the ground. "It's autumn," she said.

"Yes, I know. I caught a glimpse of the outside world yesterday," Ben said.

"I love autumn," Margot said wistfully as she sat on the floor beside Ben in the attic. "I always have. I love the jewel colors of the leaves and the cool weather."

"Me too," Ben said.

"I miss going outside so much. I wish we could go out and play in the leaves like we did as children."

He smiled.

She started to cry.

"What is it? What's wrong?"

"I got my period. I'm not pregnant. I know I should be glad, but I'm not."

"Oh, sweetheart. I'm sorry. I know you're disappointed." He took her into his arms. "I know you want a child. But considering our circumstances, maybe we should just take it in stride and realize that this is the wrong time and that God knows what's best."

"You mean maybe God doesn't want me to have a child?"

"Maybe not now. Perhaps things will be different soon. But how could you raise a baby here in this attic? I've been worried about it since you missed your period. I didn't want to say anything because I didn't want to upset you, but how would we ever keep a child quiet? You know how hard it is to keep a little one from crying. I think it would be impossible to hide. We would be caught, and then our child would be at the mercy of the Nazis. We would too," he said, touching her chin.

"Yes, I suppose you're right."

"Someday, you will have another baby. You'll see. When the time is right, God will give you another child."

There was a long silence during which he gently wiped the tears from her face with his thumb.

"Look at you," she said softly. "You're a mess. Your hair and your beard have grown so long. You look like a rabbi." She laughed.

"Yes, my hair and beard are out of control," he agreed.

"You are still handsome."

"You think so? I never thought I was handsome. Good looks were never my strong point," he said.

"That's just not true. You are very handsome. And now, maybe even more so."

He leaned over and kissed her. "No matter what happens. No matter how this all ends. I will always be grateful to have had this time with you."

She reached over and held his hand.

"Can you remember the first time we worked together on a project in the lab in science class?"

"Of course, I remember."

"I couldn't believe that you chose to work with me. You know that everyone always thought you were the most beautiful girl in school. And me? I was a quiet, nebbish boy."

"What's a nebbish boy?"

"A withdrawn, introspective boy. Bookish. I was not outgoing like you. But you liked me anyway. I remember how I felt when you asked me to go to the dance. Do you remember?"

"Of course, I remember." She laughed. "I waited for you to ask me to that dance. I waited for a week, and when you didn't, I knew I would have to ask you myself if I wanted to go with you because I knew you were just too shy."

"I was. I was so shy and so introverted. I can remember when you asked me. I was so happy. In fact, I was walking on clouds for days. It was beyond my comprehension that someone like you would be even the least interested in someone like me."

She leaned over and kissed him. "I love you, Ben. I loved you when we were schoolmates. And I love you even more now. I always will. My sweet, nebbish boy."

He laid her down carefully on one of the blankets, then he kissed her again. She sighed and brushed the hair out of his eyes. He kissed her again. And then he took a condom out of his pants pocket. "What is that?" she asked.

"It's a condom. I had Frau Danner get them for me. She bought them on the black market because Hitler didn't want any restrictions on pregnancy as far as his Aryans were concerned. He wants them to keep producing Aryan children. The allied soldiers use these. They prevent pregnancy."

Margot looked at the condom. "I guess it is probably best if I don't get pregnant."

"Did I ruin the moment?" he asked.

"No, you couldn't ruin the moment. Every moment I am with you is precious."

He kissed her softly. Then he made love to her.

After it was over, she turned over and stared at the wall. "What's wrong?" Ben asked.

"Oh, it's nothing."

"Yes, it is," he said. "I know you feel guilty about Max and that you miss him. So, I've decided that I am going to go out and go to your apartment. I know Max, so unlike Frau Danner, I'll be able to find him. Once I do, I'll tell him where you are and that you are safe."

"Oh, Ben? I don't know if you should. It's so dangerous."

"But I must do this for you. Max should know where you are, just in case something happens to me."

"No, I don't want you to do that. You just cursed yourself. Say a prayer quickly."

He said a prayer in Hebrew. "There, does that make you feel better?"

"I don't like it when you say something might happen to you. It's bad luck."

There was a long silence. Then he said, "I have an idea."

He leaned on his elbow and looked down at her. "I was thinking. You still have your papers that say you are not Jewish, don't you?"

"Yes, I still have them," she said.

"Maybe you should leave Berlin. Go to another city. No one would know you there. You could say your husband died in the war and that you couldn't find work, so you moved to another city."

"And what about you? Would you come with me? You don't have papers, do you?"

"No, I don't. I've tried to have Frau Danner buy them for me on the black market. But I haven't been able to get anyone to make them. So, I'll stay here, and you should go. I'll stay in hiding, and when the war is over, I'll find you if it's ever over. But you would be safer that way."

"Hiding in plain sight?"

"Exactly," he said, smiling at her. "Now, even after you're settled in another place, you still cannot get in touch with Max because of Trudy. If she sees you or sees a letter from you and knows where you are, she will report you. I have no doubt about that."

"Neither do I," Margot said.

"But it would make me happy to know you were living a normal life outside."

"I don't want to leave you, Ben. I don't want a normal life without you. I want to stay here with you."

CHAPTER 53

By the time Christmas arrived, Trudy had grown meaner and edgier than usual. Max didn't know why, but he tried to stay out of her way. Trudy was miserable. She hadn't heard from Peter. To make matters worse, she had spent all their savings on her trip to Munich, so Max didn't have enough money to buy her a gift. She loved beautiful things, and Max always fell short. Her interest in him had waned long ago, but now he was becoming an annoyance to her. And she hated him for always being around. To combat this feeling of being trapped with a man she thought of as a failure, Trudy began staying out late at night. She went to taverns, flirted with men, and sometimes went home with them. Then, one morning, she came home from an evening out and went to speak to Max. He was awake and getting ready for work. Trudy was unashamed and unapologetic for having been out all night. She glared at Max and then insisted that from now on, he must sleep on the sofa. To her surprise, Max didn't argue. In fact, he agreed readily. He didn't care. He preferred not having to lie with her. But all of this was not satisfying for Trudy. In the back of her mind, she was upset that Peter had disappeared and constantly worried that she would have another experience like the one she'd had with Klaus. So, although she always went home with different men, she could never quite relax.

The winter was harsh. Even as a child, Trudy hated winter. It was cold, and she despised the snow and ice. It was difficult to walk in high heels with patches of ice hiding just beneath a thin layer of newly fallen snow, making going out at night difficult. Even so, if the weather wasn't too bad, she dressed and braved the cold to go to a nightclub or a tavern each evening. She couldn't seem to fill an emptiness inside of her. It was an unbearable loneliness, and she now realized it had always been there. Somehow, when she saw how happy Margot was with Max, she believed that Max was the solution to her problem. She thought he could fill the emptiness inside of her. But now that she had him, he had failed to make her feel complete, and she had no idea what would make her feel fulfilled. Then, one afternoon in late February, she received a telegram while Max was at work. She opened it quickly and smiled with surprise when she saw it was from Peter. Her heartbeat quickened as she read it. It was short and to the point.

> *I'm going to be in Berlin next month. March 3rd through the 10th. I would like to make arrangements to meet with you. Dinner perhaps? I have not been in touch because I had some things to take care of before I could meet with you again. However, I am ready to proceed with the arrangements you and I discussed before you left Munich. Please send me a telegram and let me know where and when you can meet.*

I thought he was gone forever. I never thought I would hear from him again. She bit the tip of her nail and let out a laugh. "He wants to see me," Trudy said aloud. She was excited to hear from Peter, but she decided not to answer the telegram right away. She would make him wait for a week before she answered. *It will serve him right to spend his time wondering if I will answer or not. Let him see what it feels like to wait for me the way I have been waiting to hear from him.*

Two days passed, and although Trudy had planned to wait a week before contacting Peter, she started to worry that if she didn't answer sooner, he might lose interest. So, she wrote a telegram telling Peter she would be available to meet with him. When she finished composing her message, she took some money from the jar Max kept in the kitchen and stuffed it into her handbag. Then she dressed warmly in a dark green wool dress she'd purchased several years prior and slipped on her coat and hat. Early that morning, a soft, downy snow had begun to fall. As she walked to the bus stop, the white flakes covered her hair and shoulders, reminding her why she hated winter. As she waited on the bench for the bus, Trudy cursed at the flakes. *They will wet my hair and take out all the curls. I don't know why I even bother to pin-curl my hair in winter. Well, at least the snow isn't sticking. It's melting as soon as it touches the ground.*

CHAPTER 54

Peter sent another telegram where he arranged to meet with Trudy on a Friday evening at a quiet and intimate restaurant a few streets away from Trudy's apartment. She was excited to see him again. When the evening of their meeting finally arrived, she was dressed in the finest winter dress she owned. It was a deep burgundy colored wool dress that was just tight enough to show off her curves. Her hair was curled, and her dark eye makeup and candy apple red lipstick were carefully applied. She left the apartment before Max got home from work, leaving him a note that she would not be home that night. Then she walked to the restaurant. When she entered, the owner told her to sit anywhere. She chose a booth at the back of the restaurant. Then she ordered a coffee and waited. It was over half an hour from when they were scheduled to meet, and Peter had still not arrived. Trudy was hurt and disappointed, silently cursing Peter for standing her up and condemning herself for believing in him. She glanced up at the clock on the wall again for the tenth time since she arrived. Then she motioned to the owner and was about to ask for her bill when Peter walked into the restaurant. He stood in the doorway momentarily, shaking the snow off the shoulders of his uniform. Her breath caught in her throat when she saw him. *How*

could I have forgotten just how handsome he is? I always knew he was, but I forgot just how breathtaking his looks are. And when I look around the restaurant, I see that everyone's eyes are glued to him. He looks so powerful and divine in that black uniform. It fits him so well. Peter glanced around for a second and saw her immediately. When he did, he smiled. *His smile lights up the room.* She returned his smile. Her lips trembled, and she was so excited to see him that she thought she might faint.

"It's been a while," he said as he sat in the booth across from her.

"Yes, I guess it has." She tried to act as nonchalant as possible. What she really wanted to say was, "At least you could have sent me a telegram. I was very upset about not hearing from you for such a long time." But she would never allow herself to appear that vulnerable.

An older man who was their waiter came to take their order almost immediately. He seemed nervous and didn't want to do anything that might cause the SS Officer to be angry with him. Trudy wondered if he was a Jew trying to hide. But she didn't want to bring that up right now. She wanted to hear what Peter had to say about her future with him.

Peter paid no attention to the waiter. He placed a dinner order for them without consulting Trudy about what she wanted. While taking their order, the waiter dropped his pencil. When he bent to pick it up, his face was close enough to Trudy for her to see the sweat on his brow. *I'm probably right about this old man. Maybe later in our relationship, I'll tell Peter my thoughts, and he can come back here and investigate this man. If he does find out that the waiter is Jewish, Peter will be very impressed with me.* She didn't mind that Peter didn't consult her before he ordered their meal. He ordered plenty of food and, to accompany it, a pitcher of beer.

Until their food arrived, Peter talked nostalgically about their time together in Munich. He brought back pleasant memories that made Trudy smile. But she was too nervous about her possible future with this man to concentrate on the past. She was anxious to hear what had kept him away for so long and if there were any changes to what he was expecting in their future. But he never mentioned a word about any of it. So, when the food arrived, she was too nervous to eat. Finally, after he'd finished his meal, Peter devoured a large slice of chocolate cake accompanied by a cup of coffee. Then he sat back in his chair. A smile came over his face, showing off his strong jaw and high cheekbones. "That was good food? Yes?" He wiped his lips with the napkin and laid it on the table.

"Yes, very good." She hoped her voice was not betraying how nervous she was.

Peter lit a cigarette. Then, like an afterthought, he said, "Would you like one?"

"No, thank you," she said, but she would have liked one. It would have helped calm her down. But she couldn't remember whether he knew that she smoked occasionally. Most men, especially men of importance like Peter, would not have approved of a woman smoking. *The great and mighty Führer doesn't think good Aryan women should smoke. He doesn't think men should smoke either, but they all do, and he forgives them. But women are different, and they are not forgiven easily. Rudy used to say that it was disgusting for a woman to smoke.*

Peter inhaled deeply. Then he motioned for the waiter to come to the table. "Two glasses of schnapps," he demanded.

"Yes, sir."

"May I have a coffee as well?" Trudy asked Peter.

"Of course," he said. Then he turned to the waiter. "Bring one coffee, too."

Peter sat watching Trudy and smiling. They didn't speak until the drinks arrived. He sipped schnapps and said, "So, I missed you."

His tone was casual. It didn't sound sincere, yet because Trudy wanted to believe what he said, she let his words into her heart. "I missed you too."

"Like I said, I had some things to take care of before I could get away and come to Berlin to discuss our arrangements."

"Yes, that's what you said." Her eyes were cast down as she stirred her coffee.

"Do you remember what we talked about before you left?"

She nodded. He made it sound more like a business arrangement than a romantic affair. "I remember."

"Well, I'd like you to find an apartment. Let me know how much it will cost, and, as I promised, I'll take care of it."

She nodded again. She wanted to ask what it was that had kept him away, but there was something in his manner that told her not to.

"What about your live-in boyfriend? Will he be a problem?"

She hadn't thought about Max at all. What if he did cause a problem? What if he refused to let her go? She couldn't be sure of what he might do. *I don't think he loves me. But I don't know for sure. He's very hard to read. Even if he doesn't love me, he might punish me for causing him to lose Margot and make it hard for me to leave him.* "Oh, don't worry about him," she said, trying to sound as if she were confident that Max would not be a problem.

"Are you sure? I don't need trouble from an angry ex-boyfriend."

"I'm quite sure," she said. Then she got an idea. "But just in case, perhaps you can help me make sure I am rid of him."

He cocked his head. "What do you mean? I am certainly not going to kill another party member for you."

The coarseness of his tone and the delivery of his words hurt her feelings. She didn't want Peter to kill Max. He wouldn't need to. But his lack of devotion and passion towards her made her feel like she hardly mattered to him. "I would never ask that of you," she said sincerely.

"So then, what are you saying?"

She looked into his eyes. *Once we are together as lovers again, I am sure he will be more devoted to me. I know he cares. He would never have wanted to see me again if he didn't.* She tried to convince herself. "Hear me out. Max, my current boyfriend, used to be married to my adopted sister. When I found out that my sister's birth mother was Jewish, I threatened to report her. My parents had kept it a secret. Which I know was wrong, but they are old now, and it wouldn't do any good to punish them."

He was listening intently.

"Anyway, when Max discovered my sister, Margot, was Jewish, he got scared. He said he no longer wanted to be married to Margot now that he knew the truth about her. Max and I had been friends since we were children. I always knew he preferred me to Margot, but he gave in and married her because I was unavailable. However, after my husband died and Margot was gone, I was available, and the truth is I felt sorry for Max. We both needed to pay rent and couldn't afford it separately, so we moved in together. At first, I believed he was telling the truth, that he didn't know Margot was a Jew. But as time passed and we were together, I started to see that he seemed to be sensitive to Jews. He liked them and felt sorry for them, too. So I began to believe he knew the truth about Margot all along. I wouldn't be surprised if he knew she was a Jew when he married her. And if I hadn't found out about her and brought it all to light, he would have stayed with her." Trudy stretched the truth for her own purposes.

"Hmmm, that's very interesting," he said.

"That means he broke the law. Correct?"

"Yes, correct."

"And there is something else," she said coyly.

"Tell me. What is it?"

"Well, before I met you, I was seeing this young man. He was a nice man, very devoted to our fatherland. Then, one night, he turned up dead. I am not sure, but I think Max might have been responsible."

"Oh, really," he said, unmoved. "Are you afraid for me?"

"Oh no. You are too powerful. Too important. Poor Lucas, that was his name, was only a policeman."

"But you have no proof?"

"No, I don't."

He nodded. "That's all right." He said.

Trudy thought about telling Peter that she saw Max kill Rudy, but she was afraid that somehow she might be accused of being a part of Rudy's murder. She preferred not to take that risk. Instead, she asked, "Can I assume that is enough to have him arrested, at least taken away for a while?"

Peter smiled. "Why, yes, it certainly is. I could pull a few strings and see to it that he doesn't bother you anymore. He sounds like the kind of weak-minded fellow the Party is better off without."

"I quite agree," she said.

He paid the check, and they left the restaurant and went to his hotel room, where they spent the night together. In the morning,

Trudy awakened to find Peter gone and an envelope with her name on it on the nightstand. Inside were several Reichsmarks and a note that said:

This money is to put down on your apartment. Once you find a place, send me a telegram, and let me know the address.

Trudy put the money and the note into her purse. Then she put on her coat and left. Max had already left for work when Trudy returned to their apartment. She took off her clothes, showered, put on a fresh dress, and reapplied her makeup. After a quick cup of black coffee, she searched for her new apartment. After boarding a bus to a higher-priced neighborhood, she began searching for a place to live. It took several hours, but she found a nice one-bedroom apartment on the third floor of a tall, well-maintained brick building. This was a far nicer apartment than she and Max shared, and the price reflected it. Still, it was not nearly as lovely as the house she had lived in when she was married to Rudy. *Perhaps, after a time, Peter will fall in love with me and love me enough to divorce his wife. Then we will marry and have a house as nice as the one I had with Rudy.*

It was already getting dark when Trudy arrived back home. She was hungry. So, she began searching her cupboard for something to eat. *Potatoes, three potatoes. She* counted them out loud: an onion and a spoiled cabbage head. Trudy began to slice up the vegetables to fry in a little oil for dinner when there was a knock on the door. Trudy opened it to find a young man with a telegram. "Thank you," she said, taking the telegram and handing the young man a coin for his troubles.

Quickly she opened the telegram, hoping it was from Peter saying he wanted to see her tonight. But it wasn't. It was from the police. Trudy sat down at the table and read it. The telegram said Max would not return to the apartment that night. He had been arrested. He'd broken the racial laws. Trudy thought of Peter. He had certainly kept his promise. He'd gotten Max out of their way. Trudy felt her face grow hot. Then, a jab of guilt shot through her. For a second, she shuddered as she thought of Max in prison, and she remembered how they had all been friends when they were children. *But even so, Max was never really good to me. After all, he chose Margot over me. I don't believe he ever really loved me. I believe that if he knew where she was, he would have left me in a minute for her, even knowing that she's a Jew.* Trudy tried to justify what she had done. But there was a sick feeling in her stomach. Her head ached, and she reached up and rubbed her belly. *Well, if nothing else, I am glad that's over. Max is gone, and there's not a thing I can do about it, even if I wanted to. Besides, it's all true; he was married to a Jew, and he did break the law. And, although the authorities don't know it, he murdered an SS Officer. So, in truth, Max got what he deserved. Now, I am free to pursue things with Peter.* She sighed and picked up a cigarette. Then she took the whiskey bottle from the kitchen shelf and poured herself a glass. Trudy almost never drank whiskey straight, but she did now. It was hot. It burned her throat as it traveled down. A single tear fell from her eye. "I'm sorry, Max," she said aloud, but no one was there to hear her. "I'm sorry for everything I did. And I am sorry that it ended this way. But I cannot spend my time feeling sorry for you. I must get on with my life. You did, after all, break the racial laws." She lit the cigarette and took a puff. Then she closed her eyes and pictured Peter in her mind. And she smiled.

CHAPTER 55

The old lady died in her bed on a cold morning in mid-March. Frau Danner's generous heart gave out due to worry, old age, and constant pressure. It was several days before Ben and Margot realized something was not right. They were completely out of food and water. By the time Frau Danner had not come to the attic for a week, the sweet, sickly smell of death began to penetrate the air. Ben, having been in medicine his entire life, knew the smell. "I am going to go downstairs and see what is going on. I'll be back as soon as I can, and I'll bring up whatever food I can find."

Margot nodded. "I know you must go. And although I'm not familiar with this sickening odor. I am afraid it's the smell of death."

He didn't answer.

They waited until it was dark outside. Then Ben kissed Margot softly and quietly emerged from the attic. Margot watched him go. Then she closed the door and sat down to wait for his return. She prayed silently that Frau Danner had left all the shades and curtains drawn. Her senses were heightened as she waited alone in the darkness for Ben's return. Outside, the roar of a Gestapo siren rang out. It startled Margot, and she let out a loud gasp. But to her relief, the siren passed by the house. It seemed like Ben had been gone for hours, but it was only fifteen minutes before he returned. He carried a heel of moldy bread, a bottle of water, and a soft potato. He put them on the ground. Then, he softly said, "It's as we suspected. Frau Danner is gone. It seems she didn't suffer, though. It looks like she died in her sleep."

"What are we going to do?" Margot asked.

There was a long silence. "For right now, we must eat," Ben said.

Margot did as Ben told her to do. She took a few bites of the hard bread. Then she asked again, "Ben, I don't know what we can do now. We have no way of surviving. We have to get out of this attic before the Gestapo finds her and comes to confiscate the house."

"Not necessarily. I have an idea, but I will need Max to help me. So, I will go out tomorrow night when it gets dark, and I am going to your apartment to wait for Max. What time does Max return home from work?"

"About seven. Sometimes later."

"Well, I will try to go earlier, just in case. Once I get there, I will hide in the alley, watch, and wait for him to come. I will tell him where we are and what is happening when I find him. Then I'll ask him if he will help me bury Frau Danner before they find her."

"We'll have to ask Max to get us food on the black market. We don't have any ration cards."

"He will also have to tell them that Frau Danner is a friend and that she has gone to visit her daughter but will be returning. That should keep us safe for a little while. Don't worry. I know he'll do his best to help us."

"Yes, Max would do anything to help us survive. Do you think Trudy already turned me in? Do you think the Gestapo have my name somewhere and that they are looking for me?"

"I don't know. But I guess that Max has agreed to live with Trudy in exchange for her promise to keep quiet about you as long as he stays with her. My guess is that he is doing this for you."

"That sounds like Max," she agreed.

"He is protective of you, just like I am."

She was silent for a few minutes. *I love these two men with all my heart.*

Then she said, "But it is only a matter of time before someone, a friend or neighbor of Frau Danner's, will come to the door. What then? Someone will eventually come in and find out that no one is living here. They will tell the authorities."

"Like I said, if Max goes to the police and says that Frau Danner is visiting her daughter, it will buy us some time."

"Yes, but not forever."

"No, not forever," he said firmly. "Margot. All along, I have been trying to tell you that you have papers that say that you are Aryan. If Trudy has not alerted the authorities, you can pose as Frau Danner's niece. I will ask Max to get us some bleach for your hair. We'll make you blonde. The Germans love blond hair. You will live downstairs. When anyone looks for Frau Danner, you will tell them she has moved to France to live with her daughter. But this is only if Trudy hasn't reported you. If she has, you must get out of Berlin as quickly as possible."

"No, I can't. I won't leave you. If I can live downstairs, will you stay here in the attic?" she asked.

"Yes, I will stay here."

She closed her eyes. "I am afraid for you to leave this house. I would rather go out and find Max myself."

"I'm afraid, too. I'm not courageous, but I can't let you go near your apartment. It's even more unsafe for you. If Trudy happens to see you, she'll turn you in. The Gestapo will believe whatever she tells them because she is one of them. Trust me, this is the best way for us to do this."

"Oh, Ben. You are always trying to protect me. I hope this is the right choice. I just don't know."

"I know it is." He took her into his arms. "And..." he said softly. "Don't worry about what happened between us. I don't want to hurt Max either, and so he need never know about you and me."

She felt a hot tear on her cheek. "I never wanted to hurt him."

"I know that. Believe me, I know you love both of us. I under-stand. I always understood, even though it hurt me to know that I could never marry you. Circumstances caused us to do things in an unorthodox way. But I have always known that once Max is back in your life, you must make him your priority. Even so, I am grateful to have been your lover, even if only for a short time."

The following day, Margot was nervous. She knew that Ben had to go and find Max as quickly as possible. They could not put this off. They must bury Frau Danner before anyone comes to the door and catches a whiff of the terrible odor.

"We don't have a clock," Ben said. "But it's getting dark, and I don't want to miss Max. So, I am going to go now."

"Not yet," Margot said as she stood and walked towards him. She put her arms around his neck and pulled him close to her. Frantically, she undid the zipper on his pants. Then she lay down and pulled him down beside her. He didn't say a word. But she saw him reach up and wipe a tear from his cheek. She was crying, too, as he entered her.

"We were never meant to be together. The odds were against us from the start. And yet, my love for you was always stronger than my logical mind, and I always hoped that someday you would be mine," he said. "Even though it was only for a little while, it meant more to me than anything else I have ever done. I love you, Margot," he said.

"I love you too."

A bead of sweat or a tear fell on her forehead as they finished together.

She was weeping hard now. He didn't tell her not to cry.

"It's getting late. I have to go," Ben said.

"Now?"

"I'm afraid so." He stood up and zipped his pants.

She stood up, too, and gripped his arm tightly. They stood face to face for a minute. Then she pulled him close to her again, and she kissed him hard. "Be safe, Ben." That was all she said, but her heart felt like it was breaking into a million tiny pieces.

Ben nodded, then he turned and left the attic.

Margot's heart raced as she listened to his footsteps on the stairs. Then she heard the back door to the house open and close. "Please, dear God, please let him be safe. Please don't let anyone see him or hurt him."

There was nothing to do but wait. Margot thought she might go mad, not knowing what was happening outside. She took a deep breath and tried to calm herself. But her mind was playing tricks on her. She couldn't stop imagining terrible scenarios. *Stop it.* She warned herself. *Ben is smart. He'll be careful. He'll be safe.*

CHAPTER 56

When Max arrived at Dachau, he couldn't believe humans had created such a terrible place to imprison their fellow man. It was a horrific, dirty, and demoralizing prison. He quickly learned that not only were there political prisoners, criminals, and communists, but there were also homosexuals, Romany, polish people, Jews, and an entire block that housed priests. The men were given barely enough food to sustain life. Since Max was a large, muscular man, immediately upon his arrival, he had been sent to work as slave labor. When he first arrived after a long ride on a very cold weekend in the back of an open truck at gunpoint, the first thing the guard who assigned work said when he saw Max was, "This one is strong. He's built like an ox. Put him on a crew that's building roads. He'll be a good worker if he knows what's good for him." Max had no choice but to follow the rest of the men assigned to 'road work.' It was a grueling job, and he knew it would be an almost impossible feat during the winter. Wearing only a flimsy uniform, he tried to reason with the guards on his first day of work. He tried to explain that this work was far too difficult, considering the weather. This attempt at having a rational discussion with the guards led to a terrible beating for

Max. He was left with a deep gash on his cheek. When he returned to his block that evening, one of the other men walked over to him.

"You're bleeding pretty badly," the prisoner said.

Max studied the other prisoner. He wore a yellow star on the breast pocket of his uniform. And although he was skinny from lack of food, he was still a bear of a man, large and hairy, with thick muscles that ran through his large neck and upper body. Max wondered what he had been like before he'd been imprisoned and starved.

"I'm Kaz," the large man with the yellow star said.

Max nodded. "I'm Max."

"Let me help you get this cut cleaned up as best as we can. Yes?" Kaz called out across the room. "Adrien. This fellow over here has a deep gash on his face. I'm afraid it will get infected if we don't clean it up. Do you have some alcohol?"

The man who answered to the name of Adrien was a tall, slender fellow with a strong jaw and a Grecian nose. When he stood up from the floor where he had been sitting and stretched out his back, Max could see that he, too, wore the yellow star indicating that he was a Jewish prisoner. Then he walked over to where he slept and pulled a small bottle from beneath the straw. Slowly, he ambled over to where Kaz sat beside Max. "Who's this fellow?" Adrien asked, indicating Max.

"A new man. They just brought him here yesterday."

"You came only yesterday, and already you have an injury?" Adrien said. "*Nu*, so, what happened?"

Max shrugged and said, "I tried to reason with one of the guards."

"Don't make me laugh. You can't reason with them. I'm surprised you're not dead," Adrien said, shaking his head. "All right, let's clean this wound. Now, lay back. I'm going to pour a little of this vodka over your cut. It's going to sting like hell. But it will kill the germs."

"Vodka? How did you ever get vodka in here?"

"We have our ways. Never mind about that. Right now, although I hate to waste vodka, I will have to use it to clean that up. If I don't, you'll probably die from infection."

Max laid back, and Adrien poured some of the liquid into Max's cut. It stung more than he thought it would, and Max involuntarily let out a short cry. "Be quiet," Adrien said. "We don't want the *Block-führer* to come here and see this vodka."

Max nodded as his body shivered from the pain.

Then Adrien turned to his friend. "Eh, I hope this works. If not, it was a waste of good vodka."

"How do you keep the others from stealing your vodka?" Max asked, still wincing from the pain.

The other man smiled wryly and shrugged. "I'm the only doctor on this block. They all know that if they are injured, they are going to need this alcohol. If they drink it, they won't have it. So, they try to refrain. But occasionally, someone loses their constraint, and I find my bottle empty. Thank God that didn't happen today."

Kaz pointed to the doctor and said, "This is my friend Adrien. He used to be a very respected doctor. But now, he's a prisoner. Like the rest of us. His medical career was impressive, but that was in another life." Kaz's tone was sarcastic.

"I'm Max," Max said to Adrien.

Adrien nodded.

"It's too bad we had to meet in such terrible circumstances." Kaz shrugged. The sarcasm was still in his voice. Then he turned around and searched for another fellow. When he saw the man he was looking for, he called out to him, "Hymie," He said. "You got a needle and thread? This looks like a deep gash. I think Adrien is going to have to sew it up."

A small man hunched over with what appeared to be a hump in his upper back walked over to them and took something out of his pocket. "Here. Use whatever thread you must, but I need to have the needle back when Adrien is done." He handed Kaz a needle and thread.

"Hymie works in the tailor shop sewing uniforms for the pigs who keep us prisoners in this hell," Kaz said.

Max just nodded.

Adrien walked over and took the needle and thread from Kaz. He poured a little vodka over them.

"Those men are Jews." A man who was sitting on a cot across the room from them called out to Max. "Adrien's in here because he's a

235

Jew. And I wouldn't trust him to doctor me up. I would be afraid he would kill me because Jews hate everyone who isn't one of them. And Kaz and Hymie are Jews too."

"Shut your mouth. You're nuts," someone else said. "I'm trying to get some sleep. Nobody cares what you have to say."

But Kaz was clearly annoyed. He straightened up to his full six feet five inches and looked over at the man who had just spewed hatred towards him and his friends. "Yeah, and so exactly what does that mean to you? What does it mean to you that we're Jews? Why don't you tell me, you slob, because I want to know what you have to say before I kill you," Kaz said as he walked over to the man who was sitting on the edge of a cot. He got as close to the man's face as he could, pointed directly at his nose, and growled. "Does your hatred for Jews mean enough to you for you to fight me over it? Because I'd love to beat the living crap out of you. I'm in the mood to take my misery out on someone, and you would be the perfect candidate."

"I didn't say anything bad. All I said was that you were Jewish." The man was shaken and afraid of Kaz, who was far bigger than himself. He had spoken out before Kaz had confronted him, but now he was nervous and suddenly overly apologetic. "All I said was that you're all Jewish," he repeated. "Well, it's true. You are, aren't you?"

"That's not your business. We are good men, and I'm ready for you if you want to fight. I don't care what you think of me. You don't mean a thing to me. But when you say something about my friends, it means you're looking for a fight. And I am just the fellow to give you what you want. So, little man, just so we're clear, you should have no doubt in your mind that I would kill you just as soon as I look at you. You understand me? Here's a good piece of advice from this Jew: just keep your mouth shut if you want to live another day. Do you understand me?"

The man was clearly unnerved. He nodded. "I'm sorry, Kaz. I didn't mean it." Then Kaz nodded and walked back to where Adrien and Max were working on Max's wound.

"Everybody in here has something to say," Kaz said sarcastically. "The less you get involved with other people, the better off you'll be. There are a few good fellows. But there are plenty of prisoners who would turn on you for a morsel of bread. My advice to you, Max, is to keep your mouth shut and keep to yourself."

Max nodded.

"And another thing. Next time, no matter what the guards say or do, don't try to argue with them. They can't be reasoned with. Your life means nothing here. And these guards would just as soon kill you as talk to you. So, remember that if you want to survive. Stay quiet."

CHAPTER 57

W hen Ben walked outside for the first time in many months, it felt strange to him. The air was so fresh and clean, and the sky was so beautiful as the sun set that it almost brought tears to his eyes. He'd forgotten how incredible the world truly was. And he wished he could share these moments with Margot. He would have liked to point out the slight purple in the sky and the crunch of the leaves as he walked. She would have enjoyed this outing. But, of course, it was not an outing. It was a necessary venture. And as he walked along admiring everything he saw, it seemed he'd been closed up in that attic for a lifetime. It was cold outside, so before he left, Ben took an old coat that he found in Frau Danner's closet and put it on. It was a man's coat, and so he assumed it might have belonged to Frau Danner's dead husband or perhaps to the Jewish fellow who was her daughter's lover. The cold wind blew into his face, and although he loved the fresh smell of it, it felt like tiny sharp razor cuts on his delicate skin as he walked towards the apartment where Max and Margot had once lived. He sighed as he walked along the familiar streets to the building where Margot had lived. This was the same apartment where he had nursed little Erik through some terrible seizures. He remembered the little boy, and his heart ached. But there was no time for sentiment. He had to be very careful. Every nerve in his body was on high alert. He wore no yellow star on his coat and had no papers in his pocket. All it would take was for one bored Nazi to decide to question him, and he would be under arrest. Although he did what he could to stay out of heavily populated areas, he was not alone. He still saw some people who seemed to turn and look at him suspiciously. *Am I just imagining it, or are they really staring at me? How could they know I was Jewish? My hair and eyes are dark, but many people have those physical traits.* He tried to rationalize things to calm himself. But then a couple of young Nazis came out of a beer hall, obviously drunk, and one of them happened to glance his way, and their eyes met. Ben felt a shiver run down the back of his neck and down his spine. He turned and ducked behind a building. *I am sure he could tell that I am Jewish. I am so pale. That Nazi probably noticed how white my skin was. Surely, that's an indication that I have been in hiding because only someone who had not seen the sun for a long time would have skin this colorless.* His breath was shallow, and his heartbeat was so rapid that he knew his heart was beating too fast. Pain shot down his left arm. *I am so dizzy and lightheaded.* His vision was blurred. *I pray I don't have a heart attack out here. Margot would never know what happened to me. She would be waiting and worrying, and I wouldn't be able to get back to her.* He thought.

Hiding in an alleyway and leaning against the back of a building, Ben tried to slow his heartbeat by breathing slowly. He squatted down and put his head between his legs, forcing himself to breathe deeply, in and out, in and out. Several moments passed before he felt the dizziness subside. Ben could've stayed there longer with his back pressed against the cold bricks of that building, but he knew Margot was waiting for him, depending on him, to find Max and get help. *I won't let her down. I would rather die than let her down.*

He mustered up all his courage, his strength, and his energy and looked out to see if any more Nazis were coming out of the bier hall. *I wish there was some better way to get to Max's apartment. But there isn't. I must pass that beer hall.* He glanced around nervously. The street was empty, at least for the moment. *I must go now before anyone else comes, and I must hurry.*

Ben tucked his head down. Then he walked quickly, passing quickly by the beer hall. No one came out. But he continued to walk as fast as he could without slowing down or looking back. Relief came over him as he approached the corner. He was just about to turn and head to his destination, less than a full street away, when a voice like thunder roared out, "Hey you, there. Stop."

Ben wasn't certain that the man was speaking to him. And he dared not look back. His courage was waning. He felt weak, like less than a man. In his mind's eye, he saw himself falling to the ground and weeping. Ben pushed that thought from his mind. *I must be brave. If not for myself, then for Margot.* The fear in his heart was so overwhelming that suddenly, his feet refused to move. It was as if he were paralyzed right there on the street in a small neighborhood in Berlin.

The Nazi came up behind Ben. "Papers," he demanded.

"I forgot my papers," Ben said, his voice cracking. "I was just going to see a friend. I forgot them."

"You forgot your papers, now did you?" The Nazi was smiling, toying with him. He could feel it. But he had no idea how to fight back, how to get away from this man who was armed and who would easily take his life without a single thought. For a moment, Ben reflected on all the people he'd saved from death, being a doctor, a healer. Then his thoughts turned to all the other Jewish doctors that the Nazis had murdered. He wondered how many people they would have saved had they lived. This thought made him feel foolishly giddy. It was as if his soul was floating above the ground, watching. His fear of the Nazis seemed to dissipate like water that had turned to steam, and he began to laugh. "You are all fools," he said. "Idiots."

"How dare you? Are you mad? You must be a madman. You look like a Jew."

"Oh, and what does a Jew look like?" Ben said. *I must be temporarily out of my mind.* He thought, but even that thought was amusing, and he laughed aloud.

"Like you. You look like a typical Jew. And you're laughing like an idiot. So that's an indication right there," the Nazi said. He pulled his gun, and without even thinking, he shot Ben in the stomach. "There, how do you like that, you arrogant Jew? I'm not going to kill you.

Nope. I am going to let you suffer and bleed out right here on the street like the swine that you are."

Hot, sharp pain ripped through Ben, sobering him and bringing him out of his hysteria and back to reality. He was not laughing anymore. He closed his eyes and thought of Margot. *I must get back to the attic before I die. I must tell her what to do so she will be safe. She will listen to me now that I am dying, and I will no longer be a problem for her.*

Ben watched the young Nazi walk away. He never turned to look back. But once he turned the corner, Ben knew his time was limited, and even though he was weak, he must get up.

Getting up from the ground where he lay in a pool of blood was the most difficult thing Ben had ever done in his life. The pain bore through him like a steel sword, stealing his breath and every ounce of energy he had left. Soon, he knew this injury would take his life. Ben was a healer. That was his gift, and he had saved so many others. But he knew by the amount of blood he had lost and because he lacked the proper resources that he would not be able to save himself. *Perhaps this is what is best for Margot.* He thought as he struggled to get back to the attic. *With me gone, she will leave Berlin. She can use her papers in another city to start a new life. My death will be worth it if it gives her another chance.*

He moved as best he could, still hiding in the shadows, knowing he must not be seen. It was essential that he get back to Margot and tell her that he was going to die because if she thought he was alive, she would wait for him to return to her forever. Clutching his wound, his hand covered in blood, Ben finally made his way back to Frau Danner's house. When he entered, he climbed the stairs to the attic.

CHAPTER 58

Sitting alone on the cold concrete floor, Margot heard the front door to the house open, followed by strange-sounding footsteps on the stairs. *It doesn't sound like Ben or Max. Both of them were light on their feet. They were able to climb stairs effortlessly. This sounds like an old man.* She thought as terror ripped through her. The attic door opened slowly, and Margot cowered in the corner. Then, in the moonlight that filtered through the window, she saw the unmistakable shadow of his face. "Ben," she said, standing up and running towards him. The dark had hidden his wound, but when she got closer, she felt the hot wetness on his stomach. "Ben?" she said again. "You're hurt?"

He nodded. "Yes. I got shot."

"You need help." She was crying.

"There is no one to help. And there is not enough time to waste. You must listen to me," he said, trying to be as strong as possible for her sake. "You must listen very closely to what I am about to tell you and do as I say."

"Ben…"

"Margot, I don't have much time. I can't debate or argue with you right now. You must do as I tell you."

This was not like Ben. He'd always respected her thoughts and opinions, and he'd never before told her that she must obey him. If he had not been wounded, she might have argued. But as it was, she knew he was very serious. So she took his hand, not even paying attention to the blood that covered it, and held it close to her cheek. "What do you want me to do?"

"I'm dying," he said as gently as he could.

"No…" she shook her head violently. "No, I refuse to believe that. I won't let you die. I won't." The words barely came out through her cracked voice.

"It's true. You must believe me, Margot. I am going to die. And I don't have much time left." He took a ragged breath. "So you must listen carefully. Do you understand?"

"Yes," she nodded, but tears streamed down her cheeks.

"When I die, I want you to go downstairs and take a shower. Get every stitch of blood off you. Then, I put on a dress from Frau Danner's closet. Pack a few of her things in that little valise she kept by her bedroom door. Take all the jewelry and money I have saved. It's right over there in that box on the table."

She saw the box in the moonlight. "Ben, you can't die. I can't live without you."

"I'm not done speaking," he said almost harshly, and she knew it was because he was in pain. "Take that stuff. You are going to need money to start your life over again. Sell it as you need to and use it for bribes if you have to. But survive. Do you hear me? Survive."

She nodded, "Yes."

"All right. Good. Now, the first thing you must do is get out of Berlin. You must go where you won't be recognized just in case Trudy has alerted the authorities about you. Go to another city, perhaps even to Austria. Now, I know you have papers that say that you are Margot Kraus, an Aryan. Use those papers to start over. Never again mention the fact that you might have Jewish blood. When you get to your new city, and people ask you why you left your home, tell them that your husband was in the German army, that he was killed in the war, and that you needed a fresh start. You needed to find work, so you came to a new city."

"Ben. Oh God, Ben." She was weeping.

"I know, love. I know. I wish more than anything that I could protect you." He shook his head. "I never found Max. I never even got to your apartment. I failed you. The last thing I wanted to do was fail you. But I did."

"No, you didn't fail. You never failed me, Ben. I love you. I always have."

He laid his head on her lap. Softly, he whispered, "If only things could have been different for us. This time with you in this tiny room has been the best moment of my life. You will never know how grateful I am to have shared it with you. Your laugh brought me sunshine when I hadn't seen the sun in months. The soft touch of your hands warmed my heart when it was so cold outside you could see your own breath." Then he squeezed her hand with his last ounce of strength. "Be safe, Margot. And no matter what happens, know that I always loved you and always will." Then Ben closed his eyes for the last time. He would never save another life on earth.

In a broken whisper, tears streaming down her face, Margot leaned down and kissed Ben's forehead. "I will always love you, too. Now and forever."

CHAPTER 59

argot was trembling. It was all so unreal. *Ben cannot be dead. He just can't.* "Oh, Ben, my sweet Ben." She wept openly until her throat ached, and she had no more tears left to cry. It was almost dawn before she stood up from where she sat with Ben's hand still in hers. She knew that she must follow Ben's instructions if she was going to survive. After she placed a soft kiss on Ben's cold lips, she stood up and made her way out of the attic. Margot knew that Ben was right. She would be much safer once she was on a train on her way out of Berlin. Her papers were valid. But here in Berlin, she was still in danger. She might see Trudy or someone whom Trudy had told about her. She had no idea if her sister had reported her to the police and if the police might be looking for her. Margot considered risking waiting outside Max's job for him to arrive at work. She wished she could find him and take him away with her. But it was too risky. If the police were looking for her, they would probably be watching at Max's office. *No, I'll follow Ben's advice. It's best if I get out of town as soon as I can. I'll catch the first train out and go wherever it's headed. When this war is over, if it is ever over, I will return to Berlin and find Max. But for now, I must do what Ben told me to do. I must remind myself that I am strong. I can do this. I* can start over on my own in a new place. When Ben was with me, I didn't want to leave him. I felt safer with him than I would have alone. And I would feel safe with Max if I could find him. But that feeling of safety is not real. No one can protect me from the Gestapo. The only chance I have to survive is to use my wit and self-reliance. The idea of possibly never seeing Max again hurts my heart. I love him. And I loved Ben. However, the time has come to leave here, and I know that this is what I must do.

Margot quickly showered, packed, and dressed. She took the valuables that Ben had left for her and stuffed them into her handbag for the moment. But she knew that they were not safe there and she would have to find a more secure place for them. *I wish the old woman had some makeup. Just a bit of lipstick that I could smear on my cheeks would really help me to look a little more alive. I am so darn pale and white.* But there was no lipstick to be had. She bit her lip and smeared the blood on her cheeks to make her look less colorless. Then she sat down at the table in the kitchen and glanced around. The shades and curtains were shut tight. *I think I am safe here for the moment. Where would Frau Danner keep a needle and thread?* There was no way to determine. *I would like to sew these valuables into this coat. I can tear a thread out of the lining of the coat and use that. But I still need a sewing needle.* She thought as she got up and searched the house. But she couldn't find a needle anywhere, and the sun was rising. Finally, she decided to tuck the money and jewelry that Ben had left into her bra and leave the house. The earlier in the morning that she arrived at the train station, the better.

It wasn't as early as she would have liked; it was morning but past sunrise, and Berlin was buzzing with people on their way to work. Years ago, before the Nazis came to power, the streets would be filled with bicycle riders, but now the Nazis had confiscated all the bikes, and very few riders were left on the streets. The buses were crowded, and so were the sidewalks. It had been months since Margot had been outside of the attic. The sounds of horns honking and people rushing through town unnerved her. Her eyes searched the crowds frantically for any trace of Trudy or Max. She didn't see either of them. When she got to the bus stop, many people were waiting for the next bus.

Judging from the crowd, Margot assumed she would not get on the next bus. She would have to wait for the following one. Rather than stand outside at the bus stop, she decided to walk the two miles to the train station. Keeping her head down, she hurried through town. She had been in good physical shape before she'd spent so many months inactive in the attic. In those days, a two-mile walk would not have phased her. However, now her feet and legs ached from the effort. The suitcase she carried was not heavy, yet it felt overwhelmingly so.

When Margot finally arrived at the train station, she was out of breath, tired, and hungry. *I must get something to eat, or I might faint.* Although she hated to spend the money, she bought a single roll and a cup of ersatz coffee from a vendor. It tasted like heaven. Trying not to gobble the food, she forced herself to slow down as she studied the train schedule. A train was leaving for Munich in three hours, another for Nuremberg in two. Then she saw that a train was leaving for Frankfurt in forty-five minutes. *Frankfurt it is.* She thought as she approached the ticket booth to buy a one-way ticket.

"Papers," the man in the ticket booth demanded.

Margot steadied her shaking hand and showed him her papers. Her heart was pounding as she waited. But it was only a moment before he returned her papers and ticket. She paid him. And he called out, "Next in line."

That was easy. He didn't question me at all.

CHAPTER 60

The next forty-five minutes in the busy train station were uneventful. Margot sat quietly on a bench and waited. She tried to be inconspicuous as she continually glanced around, assuring herself that Trudy was not there and that no police had followed or found her. She still could not be certain that the police were not looking for her. The loud whistle that alerted passengers that the train was arriving made Margot jump. A middle-aged woman beside her said, "I hate train whistles too."

Margot managed to smile. She hoped she didn't look as nervous as she felt. Once on board the train, Margot sat in a window seat. She watched the landscape as the train chugged along on the track. Somewhere on the train, a child was crying, and it brought her thoughts back to Erik, which in turn made her think of Max and then of Ben. *We were a family, and the Nazis destroyed us for no reason. They destroyed Ben, too, and he was one of the most devoted doctors I ever knew. How can the German people believe this government is good for their country? How can they believe that Hitler is a good leader, and how can they follow him? I made the biggest mistake of my life when I told Max to join the Party because I thought they would give Erik the medical care he needed. Oh, they gave him medical care, all right. They did what they thought he needed. They killed him.* She couldn't bear for anyone to see her pain, so she closed her eyes.

Margot was so lost in thought that she didn't notice anything until the train came to an abrupt stop. Her eyes flew open as two low-ranking Nazi officers in uniform entered the train. "Papers," one of them called out in a harsh and demanding voice.

CHAPTER 61

Max took Kaz's advice and kept to himself at work during the day. It was best that way. He saw too many men shot because they couldn't turn away from a friend who had fallen. The Nazis showed no mercy. And as the time passed, Max came to expect this of them. His friendship with Kaz and Adrien grew. The camp was a lonely place, and although friendship was a dangerous venture because it left one vulnerable, it was the only light in a very dark world. Max, Kaz, and Adrien sometimes played cards at night after the evening meal. It was a good escape, even if it only lasted an hour or so.

During the day, Max and Kaz did manual labor, but they knew that Adrien worked at the hospital. They hardly discussed his work because Max and Kaz knew Adrien was ashamed. Adrien refused to talk about how he had been forced to work under the direction of sadistic Nazi doctors doing unethical things to helpless prisoners. As often as he could, Adrien stole medical supplies from the hospital, which he used to help those in need. He'd become known amongst the other prisoners as the man to see if one needed medical care. A visit with Adrien was far safer than a visit to the actual hospital, from which few ever returned. Sometimes, the men Adrien treated gave him gifts.

This was how he got the deck of cards he and his friends played with each night. The cards were not perfect. They were a deck of fifty-one, missing the Queen of Hearts. But even so, they were a distraction for the men from their miserable existence.

The Nazi guards had been correct when they said Max had the constitution of an ox. He was physically very strong. But Margot was his one and only love, and therefore, she was his greatest weakness. During the day, he could do his work, even though he was always hungry. But it was at night when he tried to sleep that his weakness and need overtook him. Visions of her face came to him, creating such a longing that he felt the ache deep in his belly. His yearning for his wife and the family he lost was so deep and painful that sometimes he woke up with his face covered in tears. Max had been raised to be a good Christian, but as the years passed, he stopped attending church. However, now, at night, in this terrible place, he found God, and he prayed for Margot's safety. This was all he could do. He knew he had to put his trust in God. He had no way of knowing where Margot was. No way of knowing if she was alive or dead. And he had no way of finding her.

CHAPTER 62

Margot was trembling as she watched the Nazi officers begin to sort through everyone's documents. They walked slowly and deliberately through the aisles, asking each passenger on the train for their papers.

A million thoughts raced through Margot's mind. She was worried they might be looking for her, afraid Trudy somehow knew she was on this train. She tried to tell herself that it was irrational to even consider that. But fear overcame rationality.

When the Nazi yelled at Margot, she smiled demurely at the young pimple-faced boy and handed him her papers.

Although her heart was beating faster than a hummingbird's wings, she looked into his eyes briefly, then looked down and said, "I'm sorry I was staring. It's just that you're so handsome."

The young boy blushed. He was obviously flattered.

Even though Margot was painfully thin, and a few gray hairs had found their way into her long, dark mane, she was still a beautiful woman. Her complimentary words caught the young man off guard. Instead of scrutinizing her papers, he was studying her gaze. "Thank you, *Fräulein*," He said, handing the papers back to her. Then, more curious than investigative, he asked, "Where are you going?"

There was no use in lying to him. All he had to do was ask for her train ticket, and he would know exactly where she was headed. "Frankfurt."

"Frankfurt? Do you have family there?"

"No, I am just moving away from Berlin. I lost my husband in the war. He was a soldier in the army fighting for our fatherland." She batted her eyelashes. "Berlin has too many painful memories for me. I needed to get away and start over."

"Ahhh, I wish I had a little time in Frankfurt tonight, but sadly, I don't. I must return to headquarters in Berlin." He sighed. "Still, it was a pleasure to meet you. Perhaps in the future, we will meet again."

"Yes, I would like that," she lied. As he walked away, she realized she had been holding her breath.

The Nazis continued down the aisles until they came to a young man wearing a worn-out gray coat. His head was bent, and his hair was disheveled. From where Margot sat, she could not see his face. "It's him. I'm sure of it," one of the Nazis called out to the other, "I've got him."

The other officer walked over quickly. He pulled his gun, and then he grabbed the man by the sleeve. "Let's go," he said.

The man didn't argue. He stood up, defeated, and let them pull him by his arms and force him off the train.

Margot jumped a little when the train whistled and moaned, indicating they were about to start moving. Then, the train sprung to life again like a giant snake and began to chug along the tracks into Margot's unknown future.

As her heart slowed to a normal rhythm, she thought. *I've learned something today. These Nazis are just men. And I have these papers that say I am an Aryan. I can flirt and distract them if I need to. I'll do what I must to survive.*

CHAPTER 63

Although Max was a large, well-built man, Kaz made him look almost small. He was massive but as kind and gentle as a Saint Bernard dog. Max, Adrien, and Kaz became good friends as the months passed. They ate together each evening after they returned from work and sometimes spent the evenings before bed talking. Everyone on their block was aware that before the war, Adrien had been a doctor. But Kaz and Max never discussed their lives before their imprisonment. Max was glad not to have to explain that he had once been a member of the Nazi Party and that he had once worked for them at the postal service and then also at a factory designing airplanes for the war effort. He might be able to make them understand why he had been sucked into joining the Party, but he was afraid that once they knew what he had done, no one would ever look at him in the same way. Then, one night, just as they were about to sleep, two guards brought a new man into their block. The guards pointed to an open space. "Sleep there," one of them said. Then, the guards left. The new addition to their block was a skinny, red-haired, freckle-faced boy. Looking at him, Max decided he couldn't be more than sixteen years old. He lay down in the space that the guards had indicated and began to cry.

There was no shame in him. He was too badly beaten, both physically and emotionally, to be ashamed of weeping. Kaz was tired. Max knew it because he was tired, too. Kaz grunted and stood up. He walked over to the red-haired boy, and with a gentleness that should have been uncharacteristic for a man of his size, he said, "Hey, it's all right." Then he patted the boy's shoulder and winked. Then, in his regular sarcastic but gentle tone, he added, "And even if it's not all right, I can promise you that crying won't help. I know, I've tried it plenty of times."

"They killed my father when we got here. He was all I had left in the world," the red-haired boy said.

Kaz nodded. "We all have a story. I sympathize with you. I do. But if you lay here and feel sorry for yourself, you'll die here in Dachau. I promise you that. The only men who are going to survive this place are the men who can let go of the past and look to the future. Do you understand what I am trying to say to you? Your papa is dead. I am sorry. I know that it's hard to lose someone you love. I know because I, too, have lost my loved ones. But if you lay down and stop fighting, then these Nazi bastards will have won. Do you want that? The only way to win against them is to live. It will take strength, plenty of strength, mental and physical because they want to kill us all. But if you look deep within yourself, you can find that strength. And when you do, you will honor your papa. Wherever he is, you will make him proud. Stop crying, boy. Stop crying and find the strength in your soul to live."

Max heard the words that Kaz spoke, and he realized that they were not only meant for the red-haired boy but somehow they were meant for him too. *I will live. I will live for Margot. If she is alive, someday, I will find her again. If she is not, I will live to honor her memory and the memory of my murdered son.*

Kaz saw the look on Max's face, and he nodded. "Live. Life is the only thing that is important to us right now. Because as long as we are alive, we have a chance to rebuild. To defeat them."

CHAPTER 64

Margot got off the train in Frankfurt.

Frankfurt was not nearly as large or as populated as Berlin, but evidence of the bombings in Frankfurt was everywhere. The city had taken some hard hits, just like Berlin. *All of this death and destruction is because we have a power-hungry monster in control who thinks he can conquer the world.* When she first arrived, Margot looked around her, afraid she had made a mistake by leaving the big city. There was, after all, anonymity in large crowds of people, and Berlin certainly had a larger population. But it also held a terrible history for her, and although she couldn't be sure, she thought it probably was still home to her sister, Trudy, who she was sure would destroy her if she ever had another opportunity. However, as she walked down the main street, no one noticed or paid attention to her. Ben had left her enough money to find a cheap apartment, but if she couldn't find a job right away, she would need to sell some of the jewelry he left to keep going. And that worried her. She was concerned that whoever she sold it to might ask questions. If she could, she would prefer to find a job right away. In school, Margot had taken a class in shorthand and one in typing. She was rather good at both. However, she reminded herself that she was not a party member and, therefore, she might draw attention to herself if she applied for work at a Nazi-owned corporation. In the center of town, she saw several restaurants.

I've never done it before, but I am sure I could be a waitress at one of these restaurants. I'll find a place to live first, and then I'll go into the restaurants and cafés and apply. She walked through the streets searching for a boarding house where the rent would be cheap. As she continued walking through the rubble, she saw a synagogue that had been burned, and she wondered if it was from a bomb or if it was done by the Nazis. This brought her thoughts back to Ben. Margot was glad that she had been able to spend the last few months of his life with him. And she knew she would miss him and never forget how much of an impact he'd had on her life. Her heart was heavy with grief for all she'd lost, and even now, she wondered where she was getting the strength to continue. It would be easier to take her own life. And yet, she refused to give up. *If fate has it that I am going to die at the hands of Hitler and his followers, then I am going to take as many of them with me as I can.*

After walking for over two hours, she passed a large, old wood-framed home. The white paint on the outside was peeling, and the flower box on the windowsill was filled with dead plants. But right in front was a handwritten sign that read, 'Room for rent.' *This place must be very inexpensive.* She walked up to the door and found that the knocker had broken off. She knocked with her knuckles and waited. It was only a few minutes before a middle-aged woman with silver-gray hair set in pin curls, wearing a dirty cotton housecoat, answered the knock.

"Yes?" the old woman said. "What do you want?"

"I saw your sign. I'd like to rent a room," Margot said.

"You're not a Jew, are you?" the woman looked at Margot skeptically.

Margot was shocked at the question, although she realized that she shouldn't have been surprised. After all, it was against the law to rent to Jews. The woman was only protecting herself. "No. I'm not," Margot assured her. "I have papers here if you'd like to see them."

"Not necessary. I believe you. It's just that I'm required to ask. I hope you understand."

"Of course." Margot nodded.

"Follow me. I'll show you the room I have for rent."

Margot followed the woman up a steep staircase to the second floor and then down a short hallway to a door she opened with a key.

The first thing Margot noticed was a large window covered by a dusty old velvet curtain. She had spent so much time in the darkness in the attic that having an open window with a view of the outside world was a luxury. But she didn't say a word. Instead, she walked around the little room. A small bed in the corner stood looking lonely with a beaten-up three-drawer wooden dresser beside it. The paint on the walls had once been white but now had turned yellow with age. There was no mirror or pictures on the wall. There was a very small closet next to the dresser. The room contained only that which was absolutely necessary. But it didn't matter to Margot. She didn't have much, and after living with nothing in the attic, she knew she didn't need much.

"There's a bathroom right down the hall with a shower, a toilet, and a sink. If you take the room, you'll share that bathroom with another boarder."

Margot nodded.

"So, do you want the room?"

"Yes, I'll take it, but do you happen to have a rag I can use to dust?"

"Of course. I'll get you one. But first, I need payment. How long do you plan to stay?"

"I'm not sure."

"That's all right. You can pay by the week."

CHAPTER 65

I took Margot a half hour to dust the room and then sweep the floor, and it took less than fifteen minutes to move the contents of her suitcase into the small dresser. She had only taken a few dresses and underclothes from Frau Danner's room. Once she finished moving in, she left the room and headed back onto the street to search for a job.

Most of the people who owned the restaurants she went to were kind to her when she asked about job availability, but they said they could not afford to hire her. "I hardly earn enough for myself and my family. I can't afford an employee. I'm sorry," one very kind woman said to her. Margot nodded. She understood. But she kept walking and trying to find a job. Her feet and legs ached. She had not walked so much in a very long time. *I can't stop and return to my room until I find work. If I go through all the money Ben left before I have more coming in, I'll be in real trouble. I must find a job as quickly as possible.*

Then she saw a sign that read Kraus Bookseller. *My last name is Kraus. Well, it's really Max's last name. But it's mine now. I'm going to go in and meet the owners. Perhaps they are related to Max and might be able to suggest a restaurant where I could get a job.*

"Good day," a heavy-set middle-aged man with thick black-rimmed glasses said when she entered.

"Good day," Margot answered. "Are you Herr Kraus?"

"I am." He looked puzzled and suddenly nervous. "Why? Who wants to know?"

Margot smiled, trying to put him at ease, "My husband's surname was Kraus. I thought you might be related to us."

"Who's your husband?"

"Max Kraus. His parents are Heidi and Artur from Berlin."

"No, I don't know anyone by those names. I don't have any relatives in Berlin either. I'm sorry."

She could see that she had unnerved him. "I didn't mean to startle you. I just, well…" She hesitated. "I was hoping you might give me a job. I will tell you the truth. I just don't know what to do. I arrived here in Frankfurt today, and I can't find work. So, I thought if you were related to my husband, you might help me. I thought you might need help here at the bookstore."

"Are you kidding? There's hardly enough work for me. I have a family to support. I'm sorry."

"I see," she said. "Do you know of anyone looking for help?"

He looked annoyed. But then he started tapping his pencil on the counter in front of him and said, "Well, the man who owns the café across the street might be interested. His restaurant is very popular with government officials, officers, and such. So he is always busy, but he's closed in the afternoon. He's only open at night. You'd have to come back tonight if you want to see him. That's all I can suggest."

"Well, I appreciate it. I am desperate to find work."

"Go over there tonight. You are young and pretty. He might hire you."

"Thank you," she said, leaving the store.

Margot was tired. She'd been traveling and walking since early that morning. She decided to take the bookseller's advice and go to the restaurant he suggested. So, she returned to her room to rest until evening. Exhausted, she lay on the bed and fell into a deep sleep. When she awoke, she walked down to the end of the hall and took a shower. Then she put on one of the clean dresses that had belonged to

Frau Danner, and although it was matronly, she still looked pretty. Then she walked over to the café across from the bookstore. As the bookseller had said, the café was already crowded with men in Nazi uniforms. They were standing around at the bar talking, drinking, laughing. The tables were occupied by more Nazis, some of them SS.

Many were accompanied by well-dressed women. Margot's chest hurt. It was hard to breathe. With all of her secrets, she found it very scary to walk into a room filled with the enemy. *Be brave. No one will know you.* She told herself. *Besides, only businesses that will have jobs available will be places where the Nazis go to spend their money. They are the only people who have extra money to spend. So, I am going to have to get used to it.* She walked up to the bar and asked the bartender if she could speak to the owner. He directed her to a short, fat, balding man standing across the room talking to a young SS Officer. Nodding, she thanked the bartender, then she stood in the corner and waited until the young Nazi left. Once the Nazi was gone, Margot walked over, and mustering all of her courage, she smiled at the restaurant owner and said, "Hello. My name is Margot Kraus. I am looking for employment. And this is such a lovely restaurant. I was wondering if you currently need a waitress?"

The short man tapped his fingers on his cheek and studied her. He nodded, then said, "I could use a waitress, and you're a pretty little thing. Do you have experience waiting tables?"

"Yes," she lied.

"Well, good. All right. Can you start tomorrow? We open at four."

"Yes, I can."

"Be here at four, then. But…" he hesitated. "Do you have a more attractive dress? That makes you look like an old woman."

She glanced down at the frock she'd taken from Frau Danner. It was obviously a dress for an old woman. "I do," she lied, knowing she would have to go to a secondhand store first thing in the morning and purchase something suitable. *I hate to spend the money, but at least I know I will be working so I will be able to replace it.*

"Wear the other dress," he said bluntly. "And you'd better know in advance that the men who come here like to flirt. They enjoy the company of pretty women. So, I hope you're not one of those girls who gets offended easily."

"No, no, of course not. I'll be fine."

"Good. Then I'll see you tomorrow," he said.

Margot walked back to her room quickly. She was a little nervous and unsure of how far these Nazis might try to go with her. But she needed the job, so she decided to play along when they flirted with her. She must pretend that she found them appealing. *I guess I will flirt and pretend to be the Aryan Nazi lover that they expected me to be.*

In the morning, Margot asked the woman who owned the house where she was living where the closest secondhand store was. "Two streets down. When you get outside, just turn right and keep walking. You can't miss it," the woman said.

Margot nodded. "Thank you."

Finding a couple of dresses wasn't difficult. Margot tried on several dresses and decided on two. Both of them were black, and both of them were tight-fitting. Although she was very thin and her figure wasn't as full and voluptuous as it had once been, the dresses still looked stunning on her.

On her way back to her room, she stopped at a cheap general store and bought a tube of red lipstick and mascara. This style of dressing didn't appeal to her. In fact, she felt disgusted with herself at the thought of it. But she knew if she was going to earn a living at the restaurant, she must be attractive to the male customers even if they were Nazis. And she needed to keep this job until she could find another way to earn money.

That night, when Margot walked into the café, the owner turned to look at her. "Wow! You certainly look good," he exclaimed. "I knew you were pretty, but I had no idea you would look this way when you dressed up. That red lipstick was a nice touch, I must say." He smiled at her. "You'll do just fine here. Follow me. I am going to introduce you to some of the other waitresses. They can help you find your way around the place and get acclimated."

She did as he asked. As she walked through the restaurant, she could feel the eyes of the men falling upon her like lions on zebras.

"This is Tilly," the owner said, introducing Margot to a tall, slim girl of perhaps nineteen years old with two thick golden braids wrapped around her head.

"Hello," Margot said, trying to sound friendly.

Tilly looked Margot over, and Margot saw the younger girl scrutinizing her competition. "Hello," she said coldly.

"And that girl over there is Marie." The owner indicated a short woman in her mid-twenties with curly blonde hair carrying a tray with mugs of beer on it. Then he called, "Marie, when you have a moment. I want you to come over here. I have someone I want you to meet."

Marie nodded. "Sure, Klaus, just give me a minute."

When Marie walked over, the owner introduced her to Margot. "Marie will show you around." He said, "And by the way, I guess I should introduce myself. My name is Klaus. You'll find that I am a very important man around here. I'm the top restauranter in Frankfurt."

From far away, Margot thought Marie was very attractive, but once she was closer, Margot could see she was weathered. There were deep wrinkles around her eyes and mouth when she smiled. And her face looked strained. Even so, she was pretty, and when she smiled, she seemed much more sincere and nicer than Tilly had been. "I'll show you everything. Don't you worry," Marie said, winking at Margot, "you'll learn this job in no time."

Margot liked Marie almost immediately.

That night, Margot followed Marie around and learned everything she could about the restaurant. Marie was surprisingly patient; she was a thorough teacher. "You haven't waited tables before, have you?" she whispered to Margot.

"Is it that obvious?" Margot grimaced.

"Only to me. Only because I have been doing it all my life. But don't worry. Like I said before, I'll teach you."

"You're so kind. You don't know what this means to me. I really need this job, and I am really trying to do my best."

"Shhh, don't you worry. You'll be just fine."

By the end of the night, Margot knew that the Nazis who frequented the café had no boundaries. They were disrespectful in their words and deeds. They thought nothing of reaching out and grabbing at the waitress's buttocks wherever and whenever they pleased. Margot observed this as it happened to Marie and to Tilly. But the first time it happened to Margot was a few nights later. She was serving a large party of rambunctious, loud SS officers. As she walked by, trying to balance a large tray with two pitchers of beer and several heavy beer mugs, a young and handsome Nazi officer grabbed her behind. She jumped. Her response was spontaneous. As the tray fell from her hands and the glass crashed onto the floor, she spun around to see who had put their hands on her. Beer ran like a dark river of spun gold amid the broken glass. Margot gasped when she saw what she had done. She was certain that she was going to lose her job for this. Quickly, she turned to see the owner's face. He was shaking his head. His face was pale, and deep frown lines marked his brow. Then he fixed his eyes upon her. From where she stood, they looked as if they were glaring. Then suddenly, a maniacal smile came over his face. Margot saw the change in him and began to tremble. He looked almost like a different man. A madman. But then the Nazi who had grabbed her started laughing. "Klaus," he called out the owner's name, "Don't worry about it. I'll pay for it. All of it. Don't fire the girl. It wasn't her fault. It was mine. I'm afraid I must have startled her."

Margot saw Klaus's face begin relaxing. The Nazi's words had calmed him. All of this made her feel like the kind of girl whom men didn't respect, and she hated it. She wanted to say so many things, but she took a deep breath instead. *This job isn't going to be as easy as I thought it would be.*

"I'm sorry," he said, but there was no sincerity in his apology. "Please forgive me. I shouldn't have taken such liberties with you. I should have been able to see that you are a lady."

Margot would have liked to slap him across the face. But she just nodded.

"I really am sorry, *Fräulein*. You see, I would never want to cost you your job."

"It's all right, really," she said, annoyed with him. "Excuse me, I must get a new tray of beer for that group waiting over there."

"I can help," he said. "Please let me help you. It's my fault. I'd like to make things right. By the way, my name is Kurtis." He didn't wait for her to answer. Instead, he stood up and went over to the bartender. After he laid down a few Reichsmarks, he said, "That's for the tray the girl spilled. Now, please remake the tray, and I'll take it over to the table that's waiting."

The bartender shrugged. "Sure," he said.

The young officer brought the tray over to the others who were waiting. One of them laughed. "You make a hell of a waitress, Kurtis. You'd look good in a skirt."

"Shut up," the officer who had been called Kurtis answered the other officer with a slap on the shoulder. But there was no trace of animosity between them. In fact, there was a good-natured, easy banter. After Kurtis laid the tray on the table, all the men reached for mugs and poured themselves beers. Then Kurtis turned his attention back to Margot, who didn't realize it, but her mouth was hanging open a little. He laughed. "The look on your face tells me I must have surprised you? No?"

She nodded. But she wasn't sure if he meant she'd been surprised by his grabbing at her or carrying the tray of beer. Either way, it didn't matter. Margot was holding her tongue. She didn't want to start an argument with him. She just wanted to get back to work. "Thank you for helping me with that tray," she said.

"Of course. It was only right. By the way, you know my name. Now tell me yours."

"Margot." *This is the last thing I need. But I can't refuse to tell him, or Klaus might fire me.*

"That's a lovely name. Would you please consider joining me for dinner after work tonight, Margot?"

"I'm sorry, I can't. I'm working until late tonight."

"Well, tomorrow then. I must return home on Friday as I am in Frankfurt on holiday. But I must return to work on Monday. But I have a few days left here in Frankfurt, and I would love to have dinner with you before I go. I'm sorry I was so crude. Can you forgive me?"

"I forgive you," she said in a matter-of-fact tone. "But I don't have time for dinner. I am sorry."

"Oh, sure you do." Klaus walked over to them. He'd been standing close, listening to their conversation. "She'll be available tomorrow night. I'll give her the night off with pay. How about that, Margot?"

She smiled wryly.

"By the way, Kurtis, did I hear you say you are going to be returning to Dachau on Friday? Are you still stationed there?"

"Yes."

"Are you still a guard at the camp there?"

"I am."

"I hear it's a good job. What's your rank now?"

"*Kommandoführer.*"

"*Kommandoführer* Kurtis Richter. It has a good ring to it." Klaus smiled and nodded. "You're going places in this world, Kurt. I can still remember when you were just a boy, and I would see you and your mother at the market. You were such a bad boy. You never gave your mother a minute's peace. You ran through the market, and she was always chasing after you. Well... Just look at you now. You have a big important position. Your family must be proud."

"Ehh, I suppose they are. I must admit, it is a good job in that it pays well, but it's still a prison. And because I am in a prison, I have to watch my back at all times. Jews, political prisoners, and criminals surround me. A man has to keep his wits about him and always remember to be careful."

"Well, you are a smart fellow. I have no doubt that you will go far in the Nazi Party. And don't worry, Margot will be off from work tomorrow night, so she'll be available to have dinner with you."

Kurtis smiled, "Thanks, Klaus," he said, then he turned to Margot. "So, it's all set. You have dinner with me tomorrow night," he said.

Margot saw the look on Klaus's face, and she knew she could not refuse. "Yes, sure," she answered.

"Good. I look forward to it." Kurtis smiled.

CHAPTER 66

Kurtis was precisely on time. His blonde hair was combed, and his perfectly fitted black uniform was pressed. Margot had agreed to meet him at the restaurant where she had just begun working. He sat down at the bar to wait for her. Fifteen minutes passed, then a half hour. Kurtis glanced at the watch he'd received as a gift from his superior officer and frowned. Margot was late, and he was secretly both angry and intrigued at the same time. *If she doesn't show up, I'll punish her. I'll show her the power I have. I'll make her sorry for treating me this way. I'll make sure Klaus fires her. How dare she think she can stand me up? She's far from the prettiest girl I've ever dated, and yet there's something about her that draws me to her.*

Trying to look casual, he glanced out the window. No sign of Margot. His anger was bubbling like a pot boiling. But along with the anger, he found he was filled with desire. Undressing her in his mind, he yearned to take her to his bed and fulfill this passion he'd seemed to be developing for her before he left town. *I don't need this sexual desire hanging over me while I am gone. It could be a distraction. I think it will be best to have her quickly and then put her aside. That way, I can concentrate on my job when I return to Dachau.*

Margot finally arrived forty-five minutes late. A light dusting of newly fallen snow covered her dark hair. "I'm sorry I'm late," she said as she walked up to him where he sat at the bar.

"Oh, it's all right. I lost track of time." He smiled, and upon seeing her, all the malice he felt was gone. "You look beautiful," he said.

She wore the other black dress she'd recently purchased for work. These two garments were all she had except for the things she'd taken from Frau Danner.

"I don't think we should dine here," he said. "You work here, and because of that, it would be uncomfortable. Why don't we go somewhere else? I know a quiet little place a couple of streets away."

"All right," she agreed.

"It's not far. Shall we walk, or shall I drive? It is rather cold, and it's snowing. You'd probably be more comfortable if I drove."

"I'd prefer to walk," she said.

She doesn't trust me. She's a smart girl. She's cautious. She doesn't know me well enough to get into my auto. "Then we will walk," he said, smiling. Linking his arm in hers, he said, "So tell me a little about yourself."

She'd hesitated for a moment. "There isn't much to tell."

"I don't believe that. I think there's plenty. But, if you want to remain a mystery, that's your prerogative. I won't push you. I don't want you to do anything you don't want to do."

CHAPTER 67

Margot found Kurtis to be charming, but she didn't trust him at all. And she hoped he would find her boring and lose interest in her as quickly as he had become fascinated. They were seated in the corner of the restaurant at a very private table with a single candle and a white tablecloth. Kurtis ordered a bottle of Riesling wine.

"I only use German products," he said after placing the order. "I only buy German products. I drink German wine and, of course, German beer. I eat German food. My clothes and my auto are all made right here in the fatherland. We are fortunate to live in such a country. Don't you agree?"

"Yes, of course," she said nervously.

"And much of the time, we have free labor to produce our goods. But, of course, that is the way it should be. Aryans are superior to all others; therefore, others have been put here on earth to serve us."

Margot wanted to ask questions about this free labor. She wanted to argue about Aryan superiority. But she knew that she dared not. If she questioned him, he might see into her heart and know that she hated the Nazi Party.

He didn't care that she didn't say anything about slave labor. He was too busy staring at her. "Has anyone ever told you that you would look lovely in blue?" he said dreamily.

"I'm sorry? I don't know what you mean."

"I mean, blue is your color. You should wear it."

She nodded. "I'll remember that the next time I go shopping."

"Ahh, and when is that?"

"I don't shop much. I can't spend money frivolously. I need every Reichsmark I earn just to get by."

"Well, I think we should go shopping. You and me. I would be happy to buy you something blue. A dress, perhaps?"

"It's very kind of you to offer. But I am sorry, I really don't have the time. I have to work so I can pay my bills." Her tone was colder and more abrupt than she had anticipated. *He is trying to be nice. I should be careful and not be so rude. He has the power to make my life miserable. I should remember that.* She thought, but she was finding it difficult to be kind to him.

He didn't seem at all discouraged by her aloof manner. In fact, if anything, he was more intrigued. "I hope I didn't insult you. I wasn't planning on having you pay for anything. It would all be my treat."

Be nice. He means well. I must try not to anger him. The owner of the restaurant where I am employed likes him. So, he could cause me lots of problems at work. "How kind you are," she said as sincerely as she could manage.

"Am I?" He laughed. "I am going to tell you something about myself, Fräulein. I am going to give you a little insight into my character. The reason I am successful is that I am the kind of man who goes after what he wants. And, just to be clear, I always get what I go after. From the first time I saw you, I knew you were the girl for me. I can think of nothing else. Margot, over these last couple of days, I find you have become the center of my thoughts. I want you. My desire for you is so strong that I can hardly contain it," he whispered.

The powerful way he delivered those powerful words shocked her. *He's a Nazi, an SS Officer. He's the last thing I need in my life right now. I'm trying to start over, to hide in plain sight, and now this.* She was afraid of him, and her fear must have shown on her face because he took her hand and smiled, and then he said, "Don't be afraid of me,

Margot. I would never hurt you. I won't ever force you to do anything you don't want to do. I wouldn't want you that way. I will do whatever it takes to make you want me as much as I want you. If I am to have you, to really have you, then you must come to me willingly. Anything else is not satisfying. I plan to make you love me so much that you won't be able to rest until you have me. You'll see, my dear. I know what I want, and I will get it."

Her face was flushed, but not because she was flattered. She was frightened by the strength of his resolve, and she wondered if perhaps she should leave Frankfurt. He wouldn't know where to look for her if she got on a train early in the morning. *But where should I go? I would have to start over in a new town, and I've already paid for rent at my boardinghouse. I can't afford to lose that money.*

Kurtis was smiling. He had misinterpreted her blush to be a flirtatious sign. "Margot, I will make you feel more special and wanted than any woman has ever felt. You won't be able to resist me."

Her lips trembled.

The waiter walked over to the table. "Would you like to order food now?" the waiter asked.

"Yes, why don't we do that?" Kurtis said. Then he turned to Margot and asked, "Are you hungry?"

She nodded. She was hungry, but she doubted she would be able to eat. "Yes."

"Good. What do you feel like eating?"

Margot shrugged. "Whatever you'd like."

"What do you suggest?" Kurtis asked the waiter.

The waiter rambled off several suggestions. Then Kurt placed an order. "Consider yourself fortunate that I have chosen you, Fräulein. I am quite a catch."

Even though she was afraid of him, and she had witnessed first-hand the terrible things the Nazis could do, she couldn't help but laugh at his comment. "Are you?" she asked sarcastically. Then, she immediately chastised herself internally for that comment.

"Oh yes, I am. Besides being handsome, financially stable, and a rising figure in the Party, I am charming and incredibly good in bed."

Now she was laughing outright. *What's wrong with me? Is this nerves? I can't stop laughing. I must stop. He's going to get angry.* But she couldn't stop.

His eyes narrowed. For a moment, he glared at her. Margot shivered, but she continued to laugh, a loud, nervous laugh. Then, instead of being angry, he too began to laugh. When the laughter broke, and both of them were red-faced and spent time trying to catch their breath, he said, "And besides all of these very desirable traits, I am also very humble."

They both began to laugh again. By the time their laughter was spent, the food arrived.

CHAPTER 68

I t had been a cold, dark day when the sky was the color of mourning doves. On days like these, Max battled depression. His thoughts were memories of Margot combined with worry about her well-being. He hated himself for being helpless and powerless to do anything. He couldn't help but wonder if she was dead. But he believed that they were so close that if she were dead, somehow he would know it. He would feel it in his heart, in his bones. In these times, his hatred for Trudy grew deeper and darker. He blamed her for ruining his life, and sometimes he fantasized about killing her, about choking her with his own hands. The thought of it gave him a strange sense of relief.

Max waited for Kaz to get in line for dinner that evening after work. But tonight, Kaz was late returning from his work detail. This was highly unusual. Kaz was usually one of the first men to return to his block. Max began to worry as he sat on his bed of straw, waiting.

Kaz was limping when he returned from his work detail. Max noticed it right away. "What happened to your leg?"

"I fell," Kaz said. He shrugged. "All right, I didn't fall. I was pushed. One of the other men, a *kapo* from another block, gave me a push. He was a small fellow. I should have been able to withstand it, but he caught me off guard. I'll get back at him."

"I don't care about him. I'm concerned about you. And from the way you're walking, I think we'd better get Adrien to look at your leg as soon as we can. It looks like you're in a lot of pain."

"I am. But I am strong. I can take it." He smiled and winked reassuringly at Max. But even as he did, Max could see in Kaz's eyes that he was hurting.

Max shook his head. "What are we going to do? You can hardly walk. Are you going to be able to go to work in the morning?" Max was clearly worried. He knew that if Kaz couldn't keep up with the others when he went out to work the next day, he would be shot.

"Oh, Max, when will you realize we have no choice? I have to go to work in the morning. It's not like I can call the boss and tell him I am sick, right? So, I'll work." He smiled at Max. "Don't worry so much. After we eat, I'll have Adrien take a look. He'll wrap it up and do whatever he needs to do so I can make it through until it heals."

There was nothing more to say. It was time to line up for dinner, and if they were late and ended up at the end of the line, there would be nothing left in the cauldron of soup but water.

After eating a small bowl of watery soup with two potato peels, a bit of cabbage, and a slice of carrot, Max and Kaz nibbled on their heels of bread as they sat close together, trying to get warm. Working outside on the roads all day had left them chilled, and they were hoping that the hot soup would help. It didn't. They were still cold and starving.

"One of the fellows I work with on the roads said that *Kommandoführer* Richter has gone on holiday. That's a blessing," Kaz said to Max.

"Maybe he'll get transferred and won't come back," Max said. "That's how they usually get transferred, isn't it?"

"I don't know."

"Well, I think so. Stay positive. Maybe we'll be lucky and get rid of him."

"We should get so lucky," Kaz said. "The ones who are really sadistic and terrible always come back."

CHAPTER 69

The afternoon following her date with Kurtis, Margot went to work. She was tired because she wasn't used to staying out late. All day long, she hoped that Kurtis would not come into the restaurant to see her. They had not made any future plans when the date ended. He had just walked her to the door of her boarding house and said goodnight. In fact, he hadn't even tried to kiss her. Margot was hopeful that her outrageous laughing fit had caused him to lose interest.

When her shift ended, Margot left the restaurant. As she made her way back to her room, she saw several drunk couples on the streets laughing loudly, as well as a Nazi officer with a young woman pushed up against a building in an alleyway. Her face turned red, and she looked away. *Max, I miss you. I miss the life we had.*

It felt like it took forever for her to return to her room. But she felt relieved as she entered her small space and locked the door behind her. She'd eaten at the restaurant where she worked, so all she needed was showering and going to bed. As Margot reached into the dresser drawer to retrieve the house dress she'd taken from Frau Danner, there was a knock on the door to her room. *No, no, please let it not be him.*

"Who is it?" she asked.

"It's me." Margot recognized the female voice; it was the owner of the boarding house.

"Come in," Margot said, opening the door.

The woman walked into Margot's room and handed Margot a large package. "A courier brought this for you today."

"Thank you," Margot said. Her heart was beating hard and fast. *Could it be from Max? But how could he have found me?*

The nosey landlady stood waiting. "Aren't you going to open it?" she asked.

"Not right now," Margot said.

"Oh, but I wanted to see what you got," the landlady said and winked.

"I'll let you know what it is. But I would prefer to open it alone," Margot said to the landlady in a cold and detached voice.

The landlady eyed Margot dubiously, but she seemed to know instinctively not to ask any more questions. She just nodded. "All right, be secretive," she said, and then she left the room, closing the door gently.

Once Margot was alone, she tore open the paper. Inside was a blue box tied with a blue ribbon. Her heart sank. She opened the package to find a royal blue velvet dress and a note.

How about we have dinner together tomorrow night? I've already spoken with Klaus, and he said that there is no problem with you taking the night off. So, I'll meet you at the restaurant where you work at eight o'clock. And by the way, blue is definitely your color.

———

AUTHORS NOTE

I always enjoy hearing from my readers, and your thoughts about my work are very important to me. If you enjoyed my novel, please consider telling your friends and posting a short review on Amazon. Word of mouth is an author's best friend.

Also, it would be my honor to have you join my mailing list. As my gift to you for joining, you will receive 3 **free** short stories and my USA Today award-winning novella complimentary in your email! To sign up, just go to my website at www.RobertaKagan.com

I send blessings to each and every one of you,

Roberta

Email: roberta@robertakagan.com

ABOUT THE AUTHOR

I wanted to take a moment to introduce myself. My name is Roberta, and I am an author of Historical Fiction, mainly based on World War 2 and the Holocaust. While I never discount the horrors of the Holocaust and the Nazis, my novels are constantly inspired by love, kindness, and the small special moments that make life worth living.

I always knew I wanted to reach people through art when I was younger. I just always thought I would be an actress. That dream died in my late 20's, after many attempts and failures. For the next several years, I tried so many different professions. I worked as a hairstylist and a wedding coordinator, amongst many other jobs. But I was never satisfied. Finally, in my 50's, I worked for a hospital on the PBX board. Every day I would drive to work, I would dread clocking in. I would count the hours until I clocked out. And, the next day, I would do it all over again. I couldn't see a way out, but I prayed, and I prayed, and then I prayed some more. Until one morning at 4 am, I woke up with a voice in my head, and you might know that voice as Detrick. He told me to write his story, and together we sat at the computer; we wrote the novel that is now known as All My Love, Detrick. I now have over 30 books published, and I have had the honor of being a USA Today Best-Selling Author. I have met such incredible people in this industry, and I am so blessed to be meeting you.

I tell this story a lot. And a lot of people think I am crazy, but it is true. I always found solace in books growing up but didn't start writing until I was in my late 50s. I try to tell this story to as many people as possible to inspire them. No matter where you are in your life, remember there is always a flicker of light no matter how dark it seems.

I send you many blessings, and I hope you enjoy my novels. They are all written with love.

Roberta

MORE BOOKS BY ROBERTA KAGAN

AVAILABLE ON AMAZON

Margot's Secret Series

The Secret They Hid

An Innocent Child

Margot's Secret

The Lies We Told

The Blood Sisters Series

The Pact

My Sister's Betrayal

When Forever Ends

The Auschwitz Twins Series

The Children's Dream

Mengele's Apprentice

The Auschwitz Twins

Jews, The Third Reich, and a Web of Secrets

My Son's Secret

The Stolen Child

A Web of Secrets

A Jewish Family Saga

Not In America

They Never Saw It Coming

When The Dust Settled

The Syndrome That Saved Us

A Holocaust Story Series

The Smallest Crack

The Darkest Canyon

Millions Of Pebbles

Sarah and Solomon

All My Love, Detrick Series

All My Love, Detrick

You Are My Sunshine

The Promised Land

To Be An Israeli

Forever My Homeland

Michal's Destiny Series

Michal's Destiny

A Family Shattered

Watch Over My Child

Another Breath, Another Sunrise

Eidel's Story Series

And . . . Who Is The Real Mother?

Secrets Revealed

New Life, New Land

Another Generation

The Wrath of Eden Series

The Wrath Of Eden

The Angels Song

Stand Alone Novels

One Last Hope

A Flicker Of Light

The Heart Of A Gypsy